THE RELICT

SKULLDIGGERY
BOOK 1

DM GRITZMACHER

PIQUED PUBLISHING

CONTENT WARNING

The Relict contains graphic depictions of violence and gore that may not be suitable for some readers.

RELICT

Relict-1: *a remnant of a formerly widespread species that persists in an isolated area.* 2: *a relief feature or rock remaining after other parts have disappeared.* 3: *a widow*

CHAPTER 1
PRESENT DAY

"I SWEAR if I hit one more..." Ethan mutters and curses as he pivots and turns to avoid a deep jagged rut carving its way into the forest floor. He muscles the Ground Penetrating Radar, or GPR unit as it's most commonly known, around again to start yet another sweep. Shoving it from behind like the lawnmower its design most closely resembles. He pushes the unorthodox piece of electronic machinery back and forth, over and over, across the exposed dirt and broken sticks, blanketing the pine needle-covered ground. He worked methodically between a small washed-out gully and a gurgling stream tumbling down from the mountain above. Laying down a systematic grid-like pattern while keenly watching the flickering images flashing across the screen of the device.

As the GPR unit rolls awkwardly across the uneven terrain of the wooded area, the hi-tech device, like Ethan, appears to be very much out of place in the rugged Michigan wilderness. Tiny brown pine needles stick comically out of the four rolling, mud-lined wheels as they sluggishly turn. Scratches and scuffs marred the unit's red paint, and along its edges, dirt clings desperately as if hoping for an escape from such a desolate location. Ethan has to keep one eye trained on the ground in front of him at all times as he pushes forward. The litany of rotted and broken tree branches scattered on the forest floor make for constant navigational adjustments on his part.

Out of the corner of his eye, he sees the old man scowling his way again, and Ethan pointedly ignores the dour educator. Professor Danforth had invited himself along for today's fieldwork, much to Ethan's chagrin. Ostensibly, the teacher had traveled up north to spend a few days helping, offering his guidance on Ethan's research and Ph.D. project. But, so far, Professor Danforth had spent his time primarily frowning, smoking cigarettes, and pacing in the woods away from where the actual work was unfolding. Ethan was fine with that. He'd been working solitarily since the summer started, and he was anxious for the professor to hit the road the next day and be out of his hair.

Laboring by himself throughout the morning, Ethan finds the work painstakingly slow. He must continuously stop and reach down to clear the numerous pitfalls along the ground in this part of the forest. Ignoring the actions (or lack thereof) that the older, tenured professor busied himself with, Ethan's brow furrowed while peering intently at the tiny display unit at the top of the long handle. In the hours he has been working this site, Ethan has placed three small wire and white plastic flags along the timbered floor. Each flag represents an anomaly below the surface he will later explore.

Though sheltered from the worst of the sun under the shade of the lush tree canopy overhead, sweat continually drips down Ethan's face. The perspiration depositing drop after drop on the inside lens of his wire-rimmed glasses and blurring his vision as he strains to read the subtle changes reflected on the small digital display. Ethan watches closely for any indication of possible underground disturbances in the soil beneath his feet. The entire process is both slow and arduous. After just a few hours of work in the humid Michigan summertime air, Ethan is sweating profusely. The brown hair he still has left at age thirty is already completely soaked.

As he reaches the end of his latest pass across the forest floor, Ethan decides to take a break. Powering off the GPR unit, he collapses under the slim shadow of a towering pine tree. Sitting up tall, Ethan pulls his sweat-soaked t-shirt to one side with his hands. Looking for and then finding a relatively clean and dry spot, he takes off his glasses and cleans them on the unsoiled cloth. Then uses the shirt to mop at his soaked face and forehead before putting his glasses back on. He watches grimly as the old professor saunters slowly towards him, undoubtedly to once again criticize the choice of location.

"I better find some Native American artifacts soon," Ethan murmurs under his breath. "I just can't take much more of Danforth's condescending remarks about the place." Ethan sighs and leans back, stretching out his tired neck and arm muscles while placing both hands on the ground behind him for balance. As he does, his right-hand lands on what at first he takes for a long stick no different than any of the others stubbornly in Ethan's way since he started.

His fingers encircle it, and he yanks hard, intending to pull the stick off the ground and toss it out of his way. But as he draws his arm back to fling away the offending obstacle, a flash of metal catches in the tree-filtered sunlight of the woods. Pausing mid-toss, he pulls it closer to his face for inspection. A small chain or rusted metallic bracelet hangs gingerly down, swaying slightly. Now disturbed, its old corroded clasp suddenly gives way, and the jewelry tumbles to the ground. Confused, Ethan turns and looks behind him to see where he has pulled it from. The unmistakable skeletal outline of a ribcage protrudes from the forest floor just a few feet from where he had sat down. Half of it was exposed above ground; the rest was still encased in the soil. Ethan glances from the exposed ribcage to the bracelet lying curled up on the ground and then back again before turning his attention to what he still held in his right hand. Twisting it back and forth slowly, he recognizes it to be a human forearm bone. With a start, he drops it. "Oh my god… What the… Jesus!"

Frowning disgustedly, he wipes his hand several times across his moist t-shirt. He starts to push himself up to stand but then stops himself, instead reaching down for the bracelet that first caught his eye. Ethan holds it up from one end and inspects it more closely. The chain was six or seven inches long with a two-inch curved metal plate in the center. Using his thumb, he wipes the corrosion and caked-on dirt away from the face of the nameplate. Squinting, he is able to just make out each letter. Revealing the name, he reads it out loud to himself.

"Sherry."

CHAPTER 2
PRESENT DAY

THE YOUNG WOMAN driving the maroon minivan stopped at the curb and parked. In the passenger seat, a much older man pocketed the phone he'd been distractedly scrolling through during the drive. The woman, pulling chauffeur duty today for her uncle, nodded down at his bandaged and shoeless left foot. She asked, "You want that folding scooter of yours out of the back?"

The salt and pepper-haired man pulled his sunglasses off and deposited them in the front pocket of his shirt. Turning his head slightly, he appraised the concrete steps leading up to the front door of their destination and shook his head. "Nah, be worthless getting in and out of there. I'll just use my crutches this time."

Opening the passenger side door, the man hopped out on one foot before pulling the grey metal crutches from the interior of the minivan. He said to his niece, "This shouldn't take too long. But, knowing Stander, he'll probably pull me a draft. I can give you a call if you want to go do some shopping or grab a quick bite somewhere. You don't have to just sit and wait. I'm not an invalid…"

Retired state detective Tom Secrist wasn't really sure how Stander would take the news he was about to deliver. Or if he'd want to talk much about it after. But Secrist was sure of one thing. He didn't want his niece potentially seeing him fall on his ass trying to get up a couple stair steps. He'd never live that shit down... Secrist waited until the minivan pulled away before sliding the spongy, mustard-colored pads of each crutch under his arms and looking warily up at the concrete steps ahead of him.

Aptly named "In This Corner," the bar's entrance spilled patrons down three steps and a mere ten feet from a quiet street corner. Built of brick, the building had held numerous hopeful businesses over the preceding decades. Originally built at the turn of the twentieth century, you could find the building's twin in any number of small towns across the Midwest. In that way, it was both unremarkable and comforting. Seemingly always there and, over the last ten years anyway, thought Secrist, a place of easy comfort. It was old but still held its character. Most nights, like any good neighborhood bar, it held its fair share of characters as well.

Secrist, balancing each step of the way precariously, finally cleared the doorway of the bar and made his way inside. As his eyes adjusted to the indoor lighting, he glanced at the many framed black and white photos of various old-time Michigan fighters like Joe Louis and Stanley Ketchel that dotted the walls of the bar. The majority of them were glossy 8X10 autographed photos of boxers and ex-champs that had fought out of Detroit's own world-famous Kronk gym. Lights from a couple dart boards and classic arcade games blinked along one wall, and a TV near the bar was tuned to ESPN with the sound muted.

In an awkward dance with his crutches, Secrist lurched a few steps towards a booth near the front entrance. He didn't trust he could successfully navigate very far over the uneven, wood-slated floor with only a couple inches of circular rubber pad at the end of each crutch for support. As he angled himself around to sit in the booth, he could hear Stander talking with a customer in jeans and a motorcycle shirt perched on a stool at the far end of the bar. He could just make out "....as out of place as a camel in a cornfield" before the two men burst out laughing. Secrist had barely plunged down into his seat when he heard Stander call out to him.

"What the fuck happened to you? You shoot yourself in the foot taking a piss or something?" Stander was smiling broadly as he ribbed the retired detective from behind the bar. A single white towel was slung across his shoulder, and he was already drawing a draft of Guinness, Secrist's favorite beer. "Or are you just angling for some free food and drinks? Got a good sob story and looking for a hand-out?"

"Yeah, yeah, yeah… I'm a regular Tiny Tim now," Secrist replied.

"Oh no. No one would mistake you for Tiny Tim. You? You could be the guy who ATE Tiny Tim, you fat fuck." Except for the lone patron that Stander had been conversing with, the place was empty in the early afternoon of the midweek day. Secrist gave him a smirk and the finger. "Still classy, I see…" Stander responded. Then, tilting a second glass, he poured himself a beer before starting over to the table.

Russell Stander, or just Stander as most people referred to him as was the owner of both the bar and the three-story building it operated out of. Once upon a time, he had been a professional prize fighter, and even now, at 52, he still cut an imposing figure. Although just over six feet, he was built like a fire hydrant: thick neck and wide thighs with muscled arms covered in an array of colorful tattoos. He wore his wavy, little-too-long-for-his-age greying hair and bushy white mustache with the confidence of a man who didn't really care what others thought anymore. He had an ease and sincerity about him rare to find these days. Russell Stander, as anyone who spent much time with him at all would tell you, was a man comfortable in his own skin.

Stander, wearing jeans and a faded Bob Seger concert t-shirt, strolled casually over to the booth. He flipped a couple coasters down on the table that read "Round 1" before setting each glass of beer down. Sliding over to the side opposite Secrist, he slouched with his back against the bar's wall and stretched his legs out. He laid one thick arm on the table and picked his drink up with the other hand. "You are one grim-looking motherfucker today. Someone piss in your cornflakes this morning?"

Secrist snickered a little and then took a swig from his pint. He pulled the glass of beer down from his chin and used the back of his hand to wipe the beige foam out of his mustache and the smile from his lips. Delivering bad news was never fun. But having to share something so morbid with one of his best friends made it even worse. He sighed heavily, fingering the edge of his glass. "Yeah, well, not really here on a social call." Secrist took another glance around the near-empty bar before starting again. "So I always told you we'd find her someday. Sherry, I mean." He paused briefly and added, "We did."

Clearly not expecting this line of conversation, Stander swung his feet off the cushion and sat up. Now focused, he hunched forward over the table as Secrist continued. "A guy, a college student really, was up poking around Mount Arvon. I guess he was doing some kind of research or something on the Native American tribes that used to live around there. Anyway, he stumbled across some bones, and they turned out to be hers. Your sister, Sherry." Secrist looked down and then swallowed another gulp of his Guinness.

"Jesus, man… that's like just 60 miles from here. All these fucking years, and she was that close." Stander blew a big breath of air slowly from his mouth and sunk back into the booth. Shaking his head, he looked past Secrist at a spot somewhere over the detective's right shoulder but not really seeing anything. A barrage of images washed over him all at once. Christmas mornings, his sister tearing into brightly colored packages beside him in a rush. Building sandcastles together on the beach, the day Sherry got her first car, popping popcorn and staying up late to watch movies with his big sister. "I always thought that place felt kind of fucked up to me. The parks and trails and whatnot. Now I guess I know why…" Stander sighed, "You know, I hardly even remember much about her anymore. It's mostly just from old photos that I can even picture her face from." Stander turned his head and faced Secrist again. "And other little bits and pieces here and there. I can still see her bedroom, the color of it, and the music she was always playing. Just silly stuff like that. It's fucking sad…"

"What were you? Like ten or eleven the last time you saw her?" Secrist tipped his glass back again.

"Eight. I was eight when she disappeared," Stander looked away. He was surprised how, despite all the years between, the loss of his big sister still stung him so sharply. Grazed by something he couldn't quite see. But felt just the same.

"Eight? Ten? Whatever. I don't remember anything from when I was that age either." Secrist took another sip from his glass before setting it back on the table.

"I know, I know… But she was my big sister. Even though she was only a half-sister, she was the only sibling I ever had. Period. You, well, you'd think I would recall more of what she was like or something, right? But it just feels like I only have a couple fleeting memories of her... So how am I supposed to feel here?" Stander wraps his thick hands around his cold glass sitting on the table. A couple seconds of silence pass, and then he downs half of its contents in one swallow before placing the glass pint back down on the table. "I guess I just feel numb after all this time. Is that weird? Can't say I am shocked or surprised, really."

"I hear you." Secrist stared at his old friend. A friendship that had started when they both were a lot younger. The then newly promoted state detective Thomas Secrist was eagerly trying to work old cold cases when he'd first met with Stander, hoping he might hear or learn something overlooked by the original investigators some twenty years earlier. They'd remained in contact and eventually, though Stander could be a bit of a loner, became fishing and drinking buddies. They'd grown close over the years despite the lack of new leads on the Sherry Stander disappearance of 1977.

"I may be retired now, but I wanted to be the one to tell you. You know how much I tried… Hell, how much every cop around here tried to figure out what happened to her all these years." Secrist looked down at his glass briefly before raising it to his lips again.

"Well," started Stander slowly, "by the time you began working on this, I'd already known she wasn't ever coming back. So…" Stander downed the rest of his beer, rose to his feet, and walked somberly back to the bar. He slapped the man in the biker shirt, still seated at the bar across his back. Asking if he needed anything before pulling a liquor bottle off the back wall and grabbing a clean glass for himself. Returning to the table, he sat back down and poured a couple fingers of bourbon from the ornately decorated bottle in his hand. He raised the bottle questioningly at Secrist but was waved off. Stander nodded, then downed the drink in one gulp before pouring himself a second one, which he left untouched on the tabletop. "When did this guy find her anyway? Just today?"

"No, it was the day before yesterday. Craig, my last partner before I retired, he called me right away. I guess there was a bracelet found with the remains that had a name on it. It just said Sherry, but he knew right then who it was and how personal this particular case was to me. Of course, our conversation, and the one you and I are having right now, is off the record and never happened. It will likely be weeks before anything official can come out. But the county coroner owes me a favor or two, so he rushed the initial identification of the remains. They still have all her old dental records from before." Secrist paused, trying to weigh how much he should say this soon and here at the bar. "You know, from when we thought maybe she was one of those other girls from, uh… you know, before."

Stander was peering into the glass of the amber-colored liquor in front of him. After a couple moments, he looked back across the table and gave Secrist his best "what else" look. "So how did she die? When? Was she one of those other girls from before or not?"

Finishing his beer, the retired cop answered slowly. "They

honestly don't know yet. The body would be bones after all this time. Craig said they pulled some potential evidence they are still sifting through, and the coroner hasn't determined the cause of death yet. But he swore as soon as he learned anything, he would let me know. I suppose I could have waited until they had all that figured out and everything became official. But I thought you would want to know right away that she'd finally been found."

"Yeah, no… Yeah, you are right. Thanks for coming down here and telling me." Stander was motionless, staring into space once again. Recalling that awful night over forty years ago when Sherry didn't come home. The desperation in his father's eyes and the sympathetic looks of the policeman who came to their house when his dad reported her missing. After a few moments, Stander continued. "I guess it all doesn't really matter much now anyway." Secrist waited another minute in silence before pushing himself up using the booth's table and stood. He wrestled his crutches out from the seat beside him.

"I'll touch base with you again when I get those answers. Might be a phone call next time since I ain't very nimble right now." Secrist gestured down at his bandaged foot. "You know my foot had been bothering me forever. Finally got bad enough that I showed my doctor. 'Hammer toe,' he calls it. Said I needed to fix it. Re-routed some tendons and straightened my toe back out before it became permanent." Stander was nodding, but Secrist knew his mind was elsewhere. "Anyway, it was just a one-day outpatient thing followed by like six weeks with no weight on it. Four more days now and," Secrist lifted his crutches slightly, "I finally get to ditch these."

"Can I see? Where was she found at?" Stander looked a little embarrassed as he blurted his request out. But Secrist had expected the question.

"That might be a little tricky. Right now, I'm sure things are all taped off, and people are going over every inch of the ground out there. It might be a little bit before they finish all of that, but yeah. You and I taking a little look around won't really hurt anything.

We'll just need to keep all this to ourselves." He paused a beat and then added, "How about we wait until I get off these crutches? That should be enough time for all the critical work of the investigation to be completed. I'll see if Craig can let me know when the coast is clear. I don't want to get him in any trouble for sharing any of this with me. But I'm anxious to see everything with my own eyes, too. You OK with that?" Stander bobbed his head up and down in agreement.

Secrist started for the front door before stopping and turning around. "You know, once this gets out, people may come around bugging you about it. I'm sure the official statement will be vague until they get all the final results. Which could still be a while. But you know how folks around here are. No matter what they find out about when or how she died, people will want to try and tie it back to that whack job."

"Yeah, I know. Bring some of that same old shit back up again." Stander drained his glass of bourbon a second time and stood once more. He smiled at Secrist. "And don't worry about me. I won't say anything until it hits the news. Hell, when it does, it'll give the old farts around here something new to talk about for a few weeks." Secrist snorted in agreement before gracelessly shambling towards the front door. Stander followed behind and pulled open the door for him.

"So the guy who found her. Can I know who it was?" Stander propped the entrance open with one foot as he spoke. "I feel like I should buy him a drink or something."

"I bet I can arrange that. Assuming Sherry died when she went missing, he wasn't even born yet. So I doubt the guy would mind talking with us. Craig interviewed him and said he seemed like a decent enough fellow. At least he called it in versus just pretending he didn't see anything, right?" Leaning on one crutch, Secrist pulled out his sunglasses and deposited them on his face. "But let me talk with Craig and hopefully have the final results from the autopsy first, OK? I'll call you when I know more. Fair enough?"

Stander nodded and stood watch until he was sure Secrist

wouldn't break his neck going down the steps. When he safely landed on the sidewalk, Stander waved once and let the door close. He grabbed the bottle and empty glasses off their table before making his way back behind the bar as a thirsty new customer entered the tavern.

Stander busied himself with his order.

CHAPTER 3

10TH CENTURY

THE WIND SCREAMED down the valley. Whether hurriedly scattering or running from the stench of decay it carried was impossible to know. Either way, the smell was what drew them. While the four Norse riders all had witnessed plenty of death in their lifetimes, as well as the wickedness desperate men could do, the scene before them now would leave each badly shaken. Their eyes were forever seared by the sights encountered that day.

"What manner of butchery is this?" Gunnar dismounted, his face contorted as he covered his nose and mouth from the riot of rot. Ahead of him lay the ruins of a small settlement, not Norse but familiar just the same. The native peoples of the land.

"Skraelings…" Erik spat out disgustedly. "More animals than man." Erik was Gunnar's brother in spirit, if not in the flesh. The two had grown up together in these lands after traveling across the seas to Vinland as boys with their families. Gunnar was glad Erik was by his side now. The massacre before them had stolen his breath and much of his courage. "The dark-skinned ones of this place have wretched ways." Erik swung down from his horse as well, both young men casting their eyes across the torn and abandoned structures. Most already collapsed. The few cone-shaped dwellings of dried animal skins and skeletal wood poles still standing trembled under the merciless winds whipping all around them.

"Not all who lived here before us are Skraelings, Erik." Gunnar, a head taller than the others of their small hunting party, hated the derogatory name many Norsemen called the locals of Vinland. He cast his eyes over the massacre before them. "What of Nimki and his people? My father says Nimki is as wise as Thorfinn himself." Gunnar began walking silently among the twenty or so bodies spilled along the cold ground. Looking for any movement or signs of life, doubtful as that was. He called down a prayer from Ymir, the creator god of all man sees. He asked for understanding as well as peace and protection from whatever had done this.

"Thorfinn would never have let this happen to our clan." Erik, sword drawn and walking beside Gunnar, touched one of the dead with the end of his foot. Flipping it over and turning the stiff and lifeless form onto its back. The two Norsemen exclaimed loudly at the gruesome find. Hollow holes stared back at them from where the native man's eyes should be. Both eye sockets were torn, ruined, and empty. "Skraelings," Erik repeated, the word laced with disdain. "Left their dead for the beasts and scavengers of the woods."

Gunnar looked out across the remaining carnage they'd stumbled upon. After days out hunting among the wilds of these strange lands, he, like the three others with him, longed only to make it back to their people. Now, less than half a day's ride away from their home, they'd come across this unholy desecration. Though he knew others among their clan resented the black-haired people of this land, Gunnar had only been shown kindness by them in his encounters. Even trading and exchanging with groups of the friendlier natives from time to time. Bartering away a few of the simple woolen garments they'd brought with them when they'd traveled across the seas to reach this new land. Over time, his father had even befriended one of the local tribe's oldest and most respected leaders Nimki. How this small settlement of

Nimki's own people had come to their end disturbed Gunnar greatly.

"Gunnar! Erik! Come see!" Looking up, Gunnar saw the two hunters who'd remained mounted on their horses calling to them, gesturing and yelling over the howling gusts of wind. He stepped over five more bodies, each with the same empty holes where their eyes should have been. It seemed none had been spared this cruel ending. Men, women, and children were all sightless as they'd left this world. Uncared for and sprawled along the cold ground.

"What is it?" In reply, they merely pointed. Here were the half-burned bodies of three more unfortunate natives. The corpses, each decapitated with their heads missing, had been hastily piled upon a crude pyre of sorts. But the fire set had gone out before devouring most of the twisted limbs. Charred and blackened flesh was left falling from bones. Clearly, someone, or something, had attempted to destroy these three.

One of the horseback riders said what Gunnar was thinking. "Where are their heads?" Before he could reply, the second rider asked questions Gunnar had not yet thought about.

"Why are there no animals here anywhere? These deaths are days old, if not longer. Why have they not been devoured? Or been dragged off?" Gunnar, like his companions, had no answers to these disturbing questions.

"We should not be here. This is not for us to understand, and we cannot become involved." Gunnar turned and, along with Erik trailing behind him, both strode quickly back to their tethered and whining horses. Gunnar stepped across an unclothed and slack-jawed child that had likely not yet been weaned from its mother. Its stiff hands made into claws, grasping at nothing as it had died. As the four Norsemen rode out of the small native settlement, hurriedly making their way back towards their own village, Gunnar again silently besieged the great god Ymir.

Praying nothing would follow…

CHAPTER 4

10TH CENTURY

THE SUDDEN POUNDING at the door startled Gunnar, and he knocked his empty cup over. After righting it, he exchanged a puzzled glance with his father as Sassa rose to answer. After a brief greeting and apology for intruding, the older visitor turned to Gunnar.

"Better come quick, Gunnar." It was Tor who urgently pressed forward, a slight man with little hair left on top of his head. As if to make up for that, he wore a long grey beard and a smooth wispy mustache. Tor stroked his beard nervously with one hand as he spoke. "A man has been found, and we think he may be from Thorfinn's village. But we are not for sure where he comes from." It was Gunnar's father who answered first.

"Why are you bothering Gunnar with this? A lost Norse stranger? Surely you can find a room and a place for him tonight in your home. If something about him worries you, send him on." After a brief pause, he added, "I am sure you will make the best decision for us all."

Gunnar's father said this deferentially to Tor. But Gunnar and Sassa both knew well his feelings for the man. Of Tor, Gunnar's father would tell them with a slow smile, "Does not an empty vessel make the hollowest of sounds?" For although Tor was indeed the leader of the Norse village, his power came from his family's past deeds and conquests. Gunnar knew Tor himself liked the idea of being known as the leader, but rarely seemed able to make decisions without counsel. Tor meant well but showed little personal conviction. Sometimes even less wit.

"Is he hurt?" asked Sassa. "Does he seem ill or need attention?" Sassa, green-eyed, fair-haired, and Gunnar's bride-to-be and her mother Sigrid were known as skilled healers among the burgeoning Norse outposts and settlements in Vinland.

"He is unwell true enough, Sassa," said Tor. "He looks a mess and smells twice as bad. We can't really wake him fully, and he mumbles on and on. Your mother is with him now, but she doesn't know what ails him. She thinks a fever maybe, but...." Tor trailed off and looked once more at Gunnar. "He is not right for sure. Will you come and see him?" His eyes pleaded for help. It seemed to Gunnar there must be more that Tor was not saying. He glanced again at his father and could tell by his frown he was thinking the same thing. Gunnar pushed himself away from the small wood table reluctantly. He wrapped himself in a thick woolen garment before following Tor out into the chilly night.

As soon as they were outside, Tor began to speak in hushed whispers in the pale moonlight. Looking up at the much taller and younger man, he moved close to Gunnar as they walked together through the small village towards Tor's home. As if fearing he would be left behind, Tor clasped one hand on Gunnar's long and muscled arm as he began to fill him in on the circumstances surrounding the stranger's appearance.

"The man was found shortly after everyone returned from working in the fields," Tor began. "He was seen near the well at the center of the village acting strangely. Covered in blood. Talking to himself and gesturing in the air before collapsing there. Several men carried him to my home while others tried following his tracks as best they could in the descending nightfall. They said it looked like he may have come down from the mountains. But in the darkness, no one could be sure."

Gunnar stopped walking at this revelation. That was the same direction he'd returned home from several days before. Just beyond the mountain range that rimmed their village was the butchered native settlement he, Erik, and the others discovered. Fleeting images of the torn and twisted faces of the dead he'd seen flashed through his mind. Gunnar quickly pushed them aside with a shudder. Asking, "Does he carry any weapons? Is he a lost hunter or tracker?" It was not unusual for wandering travelers to follow a river until they reached civilization again. Gunnar, who was no stranger to long hunts, had used this same tactic to orient himself a time or two in the past when traveling this land.

"He had no weapons with him. But he has a pouch on him he won't let go of. " Tor looked sideways at Gunnar before continuing in a hushed tone. "He nearly bit a finger off Erik when he tried to take it from him… It must be an object of great value." The two men began the small ascent that led up towards Tor's home.

"What he carries may be of great personal value to him. But who knows what one man treasures over another?" Gunnar was weary and in no mood for Tor's whispers. "We need to leave it be. I doubt a lost man would appreciate having his belongings rummaged through by strangers." He straightened to his full height, towering over the Norse leader to impress upon Tor his feelings on the subject. "We honor him and ourselves by letting that be."

Tor's home sat upon a small hill that overlooked the entirety of the village and stood apart from its closest neighbor. Upon entering, they both briefly greeted those who helped move the stranger and remained gathered inside. Tense and scared, Gunnar knew it wouldn't take much to set the men off. His eyes briefly met Erik's, and Gunnar could tell his friend was more than ready to run the stranger through with his sword and be done with this. But if the tension and their lingering presence bothered Tor, he did not show it as he led Gunnar towards the room where the stranger had been taken.

Tor opened the wood door where the man lay. Stepping inside, Gunnar smelled the stranger before he saw him. Gagging, he nearly vomited at the sudden mixture of blood and death that hung heavy in the air. Gunnar immediately recognized the brutal odor. It was the same stench that had first drawn them to the doomed native's village they had stumbled across only days before. Gunnar tried unsuccessfully to push from his mind the awful twisted faces of those hapless people. But, even sightless, the blank faces still stared back at him. They had haunted him ever since his return home.

Gunnar nodded toward Sassa's mother, Sigrid, as a way of greeting. He watched as Sigrid leaned over the unconscious man from the chair she sat in, wiping his face with a damp cloth. The stranger was lying across a bed in one of Tor's unoccupied rooms, his bare feet filthy and black with dirt. Candlelight flickered back and forth in the room, trying to fight off the dark shadows it created. The stranger had wiry, overgrown facial hair that obscured his features. His head was matted and crowned with long, unkempt dark hair. To Gunnar's eye, the man seemed small and unremarkable. Sleeping fitfully and mumbling incoherently but indeed clutching the brown bag, Tor had commented on. The animal skin bag seemed out of place on the man; it was not worn nor ragged like his clothing piled next to the bed. In fact, it appeared clean and well cared for. Gunnar addressed Sassa's mother as he eyed the man warily. "What do you think is wrong with him, Sigrid? Has he said anything at all?" She pulled back from the man and pointedly drew a deep breath away from the pungent smell radiating off him.

"He is feverish. Mumbles on and off, especially if you try and take that pouch from him. But I think he is exhausted as much as anything. Maybe half starving to death as well." She looked down again at the slumbering stranger. "He is all skin and bones. I don't see any sores or wounds on him anywhere. Which surprises me."

"Why does that surprise you?" asked Gunnar. In response,

Sigrid stood and moved to the stranger's clothes heaped together at the end of the bed. She gently lifted the corner of a woven sleeved garment of Norse design. The putrid smell in the room, barely tolerable when they'd entered, grew even thicker. Gunnar picked up a lit candle from the side table and held it out as Sigrid gestured where the frayed garment was black and hardened stiff. He pinched his nose shut as he peered intently at where Sigrid pointed. A moment later Gunnar looked up at her with a puzzled expression on his face.

Sigrid returned his gaze evenly. "Blood. All along his back but not his front. And one arm on his coat is just as heavy with it." She pointed at the floor where the remaining garments lay before slowly releasing her grip on the stiff, coarse shirt. Gunnar nudged the filthy and vile-smelling coat with his foot, unwilling to touch anything this man possessed. "I don't figure that any of it is his. The blood has to be days old now. Maybe more." She turned to Tor, saying, "I didn't want to leave him alone, so I left his clothes in here. Can you take them out when you leave?" Tor nodded wordlessly, his eyes still on the man. Sigrid turned back to the stranger as well. "It is a miracle the wolves didn't eat him alive smelling like that, especially if he came down from the mountains."

Tor said what Gunnar was thinking but knew there was no clear answer. "Is it another man's blood?"

"There is no way to tell if it is animal blood or not. All I know is it can't be his. As thick as it is on him, if it was a man's, I can't believe that man could still be walking. But as weak and sick as he is, I don't know how he could have recently fought a man…"

"Didn't have to come from a grown man," Gunnar spoke without thinking and immediately regretted it. Quickly adding, "It must be from some animal. He probably got lost out hunting. Whatever he killed was perhaps carried on his back as it bled out."

"But who hunts with his bare hands? Or alone in those mountains?" Gunnar could tell Tor was working himself up. The large summits bordering their village had a long history of suspicions and tall tales told late at night. Gunnar cut Tor off before his ramblings affected Sigrid. Or worse yet, the men waiting just outside the door.

"Most likely he lost any weapons or traps he had. Maybe the wolves did get at him or scared him, and he dropped everything and ran. We can know more when he wakes up. Until then, all the guessing we do doesn't mean a thing. For now, I suggest keeping any wild ideas to yourself, Tor. We'll help him as we would want any of our brothers to be aided."

Tor looked on doubtfully. Gunnar understood the unease and could appreciate his concern. He knew having a stranger in your home who has yet to speak is unnerving enough; covered in blood and maybe sick, another. Gunnar placed his large hand gently on the older and smaller man's shoulder. "It is a good thing to help another Norseman in need, Tor. Maybe you and Sigrid can take turns watching over him tonight. I am sure when he wakes, he will have as many questions for us as we do of him."

Gunnar turned to Sigrid once more and asked, "Should I send Sassa? Do you need anything from home?" Sigrid shook her head back and forth as she continued to tend to the stranger. Gunnar felt relief that Sassa would not have to be around the man tonight. He found himself hastening to leave the room and get back home. Telling himself, he was just uncomfortable in the crowded house and in the room with that stifling smell.

But once outside and alone in the fresh night air, Gunnar found little relief from his worries. As he and Tor had made their way over to the Norse leader's house, a full moon had bathed all the simple dwellings of their village in pale light. Now, as Gunnar strode quickly back home, the moon slid silently behind the gathering dark clouds above the village. As if it had suddenly grown ashamed.

Or afraid.

CHAPTER 5
10TH CENTURY

GUNNAR WOKE EARLY the next morning as the bright light of the rising sun forced its way past the wood shutters in his bedroom. Groggy and poorly rested with last night's sleep fitful at best, he rubbed absentmindedly at the raised circular birthmark on the back of his shoulder before getting dressed. Moving to the kitchen, he lit a fire that chased the last lingering cold away as his father limped slowly out of his room and joined him at the lone table in the center of the home. After a bit of small talk, they ate together mostly in silence, as was their way. Upon his return home last night, Gunnar had filled his father in on the lost Norse stranger. But he'd downplayed the amount of dried blood on the man and left out the unease he'd felt in the stranger's presence.

Gunnar's father had lost most use of his left arm and leg some years back. It had not been an accident or anything one saw. He simply went to sleep one night and woke the next morning unable to feel or use one side of his body. Sigrid had said it was not unusual for men of his age, but it still bothered Gunnar to see his father so feeble. When he was younger Gunnar's father seemed larger than life; indestructible even. Though nowhere near as tall as

Gunnar grew to be, he had been an imposing man in the village. In Gunnar's eyes, there had been nothing his father could not do.

As he'd grown, Gunnar had adopted his father's love for the strange new world they now called home. Together, father and son spent days and weeks at a time exploring and living off the land. Tracking wild beasts, hunting, trapping, fishing, and even harvesting directly from the untamed lands that surrounded their village. His father taught Gunnar how to find edible berries, roots, and plants almost anywhere. Showing him how to read the moss on the trees and rocks along the riverbeds, how to navigate waterways by the stars, where to find shelter, and build simple structures for safety or for cover. The bond he developed with his father on these trips was unbreakable.

Gunnar loved his father, and it was hard seeing him now struggle with even the simplest of tasks. Each day he seemed to grow a little weaker... But despite outward appearances, his mind was still just as alert and sharp as ever. His father was by far the wisest man Gunnar knew, and he was still well respected in their community despite the betrayal of his aging body. Before heading out to work in the fields, Gunnar fed the fire and stoked it up hot, then made sure there was plenty of wood nearby if his father needed it.

As he headed towards the fields, Gunnar decided to surprise Sassa before beginning his day's work. He cut across the small village and made his way towards Sigrid and Sassa's home. His unexpected arrival, as he hoped, clearly delighted his love. Her joyful smile briefly melted Gunnar's fears from the night before, and all felt right once again in his world. Sassa invited him in, and they embraced warmly, kissing deeply in the solitude, sheltered from prying eyes. Her softness in the early morning light emboldened Gunnar. He surprised even himself with his sudden, unplanned, and bold proclamations. The conversation and his words felt both long overdue and a revelation at the same time.

"Sassa," Gunnar started, "I want us to be joined eternally. You know this to be true." Sassa remained smiling and nodded in agreement. The topic was not a new one for either of them. "Let us not tarry any longer. I want us to be one, now and forever. The supreme god, Ymir, has once again delivered us from the cold grasp of winter. So let us do the ceremony among the early blooms of the spring flowers when all of nature can celebrate with us." Gunnar reached out and brushed the welling tears he knew were of joy from Sassa's pale face. He lowered himself to her and kissed her wet cheek.

Sassa spoke softly in his ear. "Yes, oh yes, Gunnar! Let us do this now. I watch you run through my mind as I dream. You are what I think of each night when I lay down to sleep, and you are the first question on my tongue each morning when I wake. Let's answer this question together." A sob escapes, but she smiles radiantly up at Gunnar. "You make me so happy! I can't wait to tell mother. She will be so pleased." Sassa fell into Gunnar, and he picked her off the ground, twirling her around effortlessly, both of them laughing in their shared exuberance.

Before leaving for the day's chores, the young lovers agreed that sharing the news should wait until the stranger's arrival was sorted out. Gunnar wanted Sassa to share the happy announcement with the village and not have it tainted in any way by the stranger's sudden appearance. As Gunnar trekked his way out towards the fields, his shoes grew wet in the morning dew. The morning sun left the previous night's deep frost cowering amongst shadows with spring on its way. He turned his face up to the warm morning rays as he walked, thanking and calling down a blessing from Ymir above. His smile had never felt brighter or warmer.

Later that morning, word began to spread among those working the fields that a number of goats had gone missing. The normally contented and docile animals had broken free from their pens near the edge of the village. Gunnar, joined by Erik and a few others, headed out to help search the surrounding area and round them back up. Heading out across the lowlands, the Norsemen spread out until they'd picked up the trail left by the fleeing goats. The freshly created path of trampled weeds and hoof prints was easy to follow in the thawing springtime mud. The tracks led away from the village and, oddly, seemed to be heading into a patch of trees that dead-ended at a series of natural bluffs overlooking a small valley. Climbing the incline, the group of searchers soon came face to face with one of the missing goats. It was the herd queen, an older alpha doe, and she was limping. On top of her head, one of her horns was also missing. A fresh injury, the fractured end of it jagged and splintered.

"Here now," one of the villagers in charge of the goat herd walked slowly up to the big doe. He had a simple leash prepared, and he held it out in front of him as he advanced. "Let's get you back home. See about that broken horn... Get it caught on something, old girl?" Gunnar and the others looked on as he stretched the crude lasso out. "Where are the..." But the question was never finished. As he'd reached out to rein in the escaped goat, she'd suddenly turned on him. Abruptly charging forward and head butting him once viciously in the stomach. Surprised, the villager tried to turn away but still took the brunt of the blow in his midsection, instantly crumbling to the ground. The man began to moan and clutch his belly, rolling in agony among the mud and weeds. When he pulled his hand away moments later, it was covered in slick blood. The shattered horn had torn and gouged his side. After the brief attack, the goat had merely taken several steps back. Standing and watching impassively, blood dripping down from the end of its broken horn and panting hurriedly.

As the other villagers rushed to his aid, Gunnar and Erik moved to take the injured man's place and recapture the rogue goat. But seeing their advance, the goat turned and ran up the hill, disappearing at the end of the tree line and crest of the cliffs. Gunnar and Erik reached the summit in quick pursuit. Barely stopping themselves in the slick mud before toppling over the side. Looking over the edge, at the bottom of the bluff, Gunnar and Erik found all of the missing goats.

They were all dead.

Each had fallen, been pushed, or leaped over the side of the rocky cliff. Their unmoving bodies piled close together at the bottom of the overhang. The one exception was the defiant female doe who'd just attacked her keeper. She'd partially landed on top of the body of one dead goat. But in the fall, one of her eyes had been ruptured, and it now hung from a bloody strip of meat. Her tongue was lolling listlessly in and out of her mouth while she bleated out terrible "Maaahs!" one after another.

Her front legs were shattered.

"What has gotten into these…?" Erik began as both he and Gunnar looked down at the pile of broken bodies. "She must have gone mad and led them all to their death." Erik shook his head. "Or did she push and head-butt them over the side?"

"Or they all jumped…" But Gunnar had never heard of such a thing. "Something must have spooked them. Wolf perhaps?" But they'd seen no wolf tracks along the trail or at the top of the cliff.

"I'll let the others know we found them. They'll have to get a wagon to cart them back." Erik turned and began walking back down the side of the cliff. "I'll go down and put her out of her misery," he said as he drew his sword.

Gunnar merely nodded. His eyes and ears filled with the death throes and screams of the dying goat as he turned away. He helped carry the injured villager into his home, then headed back out to the field. Looking to lose himself in simple labor and give his guarded and anxious feelings a rest. Greatly disturbed by the gruesome scene he'd witnessed, he ignored the shocked questions of those he worked alongside. Gunnar had no answers for what had happened and what he'd seen. Eventually, those closest to him gave up trying to draw Gunnar into their musings.

In the late afternoon, Tor appeared in the field on horseback. Dismounting in front of Gunnar, he strode purposefully across the yet-to-be-broken ground of the new field. Stopping, Gunnar leaned against his long-handled ax and waited for Tor to speak. As he expected, Tor did not bring up the escaped goats or how they'd been found. As always, he focused only on himself.

"Come and feast with us tonight, Gunnar. I promise there will be a large spread, and you can meet the newcomer." It wasn't really a question. Gunnar wiped his brow on his sleeve before answering.

"Very well. Is my father invited?"

"Of course," Tor exclaimed a little too brightly. "I rode over and asked him already. They'll be a few others coming to dine also."

A few beats passed. "You mean the other elders?" Gunnar said simply.

"Yes." Tor was a terrible bluffer. His smile now more like a grimace the longer he wore it. Gunnar wanted to know why Tor was calling the village elders together in council. The peace Gunnar hoped would accompany the stranger's return to consciousness evaporated. He noted the small group their discussion was drawing. He gave Tor the pass he knew he was hoping for.

"And what of the stranger?" Gunnar asked. "Is he... Feeling well?"

"As well as can be expected." Gunnar could see the visible relief on Tor's face when he hadn't pressed the issue of calling the elders together. But they both knew it was highly unusual to gather them so quickly and unexpectedly. Tor, for the first time, raised his voice so the lingering eavesdroppers would hear.

"Sigrid is with him and still aiding the man. He had some soup earlier, but he is very weak. He seems more reasonable, but we have learned little yet. He knows Thorfinn, of course, but he is part of a newer clan settlement growing between our home and Thorfinn's. I have no doubt he will be up and around soon. Until then, I will do all I can to be sure he is well cared for." Then, using Gunnar's own words from the night before, he added, "We honor him and ourselves by helping one in need." Murmurs of agreement from the group met these words.

Tor faced Gunnar once more. "Sigrid has been with him all night and this day. Have Sassa accompany you tonight so she can give her mother some relief." Gunnar nodded an agreement, and his eyes followed Tor as he turned and remounted his horse. He watched him ride back the way he had come, now wary of what the upcoming evening might bring.

Soon Gunnar gathered his things and, uncharacteristically for him, left the fields early. He wanted to get himself cleaned up and allow enough time to help his father make the long walk. He would stop by Sigrid and Sassa's home as well to let Sassa know she was expected and help her gather the things she may need. As he headed back towards the village, Gunnar wondered if he would even be able to eat. He admitted curiosity about the man, but the thought of being in the same room with the stranger was the last thing he desired. Conversing with the god Ymir once more, but now much as he did as a boy, Gunnar found himself repeating the prayers of strength and protection he'd learned as a small child long ago.

Shortly, Gunnar reached the outskirts of the little community he had known nearly all his life. He paused and took in the humble huts of wood, twig, and stone. Smoke rose from several of the dwellings, likely from baking bread for tonight's event. Or perhaps where a goose or two had been sacrificed and was being prepared.

Still standing, he imagined wrapping his long arms around every structure in sight, embracing what was his home. But his love mixed with a new and unknown fear for this place. Gunnar couldn't help but recall the blind and ruined bodies of the local native settlement his hunting party had stumbled upon. He thought again of the rancid smell and the small native child he'd callously had to step over before leaving. The way its tiny arms had seemed to be reaching out. The baby dying alone, empty-handed…

Troubled by these strange new feelings, he inhaled and exhaled a deep breath. Then, moving once more, he went to gather Sassa and his father for the feast.

CHAPTER 6

PRESENT DAY

TRUE TO HIS WORD, Secrist contacted Stander by phone that next week. They agreed to meet the following Monday morning when Secrist would be comfortable enough to walk and drive himself unassisted once again. Stander, dressed in an old Ted Nugent concert t-shirt, blue jeans, and weathered boots, was seated on the grey concrete steps in front of his bar when the car pulled up to the curb. Although overcast with clouds that threatened rain, it was a warm day and the forecast hadn't actually called for precipitation all week. The two men exchanged greetings and soon were rolling out of town.

"You ready for this?" Secrist was eyeballing Stander as he asked the question. It wasn't every day you went to the woods to see the shallow, unmarked grave of a family member missing for over 40 years. He wanted to know where Stander's head was at. "You sleep OK last night?"

"You know what they say; only a mad dog sleeps undisturbed." Stander gave Secrist his usual smartass look. "So, like always, I slept like a fucking rock." Secrist was satisfied he was pretty much his usual Stander-like-self, so he continued on.

"I know you likely have a million questions about all this and what happened. But like I said the other day, this is my first time even seeing the area myself. So let's wait until after we get up there and actually meet with the guy that found Sherry before we get into all that." Secrist paused. Deep down, he knew he was just delaying the inevitable. "His name is Ethan Glaser, by the way. I guess he's been working up in that area pretty much every day this summer. He told me he would keep an eye out for us so you can meet him."

"What is he working on up there again? Looking for old Indian arrowheads and stuff?" Stander thought that was something only kids did, or maybe Boy Scouts, but not grown men.

"Not exactly. He's a student working on his degree in Native American Studies or something like that. According to him anyway, the area around Mt. Arvon had indigenous settlements all over it back in the day. He is up there hunting old artifacts and clues about how they lived. Said he'll end up writing a paper on the original people who lived there. Before all us white men came and ruined everything." Secrist shrugged as he drove. "I'll let him fill you in if you really want to know more. I only talked to him briefly on the phone."

"I do want to thank the guy. He could have easily just left her there on the ground." Stander turned and looked out the passenger window. Secrist decided to leave him alone with his thoughts for a bit and settled in for the drive. It was only some 60-odd miles "as the crow flies" from Marquette to Mt. Arvon. However, with no direct roads between the two places, the drive would take a couple hours. But Secrist wasn't complaining. It felt good being back behind the wheel of a car and in control of his own destiny once again. He'd hated being shuttled around by his niece like an invalid over the last few weeks.

As Stander had climbed into the front seat of the car, he'd pushed aside a folded copy of that weekend's local newspaper that Secrist left lying across the passenger seat. An hour into the drive, he unfolded it and began reading. As predicted, the morbid discovery of Sherry Stander's skeleton was front page news in the small lakeside community of Marquette.

The uncreative headline read "1977 Missing Teen Found." Sherry's high school picture, which had been taken mere weeks before her disappearance, was directly under the bold print. Even in the basic two-color black and white print newspaper, it was easy to see from the photo that she had been a beautiful girl. She shared Stander's smile, and if the picture had been in color, any reader would have been dazzled by her beautiful blue eyes. Stander skimmed over the newspaper article and was gratified to see it didn't mention him at all. The writer just rehashed details he already knew by heart. At the end of the story, it promised more to come in the following days. Frowning, he tossed the paper into the backseat of the car.

Secrist's sedan continued barreling down the two-lane blacktop highway. Passing old barns and the occasional corn or bean field, they drove alongside pastures holding unimpressed cows chewing lethargically. Gradually, the fields of crops gave way to more wooded areas. Soon the trees on either side of the road crowded in on them and grew dense. Houses and most signs of civilization faded away. As they crested various hills, brief glimpses of valleys, gullies, and ravines were visible. The closer they got to their destination, the harder it was to see more than a few yards into the forest on either side of the car. The road narrowed to barely more than one lane and, though still paved, lost all its paint. After a few more turns, they began to ascend in elevation as they drew closer to the mountain. Here the forest seemed to be dominated by pine trees. Tall and skinny, mostly branchless near the ground, they soared high above the car as it made its way up the side of the mountain.

Secrist took a sharp left on a barely visible stretch of gravel road. The car rolled and rocked along muddy potholes and the zigzagging ditches cut by earlier spring rains. Soon the road ended into a makeshift parking lot. As they drove in, they saw a single older maroon Toyota Tundra pickup truck ahead of them, driverless and parked. Pulling alongside the truck, Secrist kills the engine, and both men get out of the car. Secrist groans and hobbles for a few steps, shaking his left foot out and limping a bit before gradually walking with a more normal gait.

"That must be Ethan's truck." Secrist gestured at the back of the pickup truck, which was empty except for a crinkled blue plastic tarp folded up in the corner. "Let's give him a few minutes before we head over to the site. He said he would stick close by and be watching for us."

"Sounds good." Stander pulled out his phone to make sure he hadn't missed any messages during the winding climb up into the dense forest and mountain range. Though the phone didn't show anything was missed, he noted the cellular device had no signal. Still holding his phone, he asked Secrist, "Why don't I have any bars or service? Is that normal up here?"

"Not sure about normal. But Craig mentioned while investigating up here, no one could get any cell service either. Said you have to go back almost to the blacktop road before you can get a signal." Secrist shrugged in a way that showed it didn't bother him. "Why? You need to check Facebook or something?"

"Yeah, you know me. Gotta have those likes to build up my self-esteem." Stander accepted his friend's good-natured ribbing and pocketed the phone. Opening his arms and gesturing around him in a half circle, he said, "Man, this really is out in the boonies, though, isn't it? I have been out here a few times in the past, but I don't recognize any of this. Where is the state park and all the trails?"

"Most of the campgrounds aren't really that close to here. The trails are mostly on the other side, kind of south of where we are now. No one really comes over this way much except snowmobile riders in the winter. It's kind of hard to get to this side of the peak. The few who do come up here just want to see Skull Rock and…. Ah, that must be Ethan now." Secrist waved his hand in greeting, and Stander turned.

Ethan approached the parked vehicles from the woods. The

grad student had a faded red bandanna tied around his balding forehead and was pulling a pair of leather gloves off as he walked toward the two new visitors. The three men shook hands, introduced themselves, and exchanged a few pleasantries. Each commented about the long drive and isolated area around them. After a few minutes, they began to make their way into the woods, cutting across a small game trail and stepping around a few downed trees. They followed a recent path made by the officers and coroner staff who had been on site much of the last week. Stander and Secrist somberly followed Ethan as he led them to a spot less than 100 yards from where the vehicles were parked.

They reached a patch of razed earth where the forensic team had combed over parts of the forest floor for any clues or evidence that might still remain. Brightly colored yellow and black two-toned barricade tape had been strung up and tied to several full-grown trees, cordoning off a swath of area within the woods. Secrist lifted the tape so each man could duck under it and move closer. Silently, they followed footprints stamped into the soft soil that led to a large indentation in the ground.

The three men stood over the hollowed-out earth where the remains of Sherry Stander had been crudely interred. Ethan spoke softly, repeating what he'd already told the officers who first responded. Filling the two older men in on how he'd discovered what was left of her body. He pointed to the still visible white flags he had planted in the ground nearby and their proximity to the area he'd been focused on at the time. After a few minutes, he stopped talking, and an awkward silence fell between the three men. In unison, both Ethan and Secrist slowly backed away from the gaping hole the investigators left, giving Stander some space and time to himself. In hushed tones, the retired detective and student conversed about the investigation's likely next steps and what Ethan could expect to happen over the next several weeks.

After some time, Stander drifted back towards the two other men, gradually joining the conversation and getting Secrist's perspective on the site. He purposefully avoided asking specific questions related to Sherry's death, the length of time she was buried, or any clues that might have been recovered. That could wait until the drive back home. Stander felt like he needed some time to process what he just saw and preferred to not be around someone he had just met when hearing those revelations for the first time. He also doubted Secrist would want to say much around Ethan anyway.

Ethan himself struck Stander as an honest and straightforward kind of guy. Maybe a little dorky and awkward, but that was not a big deal. Stander actually felt kind of bad for the young man. His work was interrupted for god knows how long, and who wants to be working alone in such a desolate place like this and find a body? It had to be unnerving. The woods around Mt. Arvon had always seemed creepy to Stander. Today certainly didn't dissuade any of those feelings for him. Like most Yoopers, as locals in the upper part of Michigan call themselves, Stander knew this mountain already had its fair share of old ghost stories and legends too.

Talk about spooky...

As the site visit wrapped up an hour or so later, the three men headed back to their parked vehicles together. Stander shook Ethan's hand, thanking him once again for having the courage to report his discovery. "Listen, I own a little place back in Marquette. I want you to come by and let me buy you dinner. It's nothing fancy, and our menu is pretty limited. But we do a decent cheeseburger, and I'd like to sit down and have a drink or two with you."

Secrist cut in and said to Ethan, "His place makes some of the best drinks in town. Get him to make you one of those... what are they called? Painkillers?" Stander nodded, smiling. "It's pineapple juice with rum poured over ice, and it's perfect after being outside on a hot summer day. And believe me, the way they mix 'em at Stander's place, you will soon be pain-free!"

Ethan laughed. "Sure, why not? That would be nice. I'm usually starved after being up here all day. Some cold drinks to help wash down a cheeseburger or two would hit the spot."

"Great! It's settled then." Stander stuck out his hand for a second time and shook hands with Ethan again. "I really do mean it when I say thank you. I'm grateful that I know where Sherry ended up and that I can finally get some answers about what happened to her. This is one of those things I had almost given up on. You did a good thing here, Ethan..."

Once they were back in their car and off the bumpy gravel road, Stander turned to Secrist. "Now tell me what happened to her, Tommy. How did my sister end up buried alone in the woods in the middle of fucking nowhere?"

CHAPTER 7
PRESENT DAY

"THERE REALLY WASN'T any useful physical evidence pulled from the site near the body. What little was found probably couldn't be tied directly to much of anything after all this time." Secrist began recounting the secrets Sherry Stander's skeleton had, until now, kept to itself. Details he'd gleaned from the official file conveniently left out on the desk of his ex-partner while he'd taken a well-timed, and extended, bathroom break during Secrist's recent visit to his old office. "The body itself had remnants of clothing that matched what she was reported to have been wearing when she disappeared. There were bits of jewelry that were consistent with what we knew she wore as well. In short, there was really nothing around or on the body that wasn't from Sherry herself."

Between curves on the twisty road, Secrist turned and looked at Stander, who was watching him as he spoke. "It had been 40 years, and it was not a deep grave. Most everything had washed away or had become part of the forest by now. Father Time devours the present..."

"So what are you saying? The cops can't say anything even though they have her body?" Stander had watched way too many

Dateline episodes and true-life crime documentaries on Netflix to swallow that.

"That's not what I said," Secrist started again. "I'm saying there is no other physical evidence that contradicts what her remains tell us happened to her. You following me here?" Stander nodded in agreement and sat back a little in his seat. Secrist had purposefully started the conversation this way, knowing it would answer a lot of questions upfront that Stander or anyone in his situation would have.

Secrist took a deep breath and then continued on, "The cause of death will officially be labeled a homicide. She was strangled, most likely from behind, by someone with a fair amount of strength. There is a U-shaped bone in the neck called the hyoid. It ends up being fractured in like a third of known homicides by strangulation. So we got lucky there. It made this is all, unfortunately, pretty straightforward." He paused again to let this information sink in before continuing. Stander didn't seem to have any questions yet, so Secrist went on, "Her bones tell us Sherry died at the same age she went missing, and she was buried shortly thereafter. There is no question she had remained at that same location until Ethan stumbled upon her."

"Fine, fine, fine… That all makes sense to me. But who did this? Why her?" Stander felt both enraged and defeated. He'd expected all of this. He supposed deep down he really had been expecting it for years now. When Secrist first told him Sherry's remains had been found, Stander had felt numb. But now, he could feel the sharp edge of raw emotions flooding through him. Sherry had been so vibrant, so full of life. Knowing she'd met her grisly end all alone in those dark woods, likely terrified and crying out for her family, made him sick to his stomach. Stander wiped at his eyes with hands he had to control from shaking, a little surprised and embarrassed at his reaction. But what else did he expect to hear?

"Are we ever going to know who did this to her? She was seventeen, man. Just turned seventeen and ended up tossed away in the dirt... I mean, what the fuck? What the goddamn fuck is wrong with people."

"Plenty wrong with her killer. Plenty." Secrist stared out the front windshield as he spoke. He'd known this conversation was coming and even though he'd delayed it during the drive up, Secrist still dreaded what he'd say now that the time had come.

Stander jumped at the revelation. "So what are you saying? That you know who did this?" He paused as the wheels turned in his mind. "Aw Jesus... She was one of those girls, wasn't she? That's how you know, isn't it? That crazy freaking guy? That Jimmy Tathum dude. He did this? You're sure?"

Secrist nodded.

"James Tathum killed at least two girls that we know of for sure. They caught him back in 1978, trying to grab another one. Still had her in his trunk when he was arrested. She survived and confirmed he was her abductor. That allowed the investigators at the time to get search warrants and hone in on him as the key suspect in several other cases of missing girls from around that same time. Including Sherry. Now we know he got her as well." Secrist stopped talking as he swerved to avoid a rabbit that darted out from the side of the road. "I'm sorry, Russ. I am so sorry to be the one telling you all this."

Secrist, before he'd retired, often had to speak with family members of victims. Sometimes they were strangers. Other times they were folks he knew or got to know over the course of an investigation. It was never easy, but if you wanted to be a detective, it came with the badge. Having to talk with Stander and see him like this was really difficult. But he also knew even though he would try to avoid it, the worst of what he would say was still coming. As expected, it didn't take long for Stander to ask the question Secrist didn't really want to answer.

"How do you know it was him if she was strangled? Can they tell that by the way her neck was broken? Like it was done a certain way or something?"

"It doesn't really matter anymore, does it? Doesn't change

anything. Just trust me on this, alright. We found Sherry. We know it is her. We all kind of suspected she hadn't just run away or anything."

"I told you I always knew she didn't do that."

"I know. I know. I'm just saying, what does it matter how they tie her back to Tathum? I am telling you it was him. They know who killed her, and he is dead and rotting in hell. Good riddance. Nothing much good ever came from that whacko, and nothing good comes from hearing any more about him. Bad enough I have to live with shit like…." Secrist stopped himself, fearing he already went too far. He peered out of the corner of his eye at Stander, hoping he hadn't heard him or would just let it drop. No luck. Stander was looking right at him from the passenger seat.

"Fuck you, Tom Secrist. You tell me right now what you fucking know. You owe me that. Tell me everything. You. Fucking. Tell. Me." Secrist glanced over at him and could see a vein bulging along the side of Stander's neck. He knew that meant his friend was getting wound up.

"Jesus, Stander. Calm down." Secrist took one hand off the wheel and raised it in a display of submission. "Relax, man. You'll give yourself an aneurysm. I'm just saying since Jimmy Tathum has been dead almost as long as Sherry, it's not like it matters. I am trying to save you some messed-up stuff. To be honest, I wish I had never heard and read all this from the old case files. The guy was a complete freak."

"Quit stalling and blabbering. Spit it out. How could they tell which victims were his? How do you know he was the one who killed Sherry?"

"I am not stalling. But you need to promise me you'll never repeat a word of this. I mean it. You can get Craig and me in a lot of trouble if it ever comes out that I told you." Instead of responding, Stander just gave him a withering look of sarcasm and made a crisscross sign over his heart. "Not one word. If a reporter caught wind of this… I just started collecting my pension, and I don't want any BS like this to screw that up. You hear me?"

"When have I ever betrayed anything you have ever said? Drunk or sober, I might add… Anyway, I promise. OK? This stays between us. Now, what is it?"

Secrist took a moment to gather himself. Outside the car, signs of civilization were coming back as they exited the small mountain range Mt. Arvon was nestled in. That was good because when Secrist talked about or even thought about James Tathum, Marquette's local boogeyman, he didn't like feeling isolated. The guy had been a human monster. "So you know how he died, right? That was way before my time, and you would have still been a kid. But there were plenty of rumors and gossip leaked out from some of the people involved."

Stander frowned. "All I know is he supposedly killed himself. I think you told me when you started looking for Sherry that he'd done that even before the trial started. That's all I really ever knew." Stander reflected for a moment. "One night, some guy at the bar told me the devil himself incinerated Tathum in his cell. I didn't take him seriously, though…" Stander arched an eyebrow at Secrist.

"That guy was probably just drunk," Secrist snorted. "What I told you back then was right, though. He killed himself in the county jail and never made it to trial. The story was that he did it because he knew he couldn't win with all the evidence and the witness."

"So what was the big deal then? He killed himself and saved the state a bunch of money. How is that news or rumor-worthy?" Stander didn't care if Tathum killed himself or not as long as the guy was dead. He just wanted to understand the guy's tie to Sherry. Why her?

"It wasn't that he killed himself; it was how he did it. The county jail he was being held in didn't hold a lot of prisoners or have a lot of cells. I guess Tathum ate his meals alone most of the time." Secrist shrugged, "Not really sure if that was his request or just how they did things back then. But during a meal, supposedly without anyone noticing, his food was served to him along with metal utensils. Not the plastic sporks prisoners were supposed to be served with. Tathum takes the steel cutlery, and, with no warning or signs of stress, he kills himself." Secrist looks over at Stander in the passenger seat of the car.

"He takes hold of a fork in one hand and a spoon in the other. The handles of each facing up and sticking out of his hands. Then puts both fists on the table like this." Driving with one hand on the wheel, Secrist demonstrates by pulling a pen out of his front pocket with his free hand. He encloses it in his right hand, the one closest to Stander, making a fist with the pen sticking up from it and away from his thumb and forefinger. Then puts his fist on the dashboard of the car with the pinky side of his hand pressed against the hard plastic of the car. "See?"

Stander nods.

"He then kills himself by slamming his own head down as hard as he can, face first onto the table." Secrist places the pen back into his shirt pocket and looks over at Stander. Catching the incredulous and quizzical look on his face. "Yeah…for real. He buries the end of each of the two utensils deep into each of his eye sockets. Rams them in, gouging out each of his own eyes in the process. One of them kind of goes sideways on him. Barely even got the eye and then just scraped along the inside of his skull. Doing hardly any damage at all. I mean, compared to the damage he did in the other eye and socket. That one was a… Well, a 'bullseye,' I guess." Secrist smiles grimly at the unintended pun. "Splits his eye right down the middle and ends up plunging it right into his own brain. I guess he lived, or at least his body still lived, for another hour or so before his damaged brain shut his body down completely. Jimmy Tathum died in the back of an ambulance with the end of a fork sticking out of his face."

Stander tried to conjure up the image Secrist had painted for him in his mind. He struggled with even the idea of it. "No fucking way. Are you even serious right now? How is that even possible?"

"Crazy people do impossible stuff, man. And I am telling you, he was bat shit crazy." Secrist accelerated and passed an old Ford pickup truck missing its tailgate. He swerved back into his lane and clicked off his blinker before continuing.

"When I first heard all this, I thought it must be a cover-up. Like it was some BS story, and actually, another inmate killed him. Or hell, maybe even the deputy on duty gave him the steel fork and spoon on purpose. But there were two officers that saw him, and each swore separately what happened. There was no other evidence or anything else to dispute what they said. He did it to himself. He killed himself by cramming cutlery in his eyes." Secrist shook his head. "Unbelievable, huh?"

"Kind of like that Scorpions album cover." Stander cracked half a smile despite the gruesome topic they were discussing. Now it was Secrist's turn to be confused, and it showed on his face. "You know, Blackout by the Scorpions? Rudolf Schenker's head bursting out of the glass with forks bent over his eyes?" Secrist and Stander did not share the same music tastes and what was an iconic image to Stander was obscure at best for Secrist. "Never mind," Stander relented. "So Tathum kills himself in a bizarre and creative way. What does that have to do with tying him to Sherry's murder?"

"Part of the reason the people involved with Tathum's suicide actually believed he did it that way was because of what he had done to his victims." Secrist kept talking, detailing some of the lesser-known parts of Marquette's most infamous killer.

"James Tathum was an only child. His dad was a dentist, and his mom was a teacher, so he came from wealthy and successful parents. Grew up in a big home out in the country off highway 41, about halfway between Marquette and Mt. Arvon. But, by all accounts, he was always seen as a weird little kid. Kind of a loner. Kept to himself at school, had mediocre grades, and didn't play sports or anything. The only thing he really seemed to enjoy was Cub Scouting and later Boy Scouts. He even made Eagle Scout, which I always thought was strange, knowing what we learned about him later on. But anyway, he was big into hiking, camping, fishing, hunting, and all that kind of outdoor stuff. Just loved being in the wilderness and spent a lot of time up around the Mt. Arvon area when he was growing up."

Stander cut in now. "The little freak was probably torturing animals out in the woods. Isn't that what they say serial killers start out with as kids? Pets and animals?"

Secrist gave Stander a non-committal shrug. From his experience in law enforcement, killers came from all sorts of backgrounds. He went on, "I will say, after he was caught, there were all sorts of rumors. Devil worship, animal sacrifices, that kind of thing. But that was what most of it was, just rumors and hearsay. Anyway, we know Tathum was very familiar with the area up where we were just at. He felt comfortable and at home out there alone in that small mountain range. The two other bodies that were found back in the 70s were all in the woods out that way too. The investigators at the time led volunteer searches and had cadaver sniffing dogs out there for days. But that is just a ton of acreage, and it was like hunting for a needle in a haystack. I'm amazed they found what they did at the time. My guess is the two that were found weren't buried as deep as the others. If remains are buried less than two feet down, nature's scavengers will reveal a body in a week or so. So he either rushed or was just lazy with a couple."

Secrist shook his head as he recalled the details of the cold case. "If you ask me, I am sure Tathum buried all of his victims up in those mountains. It just makes sense. He knew the woods all around the area really well and would have known how isolated it was. I'm sure he thought no one would ever find any of the bodies." This time, Secrist acknowledged to himself that he was stalling and avoiding Stander's direct question. He forced himself to finish now that he had started. In the distance, he could see some of the billboards from Marquette starting to come into view.

"So I told you he strangled his victims. That is how he killed every one of them. Even the girl he had just abducted when he was caught had been throttled until she fell unconscious as well. But the two bodies that were found back then had been..." Secrist could feel Stander staring at him. "They had been violated. And not in a normal way."

"What do you mean violated?" He paused, "You mean raped, don't you?" When Secrist didn't immediately answer or meet his eyes, Stander fell silent. He felt sick to his stomach and was no longer sure he wanted to hear the rest. But he recognized that deep down, he needed to hear everything, or it would eat him up inside for the rest of his life. Stander also realized how incredibly uncomfortable this conversation had to be for his friend. He tried to help him out, "So that's it, isn't it? What with DNA and everything you were able to ID him because he raped Sherry?"

Robotically and in monotone, Secrist corrected his friend's assumption.

"Tathum strangled each victim until they were dead. He would load them into the trunk of his car and take them into the woods around the Mt. Arvon area. Then the guy would use one of his dad's dental instruments." Secrist sighed but continued, "He used a dental tool and popped out the eyes of each victim. He scraped all around each eye socket with one of his dad's metal teeth scrapers. Each victim had telltale marks around their orbital bones that were consistent with the other known victims."

As the detective talked, the inside of the car was bathed in the afternoon sunlight. In the bright light, both men's faces appeared set in stone as the final grim details were revealed. "There... there were also traces of semen in the hollowed-out eye sockets of each of the victims." Secrist quit talking for 15 seconds while the car was stopped at a red light. He didn't look over at Stander. The light turned green, and both the driver and the car went on again.

"The prevailing thought at the time was he pleasured himself inside each of his victims." Secrist could still see in his mind's eye the crime scene photos and the empty holes in each girl's head. He hated that he ever looked at those pictures now. "Anyway, not that there was much doubt at that time about where it ...uh... originated from. But in the years since, the semen traces were tested, and it was confirmed to definitively have been from James Tathum..."

"And there were scrapes inside of Sherry's eye sockets." Stander finished for him, surprised to hear how matter-of-fact his voice sounded. Stander couldn't really begin to even process the implications of the last couple of lines Secrist just spoke. Or the next two.

"That is how they know, I mean realistically, are all but sure it was Tathum that murdered Sherry. Same scraping, strangled, and she was buried in those woods..."

Stander didn't want to hear anymore. It wasn't fair, but right now, he felt like he didn't want to hear Secrist's voice ever say anything again. The two men drove in silence the rest of the way across town. Soon pulling up to the building Stander owned, lived, and worked in. Stander opened the passenger car door but remained seated. He asked, staring out of the front windshield and unable to stop himself, "What did he do with them? The eyes, what did he do with the eyes?"

Secrist remained stoic, also looking straight ahead as he answered. "He kept them. There was a big glass jar found by investigators at the time. It was in one of his closets under a loose floorboard. He filled the jar with a formaldehyde and alcohol mixture to keep them from rotting or smelling. That was way before my time, so I never actually saw the jar, and it has long since been destroyed. But there were pictures of it along with all the original investigative notes in the files. It was like something out of an old Frankenstein movie... The notes said there were at least eight separate and unique sets of human eyes in that jar. Back then, they didn't have DNA testing. But some of the tests that were available in the seventies like matching eye color and measurements, blood testing, etc... all lined up with the known victims at the time."

"So there are still at least five more victims buried somewhere. Five more families who don't know what happened to their sisters or daughters? That is just fucked up." Disgusted, Stander pulled himself up and out of the seat of the car. The door still open and ajar, he bent over, this time looking at Secrist. "Maybe I should have listened to you. You know, to not hear all this." Stander looked to his side and across the far side of the street for a long moment, focusing his attention on a pot of withered and dying flowers left baking in the summer sun by one of his neighbors. "But if I didn't make you, it would have bothered me forever. So for what it is worth anyway… Thanks, Tommy. Thanks for showing me where she was found and for telling me everything. This is not a day I'll soon forget."

Secrist now turned his head and looked across the car at his friend. "You can forget who told you, though, right?"

Stander turned back and met Secrist's eyes. "Don't worry. I am not sharing this shit with anyone. Not exactly polite dinner conversation or bar banter that would be good for customer relations." Both men exchanged a brief smile. "And, in the end, he carves out his own eyes? What a fucking freak show…."

Stander shakes his head and slams the car door shut, waving as Secrist pulls away from the curb. Stander makes his way towards the side of his building. He treks up the outdoor flight of wood stairs alongside the old bar, unlocking and opening the door to his apartment above the tavern.

CHAPTER 8

10TH CENTURY

PREDICTABLY, Tor was already showing off his great grandfather's sword when Sassa, Gunnar, and his father first arrived for dinner. The impressive weapon was retrieved from the wall, where it hung prominently for all who came to the house to see. Tor was gesturing and speaking excitedly before the group of gathered men, including the newcomer, with the long sword in hand. The extraordinary old weapon, one that Gunnar and his father had seen many times in the past, was crafted with obvious care when forged and kept in good order by Tor's family over generations. The eye-catching sword was stamped with an intricate design that Tor liked to say made it pure and divine. But, according to what Gunnar's dad told him, the origin of the strange design was actually unknown.

As Gunnar and his father listened, Tor began to repeat the oft-told stories of his forefather's wondrous deeds and bravery. How when the sweeping fever called "Christianisation," now so favored by the ruling elite, had first begun to ravage their community, it was Tor's great grandfather who pushed to have the seafaring Norsemen explore these lands far from their ancestral home. How their clan was forced to live nomadically for years while continually searching for a better place for their children and their children's children to live. Until finally following Thorfinn's clan to this place, Vinland, clearly blessed by the supreme god Ymir, where both peace and bounty were endless.

It was a remarkable story, but one all the men listening, save the stranger, had heard many times over. It always seemed to Gunnar that Tor's version of the tale grew grander with his every telling. Embellishing, no doubt, since, as far as Gunnar knew, Tor had never actually used his great grandfather's sword himself for its designed purpose. To compensate, he would stretch the deeds of the past to match the weapon's remarkable appearance. Eventually, Tor was satisfied the newcomer was impressed enough, and the story was concluded. The sharp-edged sword rehung with a flourish before he led the assembled group into the dining area.

The wood-lined room where they would eat was tight for the size of the gathering. At the far side of the dining room, a crackling fire kept the cold of the early spring evening at bay. As Tor had promised, it was truly an inviting feast that had been prepared. Despite this, Gunnar, usually a big eater, found himself just picking at the sacrificed birds and mostly pushing the bread, mushrooms, and vegetables around on his plate. Even with the wonderful aroma the entire meal gave off, his appetite never rose.

During the dinner, Gunnar occasionally stole glances at the newcomer who had introduced himself as Vidar. He said his people's clan made their home deep in the wooded timber on the opposite side of the mountains. Gunnar had seen that dark expanse of woods from near the top of the mountain range many times in the past. It spread as far as the eye could see like an ocean of forest canopy. He had little knowledge himself of that area or where this man said he was from, but it was obvious the elders as a whole accepted this initial explanation.

Vidar had been cleaned up and well-tended before the meal, most likely by Sigrid Gunnar guessed. The stranger now wore Tor's clothes, the garments hanging loose him, especially in the chest and belly area where Tor was most expansive. Yet despite his improved appearance (and smell), the man remained somehow soiled to Gunnar.

Vidar was a small man, not outwardly intimidating at all, with a speckling of grey now taking root in his beard and in his hair. His eyes appeared very dark and skittish, never resting long on any one thing or person as the meal was served, even when he spoke directly to someone or answered a question. But by the amiable conversation that circulated the table, it appeared the others did not see the stranger's odd behavior the same way. The elders surrounding Gunnar and Sassa swapped stories with the newcomer. Each man, in turn, asked Vidar about his sea crossing, past travels, and his homeland.

The group gathered by Tor was as Gunnar had expected. A council of fellow clansmen drawn together by a shared respect, wisdom, and age. Initially, Gunnar was often present for their meetings simply because he helped his father get back and forth. He knew some of the men at the outset had resented his presence when his father became ill enough to require assistance. But his father encouraged Gunnar's participation and artfully pulled him into this select company. As more and more time passed, Gunnar began to speak his mind on the various topics of discussion as well. For the most part, he now felt comfortable and a part of the men who made up the council of their community. However, Gunnar remained keenly aware of his place and often deferred to his father.

As the dinner wound down, so did the conversation among the group of older men. Unspoken questions began to crowd the large table and took the place of the dishes as they were removed. Sigrid, Sassa, and the other women who had prepared the supper soon had everything cleared away. Only the men and vessels of wine remained at the heavy wood table in Tor's dwelling. None seemed eager to be the first to press the stranger on the topic of his arrival or of the state he had come to be in when he was found. But then again, none of the men made a move to leave the table either. The stranger, perhaps sensing the group's desire for answers, tentatively broached the subject himself.

"I want to thank thee for the kindness you have shown. I am in debt for this hospitality. Humbled by the company of such fine men." Gunnar noticed Tor sat up straighter and inhaled the stranger's flattery like fresh baked sweet bread, his chest swelling with self-importance.

"We do not often receive visitors from the other clans that crossed here to Vinland along with Thorfinn. I myself have only heard tell of the clans beginning to spread out on the opposite side of the mountains. You are the first of your people we have personally met. I know my father had encounters with the various clans over his years, and he always spoke of having a deep respect for them. So we welcome you to our village, and I welcome you to my home." With this, Tor swept his arms around the room. Clearly proud of his little speech and wanting to be sure the stranger made the connection. Gunnar closed his eyes to hide the roll he knew he couldn't stop. "I hope you are comfortable during your stay with us."

"I am beyond comfortable, Tor. I have spent more nights than I care to remember sleeping on the cold, damp soil of the ground. Trying to secure some shelter and often barely finding enough to eat. I thank you and say again I am humbled by your generosity." To Gunnar, it seemed both men were determined to out posture the other. It was Gunnar's father who seized on the opportunity to inquire more deeply of Vidar.

"We are happy to help one in need such as yourself. But, as you can imagine, we hope to understand better how you came to us." Gunnar could see Tor tensing from across the table. Clearly more interested in not offending the fellow Norseman than getting real answers. It now seemed to Gunnar that Tor had called together the elders solely to puff himself up and impress this stranger, not for their guidance. He was a fool. Luckily, the others gathered were ignoring Tor and focused on Vidar, as did Gunnar. His father swiftly cut to the heart of the manner.

"Your appearance was unexpected. Not to be unfair, but surely you realize you have many a tongue-wagging this day. Let us answer questions before they become false gossip and rumors. So I say, traveling alone across the mountains among the dangers of the forest is foolhardy. How did this come to be? Did you get separated from your companions? Are there likely to be those worried about your wellbeing?" Vidar avoided the group's gaze. He looked down into his wood cup of wine before taking a deep breath that ended in a brief coughing fit.

Tor spoke up once again. "I think Vidar is tired. Perhaps we can save these questions for tomorrow?" He grinned across the room, looking for support. But the smile was that of a dog, empty and without a thought beyond acceptance. Faltering, he added, "Of course, everyone is welcome to stay...." Mercifully to Gunnar anyway, Tor trailed off. Undeterred, his father pressed on.

"We are simple men here, Vidar. But it seems a strange twist of fate you were able to avoid all the Skraelings between your clan's settlement and ours. Finding us, fellow Norsemen, instead. Don't you think?" Gunnar's father paused reflectively before continuing. "We are blessed and gladly share the fruits of our good fortune without hesitation. But we also are not above our own fears." Again proving his wisdom and touch with delicate matters. Leaving it unspoken but making the point plain just the same: Why are you here, and should we be worried? Gunnar watched the others nod their heads in agreement. He looked on with pride as his father continued. "Where were your travels taking you, Vidar? Perhaps we can help guide or send word of your misfortune?" Vidar took a slow drink from his cup and then looked up.

"I respect your concerns and understand the oddness of my arrival." Vidar addressed Gunnar's father as he spoke. "These people are fortunate to have men such as yourselves to care for them." Vidar cast a glance around the room of wizened faces before adding, "Let me show you the reason for my travels..."

Vidar reached under his chair and placed what he grabbed gently on the table. It was the brown animal skin pouch he had with him when he was found. Held together by strong straps and strips of leather-like materials. Not new but not overly aged either, clearly having been exposed to the elements over time. A few places on the pouch had been worn and discolored, but the simple black stitches were still straight and strong. Whoever crafted it did so with care.

As Gunnar and the others watched, Vidar reached down inside and pulled the lone occupant of his carrying case from its depths. He clutched this possession tightly in his hand, seeming hesitant to release it from his grasp now that it was out in the open. Vidar's eyes darted around the men gathered at the table once more. Then, with a flourish of what appeared to be pride, he finally laid the object on the top of the table. Gunnar noticed a fine bead of sweat had appeared across Vidar's brow.

At first, Gunnar thought the object was simply a black rock. A large stone or perhaps a black gem of some sort, the size of a human baby's skull. Gunnar frowned. He pushed that morbid image from his mind and peered more closely. The item reflected the surrounding light strangely, and it had a blueish tint at its center. Gunnar couldn't tell if what he saw was a trick of the flickering candles as they burned down or not. But the core seemed to be made of a different substance. He desperately wanted to reach out and touch the thing. It seemed to beg his hand. Without realizing it, Gunnar found himself hunched forward and leaning over the strange item. He noticed Vidar was staring intently at him from the other side of the table.

"You may pick it up. It is unlike anything I have held before." Vidar was looking at and now speaking directly to Gunnar. He glanced over at his father, who almost imperceptibly nodded at Gunnar, giving his blessing.

The first thought as his fingers caressed the stone was how warm it was. As Gunnar grasped it, he felt its overall smoothness, interrupted only by several crisscrossing lines and the odd, deep blue indentation at the center. As he lifted it for a closer inspection, he was astonished by how incredibly heavy it was. He looked up at Vidar, who read the question on his face. "Yes, I also do not understand how a stone such as this could be so heavy. I have seen nothing like it ever. Where do things such as this come from?" Vidar looked around the room now as if questioning the group.

But Gunnar never heard Vidar's question. He suddenly felt himself being thrust downward as if falling from a great height. Disoriented, a white flash erupted that blinded him briefly. What Gunnar saw next, he also felt, heard, and smelled. Whether a vision or not, Gunnar could not comprehend what had happened to him. But he'd suddenly been catapulted someplace new. Abruptly finding himself standing among a group of fellow Norsemen he didn't recognize, all huddled together tightly and waiting. For what reason, he knew not. Gunnar turned to the bearded man at his side. "What are we waiting here for?" Gunnar's voice was confused, timid, and not his own. The armed man scoffed as he replied.

"We're waiting for the thing to show itself. We must wait, Vidar. Now stay silent," the man hissed. Vidar? Gunnar was confused. Why did this man call him Vidar? Gunnar gradually became aware he held a weapon in his hand, and he lifted it to his face to see what it was. The blade he grasped shined, and in its reflection, he saw not his own face but a younger, fuller version of Vidar's! Gunnar felt his legs grow weak in shock and confusion. Somehow, the black stone had thrust him back in time! Or perhaps it was showing him a vision from the past. Gunnar was unsure, his thoughts muddled. Wanting to cry out. Where was he? All he could tell was it was nighttime, and the landscape around him was unrecognizable. Where were his father and the elders? His village? But as he opened his mouth to speak, moonlight suddenly punctured the night sky above him. Illuminating the wooded area, he and the men stood facing. There, Gunnar watched uncomprehendingly as a walking horror appeared at the edge of the tree line.

Astonished at his surroundings and what crept out of the forest, Gunnar's tongue fell mute.

The thing from the forest seemed to blur and buzz like the wings of a bee as it moved. The figure, dark and distorted in the shadowed moonlight, remained motionless for long moments before accelerating swiftly forward. The unsettling scamper and hypnotic movement held Gunnar's gaze, though the thing's path was barely trackable to the naked eye. Within moments of its appearance at the edge of the surrounding woods, it descended upon a nearby dwelling where Gunnar somehow understood an ambush had been set.

The unnerving abomination's appearance was human-like, a distorted version of man. Unnaturally tall and thin, its gleaming bald head towered above the top of the doorway leading into the home where the trap had been set. The creature's skin was milky white, nearly translucent, and seemed to be lacking any hair. Its lanky body was covered by a long and filthy black robe of sorts that only punctuated the paleness of its appearance. The threadbare garment hung loosely from the disturbing frame, dragging low along the ground as it buzzed and moved in its queer fashion. The thing had gangly, bone-thin arms that extended down along its sides. At the end of these were human-like hands, each with five elongated fingers. The ends of each finger were equal in length and topped with long, yellowing nails. The ghoul was so out of proportion that the ends of each talon-like finger hung below its knees.

Gunnar was terrified! Frozen where he stood, every hair on his body seemed to rise as if hoping for a quick escape. He'd never seen or even imagined such a horrid thing before in his life. Yet the vision was equally as mesmerizing as it was repulsive. He found himself unable to tear his eyes away as the vigilant men beside him all looked on solemnly. Gunnar felt himself clutching desperately at the last strands of his sanity as the obscenity began to shudder and buzz. Becoming a blur once more before disappearing completely from their sight. He watched with unbelieving eyes as the nightmare suddenly reappeared at the door of the dwelling the men were watching.

It slinked silently inside the home. Nearly undetected.

With the trance broken, the Norse warriors around him burst from their hiding place and sprinted forward. Exploding through the same doorway haunted by the wraith just moments before.

Swept along by the urgent push of the men beside him, Gunnar ran with the group though his actions were not his own. The brave men all piled into the single-room home, surprising the fiend already draped and hunched over a fervently praying old man that Gunnar did not recognize. Behind him, the wood door was secured tightly by the last man to enter the dwelling even as the atrocity rose and turned. It loomed a head above the tallest among them as it swiveled to face the intruders. A rancid stench permeated the entirety of the small enclosed room, causing several men to audibly retch. Regardless, the drafted fighters, including Gunnar still stuck in Vidar's body, all squared up to face the nightmare.

But no face returned their disbelieving gaze.

The loathsome thing was featureless save for two shadowy holes where the eyes should have been. White and stark as bone without ears or a nose, it was seemingly without vision. Yet, remarkably, the walking blasphemy recognized instantly that it was under siege. A widening slit materialized across the blank canvas face, cracking open so wide that the growing chasm threatened to sever the creature's face in two.

Still, it went on spreading...

A monstrous buzzing and unnatural chill filled the small dark room. Jagged and sharp teeth began to fill the gaping hole. The splitting gash formed a horrible mockery of a smile. The intensity of the droning buzz increased as the thing began to raise its arms, shaking and fluttering violently with each of its haunting movements. The mouth was now cavernous, menacing, and wide. Yet all the brave men of this clan, though hardly able to fathom the madness they were witnessing, did not waver. Rooted, they held their ground. Undivided. Standing shoulder to shoulder as one.

A low hiss began to build as the specter shimmered in the flickering candlelight. But this bizarre sound seemed to embolden them, and the Norse fighters en masse sprung forward and attacked the ghoulish apparition. Letting loose with a desperate fury born out of sheer terror of this unknown thing. Bellowing, they pounced upon the creature. Hacking away with their weapons, desperate to end,

Gunnar somehow understood the evil thing poisoning their lands and desecrating their loved ones.

While defending itself, the monster ripped the arms off one man with a surprising show of strength. Turning, it clamped down on another attacker with a bite so ferocious that it crushed the startled man's skull like a grape. The unfortunate warrior's blood soaked the wall beside him in the carnage. The thing hissed in rage as it lashed out with long, cruel hands and ragged nails. Violently slashing anyone it could reach before being slowly overwhelmed by the sheer number of assailants. Black blood and gore spewed out of each injury inflicted on the contamination. Trapped, it fought on even as it began to weaken. Finally, one man was able to skewer the wraith through its black heart with his sword. Driving it down and pinning the squirming thing to the ground while the remaining men dismembered the vile creature.

They tore it apart.

None, Gunnar somehow knew, were entirely certain how to kill something so clearly not alive in any sense they could understand. All of them, equally horrified that the thing might somehow rise again, raged like a pack of wild dogs until each remaining bit of the creature quit moving. In the immediate aftermath, as the fury subsided, several men vomited violently. Whether it was from the stress and strain of the battle or the sights and smells of the fiend, Gunnar could not say. Adrenaline and lingering fear seemed to be all that kept the gathered men moving.

Once it was clear the thing had truly been subdued, others rushed in from their nearby hiding places. Gunnar, still trapped in Vidar's body, watched as the slayed bodies of those who had sacrificed everything for their people were carefully removed from the dwelling where the attack occurred. Those fallen heroes were decapitated, and their heads were quickly reduced to ash. For each had been touched by evil, and superstition was now at least as powerful as any faith.

No chance was worth taking.

As the members of Vidar's clan began to carefully inspect the remains of the monstrous fiend, a surprising discovery was made. Near the neck, between the shoulders, a mark was found that mimicked the celestial sun. The strange emblem was laid in an unknown ink of various exotic colors that blazed brightly on the surface of the pallid skin. But beyond that, the other remaining pieces of the thing held few clues or answers themselves. Each piece was wet and slimy like the underbelly of the small lizards found under rocks along a shore. What was left soon began to rapidly decay and dissolve.

The black garment it wore was now little more than a large rag - gashed, torn, and smeared in the carnage. It was quickly agreed that burning anything left, no matter how small, was the only way to ensure the thing would not rise again to seek revenge. A wood pyre was quickly constructed and set ablaze until it was deemed hot enough to cremate the contagion. What was left of the body, and the cloth it wore, was dragged over and tossed into the spirited flames. As it burned, the morning sun crept steadily over the mountains and added its warmth to the blaze as well. Perhaps blessing the resolve and bravery shown in ridding the land of such a monster. As Gunnar looked up at the burning sun above, it seemed to grow brighter until, finally, he had to close his eyes and turn away.

When Gunnar opened his eyes next, he felt a tug at his shirt sleeve as he watched his own hands turn the strange black stone over and over again. Gunnar could now see his own distorted face reflected in the shiny stone. As if inside it there was another version of himself. He felt another tug at his sleeve, and, confused, he turned and saw it was his father.

"Let some of the others look as well, Gunnar," his father said. Gunnar was puzzled. Had he just picked the weighted rock up? It felt as though what he'd just witnessed had lasted for hours. Yet no time had passed here as he'd experienced the vision? He felt light-headed and dizzy as he quickly passed the black stone over to his father. Gunnar was confused and embarrassed at his experience.

What had he seen? Where had he been?

Gunnar's father commented as he struggled to hold the stone with his one still strong and able hand. "Hmmm.... Yes... Very thick and heavy indeed... Maybe worked or carved here." His fingers traced one of the lines back to the blueish center. "But poorly done. What do you suppose it is meant to be? Is it just me, or does it not resemble an eye?" Vidar shrugged without committing one way or the other. Gunnar's father pointed and gestured at what he saw as being the indentation at the center. Then he turned it over a couple more times before placing it back on the table for the others to inspect. One by one, each man around the table held the strange black rock. Most said little as the rock was passed around.

None affected as Gunnar had been.

CHAPTER 9
10TH CENTURY

"THE RUGGED TIMBER and mountain ranges may seem foreboding from afar, but our clan has come to call it home." Vidar, after showing the gathered elders the strange black stone in his possession, began to answer the questions asked of him by Gunnar's father and the other elders. "We built our village near a large lake fed by freshwater streams running down from mountains on either side. For protection and guidance, we revere not only Ymir, but also his offspring Bergelmir, the mountain yeller. He is a deity that is good and fair in his judgments. Bergelmir always provided refuge and peace within the wonders of his mountain realm, easily sustaining all life that respected his domain and crafting the woods to provide a plentiful bounty. One that replenishes itself without exhaustion, season after season and year after year. Of course, there are dangers any place man journeys and any place man calls home. The deep wooded areas we chose to call home were no exception if one was not careful. But there, the good had always far outweighed the bad. Bergelmir continually blessed us and always saw to this."

"Or at least he had." Vidar paused to drink heavily from his cup of wine, his eyes darting from face to face before continuing on.

"It started first with the animals. After days of restlessness, several oxen broke out of their enclosure, snapping the wood fencing that had held the herd for years, only to be found in fields well away from what we considered our lands. During this same time, even our most reliable horses became skittish and no longer easily bridled or reined in, bolting if unattended or if given a chance. Hunting soon dried up also, including lands previously favored for their abundance of game. Even the chatter of birds, so constant it often goes unheard, fell silent among the thick ceiling of trees that covers much of the area. Then, within days of each other, every kept rooster, hen, and chicken had disappeared as well. Not a trace of them was ever found."

"Shortly after the animals' strange behavior began, an unexpected and intense storm rolled through our village just before daybreak. Wind whipped and howled ferociously as blackened clouds bullied their way across the lake before making landfall. But, despite the deafening roar of the rainstorm, terrifying sounds were heard coming from the large pens at the far end of our village. A high-pitched squealing that was both desperate and scared. Soon all the boars and pigs in our clans' possession were not just squealing. They were screaming like small, frightened little children. Their anguished cries echoed in the darkness of the sudden tempest. It was a dreadful sound… Unable to return to sleep, half of our clan stayed huddled under our bedcovers until the first rays of the sun made their comforting appearance."

Vidar laughed without humor before adding, "The other half simply lied and said they had heard nothing that night…"

"Yet it soon became undeniable that, over the span of the next few days, any animal with the freedom to move had abandoned the fertile land surrounding our village. The only remaining creatures were those without a choice, under protest but fenced or tethered securely in some way. These events all developed so fast that we barely had time to even speculate what prompted this peculiar behavior. Or the mass exodus of Bergelmir's forest animals. But, just as the people of our clan began to question the consequences of it all, the worst began."

"Ruthless, dark, and unseen like a plague, something profane and inhuman had come to the doorstep of our peaceful world. Swiftly and silently unsettling the very sanctity of the lands we called home. There was no more reason for it coming now than the arrival of a bad fever or sudden sickness. And like many illnesses, it was both relentless and merciless."

"In the span of six days, four families were cloaked in mourning. Mine included." Vidar lowered his eyes once, picking at a loose thread on his shirt before continuing on.

"It was the old, the maimed, and the smallest of children that were felled. All from dwellings that resided on the very outskirts of our otherwise tightly clustered community. Each violation during the underbelly of nightfall, without warning and seemingly without provocation. The stillness of the once tranquil homes pierced only by a single sharp and otherworldly shriek."

"Later, no one in the afflicted homes was able to say for sure where the sound originated from. Saying it was everywhere and nowhere as it startled family members out of their slumber. Candles and torches were quickly lit to chase the nightfall and calm fears, but the illumination had the opposite effect. For the feeble radiance of the candles exposed a cruel last vision of their fallen loved ones that would never be completely exorcised from the mind."

Vidar met the eyes of his rapt audience. "Time can heal, brothers. But not this. Not this."

"Each marred body had the same tell-tale disfigurement. Both eyeballs wrenched horribly from the head. The hollow eye sockets yawned widely and deeply down into the back of the skull itself. Cruel scratch-like marks were visible around each orbit, the single clue and only sign of violence found. The wounds were… The wounds were like nothing we'd seen before. Leaving all of us with only troubling and unanswered questions. Each clan member desperately trying to make sense of what had so suddenly befallen them."

"But why? Where had the eyes gone?" Tor interrupted Vidar, but he ignored him. Leaving the questions unanswered while he continued.

"It did not take long for our elders and leaders to agree that an unknown and strange evil was within our midst. If unchecked, surely it would continue to prey upon us until all was lost. Though unclear what our clan might have done to invite this or why the god Bergelmir had so completely abandoned us, there was no argument that swift action must be taken."

Listening intently to Vidar's tale, Gunnar began to feel as if he'd be sick. The images of the desecrated faces of the natives he, Erik, and the two others from their hunting party had seen flashed before his eyes. On the ride home, they'd all agreed not to mention what they'd seen upon their return. Gunnar convinced each that no good would come from sharing such things without explanation. Unsure if any would believe them. Or, worse yet, question their bravery and reliability in the future. In the end, they pretended to be as blind as the victims. And just as silent...

Tor spoke up once again. "Was it the filthy Skraelings? Revenge of a sort? What did you do?"

"First," Vidar continued, "the recently deceased were all beheaded. The violated heads, each in turn, burned separately from the bodies until only ashes were left. Next, we went about devising a trap."

"We were certain the monster would return in the black of night and certain we must be ready. One elder, already nearing the end of his life's journey, brazenly volunteered to be bait for the unknown nightmare. He was carefully positioned in a home that had not yet been visited and near the tree line. We gathered the bravest men among us, and we positioned ourselves in hiding with a clear sight-line and a straight path to the dwelling. Once in place, we waited anxiously and kept watch while the rest of the villagers locked themselves away in their homes. Each house posted its own sentry. All of us on edge, sleep a luxury none could afford that night."

"Time crept slowly by." Vidar paused, then took another drink from his cup before finishing his story.

But Gunnar didn't need to hear Vidar's words. He'd just lived the very same nightmare Vidar began to describe. The men of Vidar's clan hid, the chaotic hand-to-hand battle that ensued, and there was a fiery ending as the creature was reduced to ash in the cleansing flames of a pyre. By the time Vidar neared the end of his terrible tale, Gunnar's head was spinning. How had he seen this? Surely the black stone was the cause... Should he speak up? Would anyone believe him? These questions crowded his head as Vidar finished his tale, and the room fell silent. Each man around the table slowly digested both the fantastic story and the wine still being shared among them. Those who lit pipes during his telling busied themselves with the task of either refilling or cleaning them. No one seemed anxious to comment on the incredible story they had just been told. It was Bjorn, completely white-haired but among the younger of the clan's council, who broke the silence first with a nervous laugh.

"That was an impressive telling, Vidar. I am glad my wife did not hear you, or she may never have slept again," Bjorn looked around the gathering, his smile faltering slightly. He then spoke a little more cautiously with less certainty. "We have all heard similar stories of such monsters lurking among the woodlands. My father scared my brothers and me more than once when we had stayed out past dark, telling us of the strange creatures that make the woods their home." Bjorn barked out a chuckle again, "But that was just to keep us in line. I remember this one time, well, when we…." Without anyone agreeing with him or paying him much attention, Bjorn soon aborted his attempt at levity.

"Each man is free to believe what he believes, Bjorn," said Gunnar's father a few moments later. "But I would caution you to watch your tongue. There is truth in anything passed down from generation to generation. Otherwise, the lessons learned in the past would die on the vine like a withered berry. Stories and shared wisdom are things one may or may not need in life. Who is to say what paths we cross over time? And Bjorn," admonishing him now, "your father was a very wise man." Bjorn dropped his eyes to the table as Gunnar's father turned once more to the storyteller.

"But, Vidar, this doesn't explain why you appeared here in our village," pressed Gunnar's father. "Nor your arrival at night looking as you did." Gunnar noticed that a few of those closest to Vidar had, perhaps subconsciously, pulled slightly away from the man as he was speaking earlier. He wondered if they or Vidar even realized that subtle shift. Gunnar studied the man more closely, still unsure if he should share the vision he'd experienced and recalled the blinded death faces of the native villagers he'd seen. The two tragedies had to be related. How had those unfortunate souls explained what was happening to them? Were there more of these monsters here in Vinland?

Vidar clasped his thin hands together in what looked like prayer. Without wavering, he met Gunnar's father's eyes as he spoke. "The thing was vanquished sure as the sun dries the rain. We mourned our dead and cursed the arrival of what had caused us all so much pain and loss. But also felt blessed to have lifted the curse upon us, to have rewarded Bergelmir with our faith." Vidar seemed to be speaking directly to Gunnar's father, despite the others being shoulder to shoulder around the big table. "But the animals were not calmed. They were still skittish and little work could be done with them most days. The hunting remained as if we were in a drought, scarcely enough found to maintain ourselves. All was not well, and we soon discovered why."

Vidar paused and refilled his cup before continuing.

"I no longer remember who discovered it, but a small wood chest was soon found. It had been hidden near the entrance of one of the caves close to our village. The chest was well crafted but very old. Weathered with age and time, the dense wood was so dark it was almost black. The outside was covered in strange markings, and there were odd-looking symbols or writings on the lid. Figures of creatures no one could recognize were carved into the sides. Many would not touch the strange box when it was brought to the village. Some refused to even look or get close to it. After it was brought forward, there was much discussion, but in the end, everyone was in agreement. The box must have belonged to the creature. So a fire was stoked once more, but this time away from our homes on the far side of the lake. We burned the thing. Lit it up without so much as cracking the lid, even a sliver. We prayed, and we piled as much wood as we dared on the flames."

"What happened when it caught fire?" asked Gunnar directly, finding his tongue once more.

"Nothing," Vidar replied. "Maybe a little bit of an odd smell at times. Like getting a whiff of tar pulled from the bottom of a bog. A few times, we saw different colored smoke too - most likely from the ancient wood that the chest was made out of - but that was it. We all watched and let the fire burn itself out."

"That was it?" Tor asked expectantly. "And that finally ended the troubles?" He looked relieved. But Vidar did not immediately answer Tor's questions. "Was anything found when the fire died down?" In response, Vidar nodded and pointed at the black rock still resting on top of the table.

"Our elders came to believe that, whatever the thing that plagued us was, the box we found and this stone had been in its possession. Believing this black rock protected the thing's immortal soul by means of dark sorcery. For it is indestructible." Vidar picked up the object once again and then rose to his feet, standing before the clan's gathered council.

"You ask why I am here. This, this is why I left my home and came to be here." He held the black and shiny round rock aloft as he spoke. The room fell silent at this sudden revelation. "You heard the story of what happened, did you not? We did not ask for this," Vidar paused. "We did nothing wrong and you now know all that was lost by my people. Where I live will never be the same again. Never. We thought we had destroyed the thing, cast out the evil from our homes. But we were fools. It never really left us. We wanted it gone, but the cruel thing has such a strong will. A deep hunger. Vengeful! The soul of it remains, don't you see?"

A thin trail of drool began to spill from the corner of Vidar's mouth as he continued. "I have walked more days than I can remember, searching for wise men such as yourselves. But most men are fools and couldn't... couldn't see." Again Vidar turned his attention directly to Gunnar's father as he pleaded. "This thing must be destroyed! I have tried everything. My people have tried everything we know of, but n... no... nothing works!" Vidar's voice was getting louder as he spoke. "We burned the chest that held this rock and tried... We tried to smash the rock again and again. But it never breaks! NEVER!! Vidar began to run words together. At other moments, he stuttered, inflections rising and falling.

"We all knew it would come back, and I hear it. At night it s... s...sp... speaks to me. It wants me to do terrible things. It does... Don't you see, it wants back among us! In my village, we only killed the body it was using. Now it wants back in our world. And it chases me! Torments me so... It won't rest until it has its revenge on us. All of us!"

Vidar was now shouting. Red-faced, his voice shrill and piercing. He looked from man to man among the gathered. "Can't you tell? Don't you feel the thing all around us? Even in this room, no? NO!"

Vidar's eyes grew wild, and they rolled from man to man before finally focusing once more on Gunnar. "You! You feel his power, don't you?! Yes, oh yes, you do... I saw it in you when you held him in your hand. Yes! Yes! You did, yes?" Startled at this sudden attention, unsure what he really saw or what to believe, Gunnar shook his head. "You must tell them, don't be d... de... deceived or afraid, you must be brave like me... Like I was." Gunnar now leaned back in his chair, continuing to shake his head. Wanting to be far away from the table and end this conversation

"LIAR!" Vidar roared, thrusting the strange rock out towards him. Gunnar flinched, expecting the heavy stone to be hurled at him, but Vidar held it firm as he rambled. "It talks. It whispers, and I hear it. It wants out, and he wants me, don't you see? It never leaves me, and I can't leave it." Still standing, a single tear squeezed its way out of the corner of his left eye, trailing down until it mixed with the drool now hanging from his chin. Several of the elders began passing glances among themselves at the sudden outburst, taken aback at the fierceness of his words. Vidar stood shaking, his entire body quivering.

Gunnar's father never took his eyes off Vidar.

"Wh… What? Why can't you just throw it away? Down a hole or throw it in a river? I… I don't understand." Tor was clearly confused by both Vidar's actions and his speech. "Why do you keep it with you?" He shot a puzzled look at Gunnar's father, who still said nothing. "Can you, please. Just sit down and say what it is that troubles you, Vidar…" Tor now also stood and gestured to Vidar's chair. "Let us talk more. How does it speak to you? We will try to help, but you must help us understand."

Tor stole a glance at Gunnar and a second one at his father. Clearly looking for help with this unexpected turn of events. Looking back to Vidar once again, he finished, "We all want to help you and your people, but this is all very confusing… You say the monster you killed lives in this?" Pointing once more at the rock. "Still?"

Vidar exhaled deeply and sat down heavily in his empty chair, head down, not appearing to be looking at anything in particular. After a few long moments, he wiped his face with first one sleeve and then the other. Looking down in his lap, he began again. "I am so sorry for how I am acting. Please forgive me, friends. I am not myself, and I think I may have enjoyed your wine a bit much. And I am so tired. Oh, so tired… You have no idea." Finally raising his eyes once more, he appeared much calmer. His voice no longer raised in excitement. He pulled out the brown deerskin bag and carefully laid it out on the top of the table. He placed his lone possession carefully on top of the flattened bag as if to protect it from the table's surface.

"How can I make you understand…? My clan believes it can never die or be destroyed." He turned to Tor now. "You ask why I keep it with me. As long as I have it with me, I know my people are safe. Once it awakens again, it will have its revenge." Vidar gestured to the table. "We vanquished the body of the beast but not the evil. I know it is still there. I feel it." He looked once more at Gunnar's father. "I beg of you. Help me find a way to destroy it completely. There must be a way. There must! For why would the creature hide this if not so?"

"I still don't understand why you can't throw it in the sea," replied Tor. "Or just bury it very deep where it can never be found. Or maybe just…"

"That's enough, Tor." Gunnar's father cut him off, then turned to Vidar, "I speak for all at this table when I say we are truly sorry for the pain of your people. You are a brave man, as are your people." Gunnar's father paused briefly before continuing on. "Let me ask you, Vidar. There are different villages and groups of Skraelings you must have encountered from your home to ours." Vidar acknowledged the question and answered with a nod of his head. "You must have shown and spoken of this with those people at that time as well." Again a nod of agreement but followed by a downward glance. "And none could help you or offer advice?"

"They were fools. Not nearly as welcoming as you have been or as wise. Some drove me out as if I was…" At this, Vidar stopped short and said no more. Gunnar squirmed in his chair and felt his face coloring. He knew he needed to tell his father what he and the hunting party had found days earlier. The abandoned native homes, the faces without eyes, and half-burned bodies. Gunnar decided that in the morning, he would confess all they'd seen that day as well as the vision of Vidar's clan's fierce battle.

"It is a fearful tale, Vidar. Hard to cast blame, is it not? You have given us much to ponder this night, but now it grows late, and I am a tired old man. I think we all may do well with some sleep. Tomorrow we shall discuss this more. Perhaps there is a way to imprison or banish this thing for eternity. Or together we can see if someone may know of another who has the experience and can be of help."

With this, the gathered men began finishing off their drinks. Each began to rise one after another and make their way to the door, in turn thanking their host, before leaving Tor's home and heading back to their own dwellings. Tor himself seemed to grow very disturbed as the men, one by one, departed, leaving him and his wife alone with Vidar. Gunnar and his father, moving even more slowly and deliberately than usual, was the last out the front door. The late hour left him tired and worn down. Lost in his troubled thoughts, Gunnar still said nothing aloud to his father as they made their way home.

He would tell him everything in the morning.

CHAPTER 10
PRESENT DAY

AFTER VISITING the site where Sherry's murdered body had laid hidden for decades, Stander just wanted to be alone. Wearily climbing the stairs to the apartment above his bar and opening the fridge to retrieve a cold beer. When he'd originally purchased the three-story building, Stander had immediately converted the top floor into a loft apartment for himself. Gutting it completely and creating a wide-open space that left the bathroom as the only place of privacy. Large twelve-foot high windows dominated three of the apartment's walls, and the fourth wall, unadorned and windowless, was still the original brick-work. In one corner stood a modern kitchen, and opposite that was a bed tucked along the windowless wall in the room's darkest corner. Next to the king-size bed stood an antique wood chifforobe that, along with a matching bureau, held all of Stander's clothing. In the middle of the apartment was a striped area rug where a leather couch and two easy chairs sat facing a flat-screen TV mounted on the wall.

Welcoming Stander home was Frazier, his four-legged roommate of the last six years. The brown and white dog barked and wagged his tail enthusiastically as Stander smiled and bent down to greet and scratch him behind the ears. The pit bull and boxer mix licked Stander's hand and bent, twirled, and twisted his body around and around in a little happy dance. The pooch, as usual, was hardly able to contain his joy at Stander's return. The dog finally slowed its gyrations just long enough to contort itself in a U shape so both his butt and head could be petted simultaneously. Stander obliged the medium-sized canine with both hands before leading the dog back outside so he could do his business.

"Good grief, Frazier..." Stander chided him good-naturedly after watching him, nose to the ground, circle the grass area behind the bar for five minutes without success. "You going to drop the deuce or what?" As usual, the dog disregarded Stander's rhetoric. "Come on, any spot is as good as the next. Let's go. We both still need to eat, you know..." Frazier finally finished and then kicked his back legs out behind himself twice before running back over to Stander.

"You are one picky motherfucker, you know that?" Together they turned and made their way back up the stairs to their home. Stander filled Frazier's dog bowl and then cooked himself a frozen pizza before twisting the top off a second Leinenkugel Summer Shandy beer. Toasting Frazier, he told the dog for the umpteenth time that nothing hit the spot like a cold Leine.

After dinner, Stander sat down on his couch with a third beer in hand. Frazier jumped up next to him, and they both settled in their usual spots. But this time, Stander did not turn the TV on. Instead, he sipped his beer contemplatively while resting one hand on the dog, thinking about what he had learned that day. The finality of it all and the horrible truths of how Sherry's brief life had ended.

Soon he got up off the couch briefly to retrieve the one photo album he owned. Inside were pictures of his family life before everything he thought he knew about the world changed. Stander opened the old book to the middle, skipping over the endless baby pictures where both he and Sherry were posed with friends and relatives of his dad, people he never remembered meeting or ever really knew.

The binding creaked, and the pages stuck to each other as Stander peeled one page from the other. The clear protective sheets still tried desperately to cover and hold in place the colored pictures on each page. Stander stopped struggling with the old binder when he found his favorite picture of Sherry near the end of the photo album. She was seated at the edge of the bed in her room, smiling gleefully with her face pressed against her little half-brother's cheek. Both of them seemed to be bursting with joy as the camera clicked.

Stander could still remember the smell of the incense sticks she burned in her bedroom and the array of colored beads that hung in front of the girlie curtains covering the windows in the room. He recalled all the walls had been painted a light pink and that there was a dresser with a mirror that Stander remembered being hopelessly cluttered with girl stuff on top. Between her bed and the closet was a wood stand holding her most prized possession: a stereo record player with two speakers strung out on each side. Below that was a pile of records stacked half-heartedly every which way, leaning against the bottom of the wood stand. She had albums by Elton John, Barry Manilow, The Bee Gees, Glen Campbell, and others. It always seemed to Stander that when Sherry was home, the little bedroom was filled with music. The record player scratched out song after song, occasionally skipping, which would often elicit a scream of frustration from Sherry as she sang along.

Above her bed, he remembered, there had been a single feathered dream catcher. Either given to her or perhaps something she had won at a carnival or the local county fair at some point. One tiny nail holding it in place as if her dreams were only ever going to be lightweight. On the wall opposite her bed, strategically placed, Stander was sure, were various posters and pictures torn out of the teen idol magazines that she was always coming home with. Leif Garrett, Shaun Cassidy, Andy Gibb, etc... all watching over her while she slept.

Sherry had just started a part-time summer job the week before she disappeared. She was hired on as a cashier at the local K-Mart, where several of her friends also worked. To get back and forth, she borrowed the princely sum of $2,000 from their dad to buy her first car. It had been a mustard-colored Ford Pinto, and Stander vividly recalled begging Sherry daily to take him on rides in it. Hoping friends would see them and be jealous of his freedom. He had felt so grown up beside her, just the two of them with no parents to be found, cruising down the main strip of Marquette with music blaring out of the rolled-down windows. Laughing and changing the radio channels anytime a commercial would come on, their hair blowing back in the wind. In Stander's mind's eye, Sherry was smart, beautiful, and ready to take on the world back then. She had been very excited to finally have a real job and her own car. All at the age of 17.

Just two weeks after starting her new job, all of that excitement and hope for the future would be forever snuffed out.

The night she disappeared, Sherry had worked a closing shift and left the store a little after 9:00. Her car was found abandoned by a patrolman not even an hour after it was last seen pulling out of the K-Mart parking lot by her co-workers. The Pinto was parked along the side of the road and, at the time, assumed broken down. This was a time well before cell phones, and if your car broke down, you walked to the nearest house or flagged down a passing car. Stander couldn't remember if the authorities later determined Sherry actually had car trouble that night and had been picked up by someone. Or if she had simply pulled over to possibly help someone else. In the end, he supposed, it didn't really matter. What mattered was no one had seen anything. It was as if Sherry Stander had dropped off the face of the earth.

Gone and vanished.

There were a few days of forced optimism and supposed possibilities. But, with multiple missing women over the last couple of years across several surrounding counties, that false hope dried up quickly. This was the summer of 1977. Both the papers and the news on TV were constantly running stories on the Son of Sam shooter terrorizing New York City. Or reporting on the manhunt for a murderer named Ted Bundy who, at that time, was suspected of "only" killing some co-eds in Florida. Bundy had somehow escaped custody, was on the loose and could be anywhere it seemed. That same summer, there were also reports of a maniac nicknamed the Hillside Strangler who was killing women in L.A. And here in rural Michigan, within a tight cluster of six or seven small towns, women simply vanished. To a young boy barely eight years of age, it seemed no adults could be trusted. Surely every town had a killer or two, and the one in upper Michigan had taken his big sister. Now today, some forty-odd years later, Stander had seen enough to understand he had been right.

Monsters in human masks walk among us.

Stander sighed and, breaking out of his reverie, shut the photo album and flipped the TV on. The local newscaster was following up on a story from the previous week. The talking head informed viewers that there were still no new developments or leads in last week's student disappearance down in Ann Arbor, Michigan. Just like Sherry, this young girl had also vanished, last seen walking back from class at the University of Michigan campus where she was enrolled in summer classes. Stander thought to himself how some things just never seemed to change. All the news was bad news anymore. A story that barely resonated with him last week now seemed to hit very close to home.

Stander stood up from the couch, in the process disturbing Frazier, who looked up at him sleepily and yawned. Stander stretched and picked up his empty beer bottle, surprised to see it was as late as the kitchen clock confessed it really was. Frazier sat on his back haunches on the floor, and looked up at him expectantly. The encroaching darkness outside his cue that the time had come for one last trip out the door and down the wood stairway before settling down for the night. Stander led Frazier outside and as the dog once again endlessly scrutinized the grass, Stander recalled the impact of Sherry's disappearance.

No one ever came right out and said it back then. But when Jimmy Tathum was caught, and then later the corpses of two missing girls were found, it was like collectively everyone decided to stop. Stop the investigation into Sherry's disappearance. Stop expecting her to return. Stop talking about her. As if the entire town had given up and merely waited for the inevitable to be discovered. Between Sherry's disappearance and the capture of Jimmy Tathum, the year was like an awkward purgatory for a young Russell Stander.

His father, a doctor, and a man full of empathy teared up easily if the subject of Sherry was ever discussed. Up to that point in his life, Stander had never seen a grown man, much less his own father, cry before. He could remember feeling embarrassed by his dad's show of emotions, and since he never wanted to hurt his dad, Stander had avoided the subject altogether. In the end, the boy was left with no one to talk with about his loss. Certainly, his own mother, a cold and often emotionless woman whom Sherry had never warmed to, was not able to comfort or provide any support to the young boy. Not that it had mattered much anyway. Within two years, his mother would be gone as well.

One year after Sherry had gone missing, there had been a service in her honor, complete with a closed and empty casket. Stander had worn a little blue suit coat, white shirt, and clip-on tie. His toes pinched in a pair of tight, shiny black shoes with slippery soles that he had only ever worn three times before that day. He stood for the entire service slightly off-balance in the grass on the slope of a small hill. The local church pastor droned on and on while his dad cried softly next to him. The supposed celebration of life became one of hushed pity as his mother stood beside him and let everyone know "the boy would be OK."

As the service ending neared, Stander could recall watching dark shadows cast from the surrounding trees, crawling leisurely across each headstone towards them. The boy stared at them as they inched closer with a terrible feeling that everyone needed to get out of there before they reached the cavernous hole where the empty casket would be buried. He'd run to the car after, locking himself inside until his parents were ready to leave the cemetery.

Later that same night, after climbing into his bed tucked against the wall his room shared with Sherry's, Stander understood how utterly alone he was. Sure he still had a mother and a father he loved dearly, but the finality of the loss of his big half-sister left a gaping hole inside him. Stander realized now it had been right then and there that he'd grown up. He never got the extra ten years most every other kid did. Eight-year-old Russell Stander swallowed all his boyhood anger and fears that night. Pushing them down so deep that, when his own mother left him and his father that next year, he had not shed a single tear. Stander began to keep everyone an arm's length away, never letting anyone, except his father, inside his world. And with the exception of a short-lived marriage (and much later Frazier), that was exactly what he had done for the last 40 years.

CHAPTER 11
PRESENT DAY

AS ETHAN APPROACHED Russ Stander's bar later that week, he had no idea what to expect. Though he appreciated Stander's offer of free food and drinks, he anticipated the night would be somewhat somber and awkward. Despite this, Ethan figured he couldn't turn the guy down. What were the proper social graces when you find somebody's dead sister's long-lost remains?

He pushed open the glass door etched with the establishment's operating hours and name, "In This Corner." He was pleased to see that the bar seemed to have a good crowd for a weekday night, with the majority of the bar stools filled. The patrons, like Ethan, were dressed casually, with a few folks looking a little sharper as if they had arrived straight from work. Though a few of the customers turned to eyeball Ethan as he entered, the majority of men and women were focused on the bar's owner.

Stander, dressed in jeans and wearing a t-shirt with the image of a bottle cap stamped "Pop Evil," stood behind the bar as if holding court. Clearly in the middle of regaling the onlookers with a story or joke. Ethan saw behind Stander, high above the array of liquor bottles lining the back wall of the bar, hung a sign that read "The

Sweet Science." Displayed on one side of the sign was an impressive, full-sized sword that seemed to radiate under the glow of the overhead lighting just above it. On the opposite side of the same sign, under glass and set in a wood-framed shadow box, was a picture of some kids and a worn, old-fashioned-looking sling shot. The two "weapons" were in stark contrast with each other and the boxing memorabilia displayed throughout the bar. Ethan self-consciously pulled his eye glasses off his face and cleaned them on his shirt, waiting for Stander to notice him.

"I just told him, Jesus Larry, how many sets of testicles can you kick?" Stander smiled, and the saloon erupted with laughter. The customer seated at the bar stool closest to Stander chipped in as well.

"That's what I mean. These insurance companies are all the same. On your ass, if you are late with a payment. But getting money out of them is like trying to get blood from a turnip..." Other customers soon joined in the ongoing conversation with their personal experiences on the topic.

Ethan finally caught Stander's eye and gave him a little wave before moving to an empty table across from the bar. Stander nodded and held up a finger indicating he would be right there before disappearing into a swinging door off to the side. Emerging minutes later, followed close behind by a younger woman who looked to be of Hawaiian or Polynesian descent. She moved behind the bar taking Stander's place as he walked over to Ethan's table. The two men shook hands and sat down across from each other.

Looking around the bar, Ethan started, "Really nice place you have here, Russ. I appreciate your invite. Thank you."

"Just call me Stander, Ethan. Everyone in here does. They catch you calling me Russ, and you might get tossed," Stander and Ethan both smiled. "And you are welcome. Now let me get us a couple drinks and some food coming." Ethan glanced over the menu and ended up taking Stander's earlier recommendation on the cheeseburger. Before long, both men had their food and a cold draft in front of them.

Ethan pointed at the various bits of old boxing memorabilia in the bar. A pair of blue boxing trunks and a matching robe hung from a hook high above the coat rack. Several pairs of cracked leather boxing gloves and vintage boxing and fight posters hung along the walls inside the bar. "So what is with the whole boxing theme in here? Did you used to box yourself?"

"I did. When I was a lot younger, I boxed on and off. In fact, when I first bought this building, I even opened a gym down in the basement. We had our own little amateur boxing team here in Marquette for a while." Stander shrugged, "I liked working with the kids, and it gave them something to do. Especially for the kids who maybe weren't big enough to play basketball or football. Or whose parents couldn't really afford to pay for private hitting lessons or pitching coaches. Seems like to play sports these days, you need all that stuff just to make the teams..."

"I hear you. Although I gotta admit, even if I had extra coaching as a kid, I doubt I would ever have been athletic enough to make any of the sports teams at my school." Ethan patted his flabby belly, smiling, then took another drink from his beer before continuing. "We had wrestling, but there weren't any boxing gyms around. So how long did you box? Fight anyone I would have heard of?"

"You ever hear of Mike Tyson?" Stander asked. Ethan opened his eyes wide and nodded yes as he took a bite out of his burger. "I like to tell people that I fought him and took the best Tyson had back in the day." Stander appeared somber, then broke into a wide grin. Quickly adding, "But when I say that, I'm fucking lying," before laughing out loud at his own joke. The Hawaiian or Polynesian girl working the bar appeared just then with two more beers. Laying both down on coasters that said Round 2.

Overhearing, she commented, "Is Stander here telling old fight stories again? Should I have him thrown out?" She winked at Ethan. "Don't believe everything you hear in this bar, honey. Especially from the owner."

Stander waved his hand dismissively at her. "Oh Hannah, if I ever stopped lying, I'd just disappoint you." The younger lady just shook her head and swatted Stander with her bar towel as she walked past him.

"Anyway," Stander continued, "I won a few of those Tough Guy or Tough Man tournaments that used to be kind of big around here. Won some sweet prize money doing that. But officially, I only had a handful of true professional boxing matches. I found I could definitely knock guys out if I hit them just right. But also learned I am just way too slow to really be any good. Sure, I could beat the stumble-bums just making a buck here and there. But after sparring with some real pros, I knew that was likely as far as I'd ever be able to take it. So I said fuck that, I'll stay a fan and keep my face from getting kicked in." Stander said all this without a hint of embarrassment or false modesty. "I do love the sport, though. The one-on-one, your will against the other guy's will. You know, you can 'play' basketball, football, soccer, and all that. But you can't 'play' at boxing. If you do, you are likely to get your head taken off." Stander gestured in the air and made quotation marks with his hands both times when he said the word play. Then he lifted his glass in a half salute and took a swig.

After finishing eating and more small talk, Hannah cleared away the empty dishes and placed a shot glass of what Ethan presumed to be whiskey in front of them both. The coaster under each read Round 3. Both men tipped their new drinks back, and Ethan coughed a little as the whiskey burned its way down his throat. "So, Ethan," Stander began, "tell me more about why you are staying up here in Marquette all summer. Secrist said you were a student working on something. No offense, man, but you look too fucking old to be in college anymore."

Ethan laughed and grimaced, tentatively sipping at the remains of his whiskey shot. "Sometimes I think that too. But I already have my bachelor's; I finished that up years ago. However, a four-year degree in English literature doesn't really pay the bills. Turns out that degree is good for working like a dog in retail, but not much else. So I decided to go back to school and started doing a few classes here and there. Finally did enough to get accepted at the

University of Michigan down in Ann Arbor. So technically, I am working on my Doctorate in Native American Studies."

"That is a fucking mouthful," said Stander. "What will you do with a degree in that? Teach somewhere?"

"More than likely, yeah. But I have to tell you. I am really enjoying the field work I am doing right now. Makes me question if I want to spend the rest of my life in a classroom somewhere or not." Ethan finally finished the remaining thimble's worth of whiskey in his glass with a forced smile.

"Field work, huh? So that is why you are up by Mt. Arvon?" Ethan nodded an affirmative. "Why so far away from your school? That is like six or seven hours from here. You can't be commuting back and forth every day. You renting a room here in Marquette?" asked Stander.

"Yeah," replied Ethan. "I got a room out by the highway in that old Starlight motel. The rates are cheap, and they are even charging me by the week, so I can afford it while I work up here."

"Gotcha. But still, out of all the places Indians hung around, why so far up here?" Stander questioned, "What is so special about Mt. Arvon or even the Huron mountains in general?"

"To some degree, because no one has really done much research in that area. It is kind of hard to find places where that is true anymore. But also because the wilderness up that way has so much lore tied to it. The mountain itself has a long oral history and kind of mythology with local tribes that dates back thousands of years." Ethan pulled himself in closer to the table as he spoke. Obviously excited by this topic. "Native Americans lived all around here. Wisconsin, upper and lower Michigan, Canada, Ohio, you name it. Algonquian-speaking Native Americans lived in the Great Lakes area for millennia."

"Makes sense, I mean, with the lakes and all. They sure weren't going to starve."

"Exactly, hard winters but plenty of resources." Ethan went on, engrossed in the subject matter that currently occupied his days. "Some of the oldest stories and legends even speak of immigrations to and from all the Great Lakes over the centuries. Archeologists who have worked around the area in the past have found sites as far back as 3,000 B.C."

Stander had to admit that was impressive. "Seriously? So local people lived right here in upper Michigan that far back?" Stander whistled in appreciation. "So what tribes were these? Cherokee? Apache?" Stander named off tribes he knew about mostly from watching old movies.

"That far back, right around here anyway, the people were called Anishinaabeg. The really ancient sites found were fishing tribes whose settlements dotted the upper Great Lakes around Lake Superior, Lake Michigan, and Lake Huron. They hunted, fished, and were primarily gatherers who preserved food to sustain themselves over the long winters." Ethan looked across at Stander, expecting him to already be yawning. To his surprise, Stander seemed genuinely interested. So he continued, "The Anishinaabeg people were respectful to their elders and treasured their children. They conducted ceremonies for good health, giving thanks, war, funerals, and other things. Basically, good guys who really strove to conduct their lives in harmony and peace."

"Sounds like they knew the right way to live. I suppose we screwed all that up for them when we got here, huh?" Stander lifted and downed the rest of his whiskey with a smile.

"Kind of, but not right away. The Anishinaabeg lived basically the same way for hundreds of years until the arrival of European settlers in the 1600s. The Anishinaabeg had dealings first with the French, then the English, and then finally Americans. Eventually, the Anishinaabeg people slowly evolved and split into various other tribes. But their basic beliefs and way of life didn't really begin to deteriorate until the various attempts to matriculate them into American mainstream society started. They began to be placed on reservations, sent to boarding schools, etc..." Ethan stopped himself, feeling like the alcohol was beginning to make him ramble.

But, to his surprise, Stander kept asking questions. At least, pretending he wanted to hear more. "So you are looking for more old sites of this Amishnaggaa-whatever tribe?" Stander butchered the tribe's name, but Ethan didn't mind. Smiling, he corrected him.

"A-nish-in-aa-beg," Ethan slowly articulated each sound.

"That's what I said. In-A-Gadda-Da-Vida or whatever." Stander laughed after purposefully spitting out the jumbled Iron Butterfly song title from the late 60s. "That is the tribe you are interested in? Or writing your paper on?"

Ethan shook his head. "No, actually, the tribe I am most interested in is from later on. Technically, I am researching and then hopefully writing a paper on the Sault St. Marie Tribe of Chippewa Indians. The Anishinaabeg people were their ancestors. Like I said, over long periods of time, groups would sometimes splinter periodically into separate tribes for a variety of reasons. The Chippewa Indians are the tribe most associated with this area."

"And Chippewa Falls is where the best beer is made!" Stander got to his feet and pulled the empty glasses and both coasters off the table. "Be right back with some official Chippewa Falls drafts. We can't have this discussion without toasting and drinking the beer made in the town named after the Chippewa Indians, now can we?" With that, Stander made his way back towards the bar.

As Ethan looked on, Stander chatted with a young guy, probably still in his twenties. He had a shaved head and wore a tank top that showed off a barbed wire tattoo around his bicep. As he talked, Stander was simultaneously pulling two drafts of Leinenkugel beer. Ethan already knew that the brewery's home was right next to the Chippewa River in Chippewa Falls, Wisconsin. When Stander finished filling the two glasses, he walked back to their table with a mug in either hand, each with a perfect white foamy head on the surface. Stander put both handled glasses down on top of the two new coasters he had brought with him that said Round 4.

Ethan thanked him and as Stander sat down, he questioned the older man. "I hope you don't think you have to babysit me here, Stander? I know you have a bar to run."

Stander waved the suggestion off. "I got great people like Hannah who do all the real work. I just shoot the shit and make a few drinks here and there. And don't get me wrong, I do love all my regulars. But, for instance, that guy I was just talking with? He is about as sharp as a marble. So, believe me, you are probably saving my life here. Second-hand stupidity can kill!" Both men laughed and took a drink of cold beer. Stander then rekindled the same topic with another question, "So you said earlier there are a lot of old Indian myths and legends about that area up by Mt. Arvon. Are you talking about Skull Rock?"

Ethan frowned. "The only Skull Rock or Skull Mountain I know is at Six Flags in New Jersey. You know, the roller coaster." He paused, then added, "Well, that and the Nancy Drew mystery."

"It was Hardy Boys, not Nancy Drew. But I am impressed at your age you would even know either one of those book series." Stander smiled wistfully, "I grew up on those fucking books... But anyway, you're doing all this research on Mt. Arvon and never heard of Michigan's very own Skull Rock? Geez, what kind of a student are you?"

Ethan turned his palms up on the table. "So educate me then."

Stander went on. "Oh, there is nothing, really. All I ever heard was a bunch of bullshit stories when I first started coming up here as a kid. But there is a big boulder up on the mountain that does kind of look like a skull. I mean, if you look at it just right and know where it is."

"Interesting. You need to come up and show me sometime. I'd really like to see that. Maybe it was carved by one of the early tribes?" Ethan paused momentarily. "That would actually kind of tie-in with some of the early Native American legends and stories from up there. Stories were passed down word-of-mouth by tribes over time. Usually, there is some truth or fact they were based on. If there is something that resembles a skull on that mountain, it would actually explain a lot."

"What stories or legends? Where did you hear these at?" Stander was genuinely curious to hear more about the place his sister had been buried at. He studied the younger man as he spoke.

"I never really heard anything per se," Ethan began. "But early white settlers kind of reported on local tribes. Some of the pioneers were smart enough to realize what was happening to the Indian culture and their way of life, so they tried to put down on paper their stories and teachings before they were gone forever. Some of the very first writings are really interesting. For instance, did you know some of the earliest stories about zombies came from Native American folklore?"

"What? Like George Romero or Walking Dead kind of shit?" Stander shook his head. "No fucking way. I never heard any Indian zombie stories before."

Ethan laughed. "Well, not literally the same zombies that we picture now. But in old Indian folklore, there are Skinwalkers. And, of course, the Wendigo. You have probably heard of that before, haven't you?" Stander agreed he had seen that name mentioned a time or two in a book or an old horror movie he'd seen somewhere. "The Wendigo is said to be a mythical man-eating creature or a demonic evil spirit of sorts. As the tale goes, he was once a lost hunter. In some versions of the legend, he came from a faraway land. In other stories, he was supposedly native to the northern forests of the Atlantic coast and Great Lakes region of the United States and Canada. In some of the tellings, he is a supernatural creature that can curse and possess humans with severe hunger pains. The thing causes them to suffer from cannibalistic urges and a psychosis that can never be sated. It was said that many different individuals can be infected by this single, ancient evil, serving as multiple extensions of it." Ethan stopped and took another drink.

"That sounds more like a vampire than zombie to me, Ethan." But Stander had to admit it was weird to think that Native Americans here, in what would later become America, had some of the same beliefs and stories of monsters as other parts of the world. For that matter, the same stories that still scared modern people today.

"Every version is a little different. So who knows? But these tales are believed by some to be the world's first zombie stories. A myth that may have originated as a way to prevent those facing starvation in times of famine from resorting to cannibalism for survival." As he continued, Ethan began to regret where the conversation had now turned. After all, Stander was dealing with his sister's death on that mountain. He tried to change the morbid tone. "Most scholars now dismiss the tales as simple morality stories. That the Wendigo mythology was really a way to encourage moderation and cooperation within tribes."

"What would make someone in the tribe get cursed by this thing?" asked Stander.

"In some versions, all it took was just being greedy or full of jealousy. But usually, you had to have tasted human flesh. That was what tainted you and made you prey for the evil spirit. Some tribes even appointed Wendigo-slayers-for-hire. Those who were believed to be transforming into a Wendigo would be put to death."

"Sounds a little like the witch hunts and farces led by the... uh... 'civilized' white man." Stander made quotation marks in the air again with his fingers as he spoke the word "civilized." Both men drained the last of the beers in front of them. "So, do you really want to see the big rock that looks like a skull up on Mt. Arvon? Maybe at the same time, you can show me how you find all that old Indian stuff after so long."

"I'd love to see that. As I said, maybe the rock was shaped at some point. If so, I have a geologist friend who could help me date any carvings or markings on it. If it was done by Native Americans, it would be a great find to comment on in my paper." Ethan cursed and instantly regretted his lack of sensitivity. He added, "I mean if you are offering and up for it. I don't want to impose, and it can wait..." Stander shook him off.

"Save it, Ethan. It's no problem for me. It might actually feel good to hike up around there where my sister last was. Might bring me, what do they call it? Oh yeah, closure." Stander smiled grimly.

After Ethan put his mug down, he stood up. "I better be heading out of here now. I think I'll take a quick leak and then hit the road. Thanks again for the hospitality. I really enjoyed getting to know you even if it was under kind of odd circumstances." He added, "Sorry I spent so much time talking about my work. I tend to get carried away at times."

Stander let him know that he had appreciated the younger man's company. They both settled on a date and time to meet up by Mt. Arvon. Ethan tried to pay for at least some of his meal, but Stander refused. Both men shook hands and as Ethan headed back towards the restrooms, he heard a group of three middle-aged ladies calling Stander down to their end of the bar. Loudly asking if he was done drinking for the night. "Are you kidding?" He heard Stander reply laughing, "I can drown a drink of water."

CHAPTER 12

PRESENT DAY

WHEN STANDER and Ethan met again four days later, it was once again at the foot of Mt. Arvon. Stander pulled his Jeep into the same temporary parking lot he and Secrist had parked before. He spied Ethan's old maroon Toyota truck, killed his engine, and got out. Ethan waved once as Stander walked towards him but otherwise was busy fidgeting with what looked to Stander like a push lawn mower.

"Damn, Ethan, you didn't tell me you were mowing grass up here in the woods?" Stander said, laughing a bit. "That looks almost exactly like the old Briggs and Stratton lawn mower I pushed all around the neighborhood I grew up in. I hope it starts easier than that fucking piece of shit did."

"I know, I know, it does look a lot like a lawn mower. But believe me, this is way more sophisticated than that. And a lot quieter! It's actually already running and ready for a little demonstration." Ethan waved Stander over and showed him the small digital screen attached to the handle.

"Looks like a fish radar to me," commented Stander, appraising the lit-up view. "Maybe a nice bass finder."

"Actually, it is similar in a way." Though Ethan knew he was no expert, he wanted to explain the principles since Stander offered to come up and see his work. "This thing is called a Ground Penetrating Radar unit or, as it is more commonly referred to as, a GPR unit. I have it on loan from the university for the duration of my work up here."

Stander squatted down next to the GPR unit, "So how does it work exactly?"

"Basically, GPR works by sending a tiny pulse of energy into a material - in this case - the ground, via an antenna. Then the integrated computer records the strength and the time required for the return, looking for any abnormal signals. Subsurface variations or disturbances in the ground create a kind of reflection that is picked up by this baby and shows it on the screen." As he spoke, Ethan pointed out the few exposed parts on the device that could be seen.

"So a radar that bounces up weird signals if it senses something in the ground? Is that about it?" Stander asked. "Seems like a fancy-ass treasure finder to me." Stander cocked an eyebrow at Ethan and, in his best old-time prospector voice, said, "You really just looking for gold up in them there hills, boy! Ain't ya?"

Laughing, Ethan responded, "Maybe archeological gold... Actually, it can't see metal, and I also have found it is incapable of identifying bone..." Ethan kicked himself for sharing this factoid with a guy whose sister's skeleton had just been recovered from the forest floor.

But Stander ignored the comment and simply asked, "So now you come up here by yourself and just go back and forth until you see something buried in the ground. Then what? You dig it up?"

"Not exactly. I have found a few kinds of one-offs close to the surface, but usually, I will place a marker on the spot until I can determine if it is part of a bigger pattern. If I think it is part of a more substantial configuration, I will download the spot into a GPS unit until I can come back later with a bigger team of students."

Stander was puzzled. "Wait a minute. How come you can use a GPS unit, but I can't use my phone?"

"GPS devices have nothing to do with a cellular network. There are satellites up in the atmosphere that are constantly broadcasting a signal. So basically GPS works entirely off a satellite signal, not cell signal." Ethan pulled his small handheld GPS unit out of a side pocket and held it up for Stander to see briefly before returning it.

"So, anyway, if what I find doesn't appear to be tied to anything else, I will come back with a little shovel and dig it out. Usually, those finds end up being more modern stuff with no real archeological value. I am really only interested in locating old paths, high activity areas, and maybe figure out where individual dwellings stood." Ethan paused and looked over at the path he had most recently been using to reach the area he was now canvassing. "Anyway, now that I bored you to death with all the technical jargon, how about I show you. Let's go see if we can find something." Ethan started pushing the GPR unit into the timber, with Stander following close behind.

The men took turns using the GPR unit, occasionally placing a small wire and plastic white marker flag here and there. They stopped to dig in the ground several times, but each shovelful proved to be of no value to Ethan's work. A short time later, after the little demonstration ended and they'd returned the GPR unit to the back of Ethan's truck, the two men headed out in the direction of Skull Rock. Stander led the way so Ethan could see for himself the nearby natural rock formation some believed resembled a human skull.

Fifteen minutes later, Ethan and Stander stood together looking up at a small dirt embankment from a dry and rocky creek bed. The top of the slope was a good ten feet above their heads. Erosion over the years had worn away the soil unevenly along the side. Big clumps of dirt stuck out like miniature cliffs part of the way up. Broken branches and small dead trees that had been downed in the past by rushing rainwater littered the path to the top as well.

"We can either walk all the way around or pull ourselves up and over." Stander eyed the younger, pudgy man, already breathing hard, unsure if Ethan could actually do that by himself or not. "Up to you, man. But see those long dangling roots hanging down from near the top? We can grab on those to help us get up."

"And you can see this skull rock of yours from right up there?" Ethan said this a little doubtfully as he pointed to the top of the small ridge. Then added, "Will those roots even hold us?"

Stander confirmed, "It's been a while since I have been up this way. But, from what I remember, you can see the profile of the rock perfectly from right up there. It's actually the best place to see the skull. From other angles, it just looks like a big rock."

With that, Stander bounded two big strides up the side of the ridge and grabbed at a downed pine tree for support. As he moved another step higher, he grasped a handful of tree roots that erosion had exposed and left hanging. The thinner and smaller ones broke off in his hand, but the thicker ones held. Using his arms and digging footholds as he ascended, Stander soon was standing at the top and looking down at Ethan.

"Come on, man. I can give you a hand when you get close to the top." A minute later, Ethan was huffing and puffing beside Stander but looking elated at the climb he had managed to navigate up the slope. "See? Saved us like 10 fucking minutes of walking." Smiling, Stander slapped Ethan on the back and instantly regretted it. His hand was slick and wet from Ethan's sweat-soaked shirt. Stander wiped the slimy hand discreetly on his own jeans and then turned, along with Ethan, to face Mt. Arvon. Unfortunately, a cluster of trees obscured the two men's vision.

"Shit," said Stander. "I don't think those were here before. Or at least hadn't grown that tall the last time I was up this far." Stander began walking around the huddled group of tall pine trees to get a better look up the side of the mountain. But not watching closely where he was walking, he nearly lost his footing when he stepped into a small pile of animal bones heaped unceremoniously along the ground. "What the fu…? Watch your step there, Ethan. Looks like something died here." Stander gestured at the mound of near fleshless carcasses. "God, were these deer? Fawns, maybe?" Stander pushed a few of the bones around with his foot. Several of them, in varying degrees of decomposition, still had tufts of hair attached. "No, not all of them. Check that out," he said, directing Ethan's gaze to the grisly find. "That one had to have been a fox. See the red fur? And look at the teeth on the one next to it. That was obviously a beaver."

"Must be some natural predator feasting here. Maybe dragging their kills to this spot to eat?" Ethan said this distractedly, clearly wanting to move away from the spot and continue on with their hike.

"Out in the open like this? I mean, maybe..." Stander squatted down to get a closer look. He didn't remember ever seeing such a display of assorted animal bones before. It just didn't seem natural to him. He couldn't help but recall what Secrist had told him about Tathum haunting these same woods as a kid back in the 1970s. The suspicions he'd started out torturing defenseless critters before moving onto humans as an adult. These bones were way too recent to have been from him, of course. But Ethan had found Sherry's remains not far from where they now stood, just on the opposite side of Mt. Arvon. When Stander stood back up, a flash of light winked at him from the stand of trees beside the stark pile of bleached animal bones. Sunlight reflecting off of something. Stander walked into the cluster to investigate, stepping past the tangled underbrush. Ten feet in, he stopped and called for Ethan to follow.

"What did you...?" Ethan stopped midsentence. Stander didn't answer. He didn't have to. There, nailed to several of the trees, were the remains of more animals. The unfortunate woodland creatures had been stretched out, and metal nails were driven at some point into their paws. The steel heads of the nails, what had first caught Stander's attention, glinting under the dim rays of the sun rays able to pierce through the tops of the trees. Each of the animals had been crucified. The three animals were so butchered and decayed they were unrecognizable. The pieces remaining had mostly fallen along the ground of the blasphemous scene. "Jesus!" Ethan couldn't find another word to say.

"More like Lucifer, I'd say. Or at least Judas…" Stander turned from his gruesome find in disgust. Whoever had done this was long gone now. The remains are likely months old. Stander turned and followed Ethan back out of the shadowed patch of wilderness. Then took the lead once more as they continued their climb, with Ethan falling in step just behind him.

Both men talked sparingly as they made their way towards the top of Mt. Arvon. Stander tried to push from his mind the grim scene they'd just stumbled upon. He kept his eye out for Skull Rock, but Ethan actually spotted the locally famous boulder first five minutes later.

"That has got to be it," Ethan spoke and pointed up the side of the mountain. Stander turned around and then followed Ethan's gaze back the way he had been hiking, immediately recognizing it as the rock they both had trudged up to see.

"You got it. Told you it was right up this way." Stander, though still puzzling over what they'd seen, couldn't help but start to smile at his little conquest. He was slightly relieved that he had actually remembered the landscape well enough to bring the rock into sight. Squinting to bring the features of the rock into better focus, he brought his hand up to shield his eyes from the bright and blazing afternoon sun. "Damn, man, I swear that thing looks even more like a skull now than it did before." Stander brought his hand back down. "Must be the way the sun is hitting it right now."

Ethan commented as well at the clearly defined shape before his eyes. "I can see why they named that Skull Rock. The way it sticks out from the side of the mountain, it really does look just like a skull. You can see a well-defined chin and two eyes. That is magnificent!" Ethan seemed stunned at the clarity. He pulled out a small pair of green camouflage binoculars from one of his pockets and lifted them to his face. "It even looks like lines running up and down where the teeth would be." He dropped the field glasses back into the deep pockets of his khaki shorts. "Let's get a closer look," Ethan strode purposefully up the side of the mountain.

Stander followed and, like Ethan, kept glancing up at the

boulder as he walked. Expecting the shape to change dramatically and just "become" a rock again with each step. However, as they got closer, the metamorphosis Stander had experienced in the past never happened. Abruptly, Ethan stopped and turned back to face Stander.

"You are putting me on, right? There is no way that rock wasn't carved to look like that." Ethan was giving Stander a bit of a queer look. "Is this whole thing kind of a put-on? I kind of feel like maybe I am being punked here. Like maybe there is a local tradition of seeing how long you can keep us out-of-town folks believing this is some spooky ghost rock or something?" Stander shook his head no. "Oh, come on, look at that." Ethan jerked a thumb over his shoulder at the boulder in the distance. "No way Mother Nature did that, Stander."

"Look, I don't know if anyone has been up here messing with it recently or not," Stander began. "But there is no tradition of fooling people, at least that I know of anyway. And even if there was, I wouldn't be fucking with you like that." Stander stopped and looked back up the mountain. "Shit, you were the one who brought up all those old Indian legends or tales that I had never even heard before. I just thought you might want to see it. I am telling you that boulder up there has been called Skull Rock for as long back as I can remember." Stander looked back at Ethan once again. "But I will admit, I don't remember it being so clear before. As I said, I haven't actually been up here myself in years. Maybe kids have been carving on it or something. Hell, for all I know, maybe kids always have been, for that matter. But your geography friend will be able to tell you that, right?" Stander now felt a little defensive of the sightseeing trip he had led them on.

Ethan held the older man's gaze another beat and then looked back up to the top of the mountain once again. "Geologist, not geography." Turning back to Stander, Ethan held up his arms in deference. "OK, OK… I believe you. I believe that is what you think. But I am telling you that had to be carved to look like that." Ethan shrugged, "But who cares? I have to say it is cool looking.

Especially out here in the middle of nowhere. Now let's get up there and take a closer look since we have come this far. I at least want to get a picture or two."

"Geologist, geometry, geography, whatever. You know what I mean." Both men again started walking up the mountain at an angle, free from the strand of trees they had emerged from and pushing past the knee-high weeds that itched and scratched at Ethan's bare legs.

They brought themselves around until they were facing the front of the boulder and then began walking straight upwards. Now in a direct line with the face of the rock, their new perspective, and closing proximity did not diminish the effect the oddly formed rock had on them. Instead, the sheer size of the boulder made the likeness of the skull more intimidating, if anything. After a few more steps, it was Stander this time that stopped to point out a couple additional features. "Now that is really fucking freaky. Check out those trees on either side of the big rock," he pointed to help guide Ethan's vision. Both men had to peer into the sunlight as they looked up the side of the mountain.

At almost identical positions were two sagging and virtually branchless pine trees on both sides of Skull Rock. Their odd trajectory was clearly caused by slippage in the rocks and soil that their roots had previously been secured. But now, both pines were no longer standing upright as before, nor had they been completely felled either. Instead, both trees stretched out from the side of the mountain at an almost perfect 45-degree angle. That in itself was not unusual to see on the side of a mountain range. Trees often slowly collapsed forward with gravity's help as they aged, bending down the side of even gently sloping hills.

What was eye-catching and weird, however, was the two trees' closeness to the boulder with the skeletal human face. Taken together, the twin pine trees looked like two separate arms on either side of a very large skull. Appendages that appeared as if they were somehow attached to the giant skull's body were still buried under the soil of the mountainside. Both arms engaged in a struggle to pull an entire giant skeleton out of the side of the mountain. Only the tops of each tree had a few branches still attached. Those couple remaining tree limbs did nothing but solidify the illusion the two trees created. The branches each appeared as hands and fingers at the end of long and emaciated limbs. Skull Rock's protruding chin and brows above each eye hole gave the entire deception a menacing appearance.

"Whoa... I see those. You're thinking what I'm thinking, right? They look like two arms, don't they? I bet if we had been here a month before, those couple of trees would have still been standing tall. For that matter, a couple weeks from now, they would most likely be entirely collapsed." Ethan further commented on the bizarre image before them. "Kind of like those two that are lying underneath the bottom of the boulder. You see those downed trees lying on the ground on either side, don't you?" He pointed at a spot well below the irregular boulder. "Right there, those two totally look like the thing's legs, don't they?" Ethan pulled a digital camera out of one pocket along the side of his shorts. "I have to get a picture of all this before it changes. That is just way too strange to not have proof."

When he was done taking pictures, both men finished their upwards climb to the top. Ethan took more photos from various spots of the boulder and surrounding scenery. He climbed all around the rock and scampered up the face of the diminutive cliff. He found that directly above Skull Rock was a relatively flat ledge. Inviting Stander up with him, they both enjoyed the view of the gently sloping valley below them, trying to judge where their cars were parked and where they had been working earlier that day. Ethan plugged the location where they stood into the GPS unit he carried for later reference.

Eventually, Stander made his way back down from the ledge. Ethan followed a few minutes later but lingered near the skull-like face, walking back and forth and closely examining the sides of the boulder. Then he scurried once more back on top of it, inspecting the rounded top and nearly falling down the side in the process.

Stander finally asked, "Ethan, what are you doing? It is just a big rock, man. I have to admit, you were probably right about it being sculpted. Someone must be hanging around up here and carving it up." Stander casually tossed a loose stone down off the side. "Are you still going to have your expert on rocks come and verify that?"

"Absolutely! I want to get him up here for sure now. Although he might actually be able to tell just from my pictures if this was carved by man or Mother Nature." Ethan stood stroking his chin contemplatively. "But I think now I have a different question for him. See the way this sets in here, the flat ledge and space on top? Does that seem natural?"

Stander studied it for a moment, "I mean, I don't know. I guess it could be..." Stander shrugged, "But why the interest? That's not your line of work or study anyway."

"Think about it, Stander. All the lore and old tales about this mountain. The rock shaped into a skull? This could have been a very significant site at one time." Ethan could hardly contain his excitement at the thought. "If I can find it somehow ties into the Native American beliefs about this area, that would be absolutely huge. Professor Danforth would positively shit himself. God, what I would give to see that presumptuous old fart's face..." Ethan stopped himself from talking but not smiling. "You know, he tried to convince me not to look in this place, to begin with. If this turned out to be of significance for local Native Americans, there would be a ton of new information about the tribes that were localized here in the past. Plus, artifacts and cultural learnings. I am telling you, it would just be amazing."

"Well then, for your sake, I hope that is the case. I just wouldn't get myself all excited just yet. Not to be a Debbie Downer here, but this is part of a state park. You would think if it was that important someone would have found that out by now." Ethan understood what he was saying, but Stander's lack of enthusiasm hardly diminished the excitement he could feel in his bones about the place. He continued to talk about the potential finds as they prepared to start back.

Before heading down the side of the mountain, both men kneeled beside the small stream that flowed hurriedly alongside the face of the skull-like boulder. They splashed their faces and necks with some of the bubbling cold mountain spring water, refreshing themselves before starting back down. After hiking back to their cars, the two men shook hands goodbye. Stander let Ethan lead as they pulled out in their separate vehicles. He followed him along the winding roads until the cars split up as they closed in on Marquette.

CHAPTER 13
10TH CENTURY

GUNNAR SLOWLY OPENED his eyes and groggily sat up, feeling barely rested as if he had only just settled in for the night. The dinner with Vidar and the elders from the night before was still fresh in his mind. Disoriented, he clutched at the strands of his fading dreams as he rubbed the sleep from his eyes. Trying to recapture some of the images even as they slowly faded.

As was often the case, he had dreamt of being with Sassa. They had been together down at the river or at least by some river or stream. Gunnar hadn't actually recognized the flowing water or the mountain it cascaded down from. The trees in his dream were different also, similar looking but much thicker and taller. Or perhaps he was meant to be smaller in his dream…?

Pondering all this, Gunnar pulled down the heavy covers and stretched his long arms up and over his head. Yawning, he felt the familiar dull ache deep in his shoulder he often did first thing in the morning. Out of habit, he fingered the birthmark on his shoulder. His fingers traced the raised pattern of discolored skin on his back as he tried to recall more of the dream so he could tell Sassa about it. He knew she'd been talking at him as well, but he couldn't make out her words…

"Aaahhh! Yaahh!" Gunnar exclaimed loudly as his bare feet touched the ice-cold dirt floor under them. The chilly shock startled him wide awake. Breathing out deeply, Gunnar could see his breath in the dim light of the early morning. Bracing this time, he forced himself out of the soft, warm blankets he'd slept in and quickly pulled on his clothes and boots before swiftly moving out of his room and over to the fireplace. Soon he had the fire re-lit and rubbed his numb hands together greedily over the budding flames. Once his hands regained feeling and his face was warmed, he moved towards the front door, heading outside to retrieve more wood for later.

Making his way to the wood supply, Gunnar could hear the grass crunching loudly under each of his steps. He paused briefly, admiring the glistening beauty of the landscape in the morning sun and listening to the creaking of the frozen branches above his head. Stooping, he filled his arms with chopped wood before hastening back inside the now-warming house. Careful not to lose his balance on the slippery, frost-covered ground along the path as he made his way. After setting the wood pile down, Gunnar threw a few more pieces of wood on the fire before crossing the room to wake his father. Anxious to show him the gift of beauty the god Ymir had bestowed upon them this morning.

Once his mom had passed away, his father had grown accustomed to the solitude of his own room each evening. But during the winter, to stay warm, his father seldom closed the door at night. The warmth from the central room and fireplace was much needed during the long cold nights. Usually, as winter made the slow turn to spring and spring to summer, he often would begin closing his door when retiring for the night. So Gunnar was not alarmed to see the door closed now. Although freezing this morning, it had been slowly warming up recently.

Gunnar knocked on his father's door. "Come out and see the frost before it all disappears. The sun is just now hitting it." Hearing no reply, Gunnar waited a few moments and then knocked louder. "Hurry up now and come to the fire. It's freezing this morning." Even as the words escaped his mouth, Gunnar began to open his father's door. Putting together the cold night, closed door, and his father's continuing decline, he grew concerned. Still hearing no reply, Gunnar entered the room.

If possible, it seemed to Gunnar his father's room was even colder than his own had been. The door swung halfway open before it stopped and began to swing closed again on him as he stepped forward. Ducking around the slowly closing door, Gunnar saw what stopped the door from opening completely. His father lay prone across the hard dirt floor of his room. Still, in his bedclothes, face down and with one arm outstretched towards the door as if reaching for the exit.

A rising panic seized Gunnar.

Moaning, he kneeled and clutched the extended hand of his father, recoiling first at the stiffness and chill his touch encountered before immediately reaching out again with both hands. He had to get his father off the floor and over to the fire, thinking to himself, "He'll catch his death on the freezing ground." But pulling him over and towards him, Gunnar saw death had already caught his father. Blank, grey-filmed eyes stared up at him in the growing light. The life and love that was his father were long gone.

Silently at first, Gunnar began to cry. Soon whimpering sounds followed until they were drowned out by sobs. The sobs wrenched themselves from Gunnar's chest and quickly gaining in momentum and strength as reality set in. Tears streamed down his face, and the sobs soon became wails of anguish that stopped briefly each time Gunnar would run out of air. Only to start up again after the next inhale of a long shuddering breath. He wasn't sure how much time had passed because, both inside and outside, he felt cold and numb all over.

Eventually, Gunnar became vaguely aware of movement around him. He understood people had entered the room and were trying to talk with him, but he couldn't answer. Neighbors, concerned by the desperation of his cries, had come to help. Someone tried to pull Gunnar's father's hands out of his own, but he held tight. The look he shot them stopped their efforts. It wasn't until a little later, when Sassa sat down in front of him, that Gunnar really understood what was going on. She held his face in her hands and kissed his tears.

She was crying too.

Sassa was talking to him like a child, telling him his father had died, he had found him, and now Sigrid and Sassa were both here. Eventually, together, with some help, they were able to get Gunnar up off the floor. He was held and cried with both of them. Gunnar knew he should be ashamed, but he could not stop himself. Somehow he was moved to a chair by the fire, and a cup was placed in his hand. Sassa stayed with him as other friends and neighbors tended to his father's body.

Gunnar felt paralyzed.

Everywhere he looked was a reminder of his father. The cabinet he'd built his mother years before. The chair he sat in at the table. His long overcoat was hanging on the wall. His father was everywhere but no longer here at all. The enormity of the loss threatened to overcome Gunnar once again. He felt the tears and sobs climbing up his throat and clamoring to escape. Gunnar pressed the cup to his lips in hopes of washing these things back down. Gulping the liquid, he gagged and spat the drink back into the cup he was holding.

It tasted wrong.

He bent his head forward and sniffed the liquid in the cup. A sickly sweet smell rose from the drink. He looked down into his cup and saw it was goat's milk but clearly spoiled. Disgustedly, Gunnar passed the cup to Sassa, saying simply, "Rotten." Gunnar buried his head once more in his hands. Trying to block out the sounds and the light from the early morning sun, willing this to be another dream that he would soon wake from.

Not a dream, thought Gunnar, a nightmare…

After some time, Gunnar followed Sassa and her mother back to their home at the edge of the village. Both insisted he leave with them while others took care of his father's body. As the three of them walked together in the chilly morning air, Gunnar kept his head down. He thought of the meal they all shared together just the night before. Who would have expected that dinner would be the last meal his father would ever have? Gunnar thought again of Vidar. He desperately wanted to somehow blame the man for his father's death. But he knew his dislike for the man and his own grief were clouding his emotions.

As he sat in Sigrid and Sassa's home, he tried pushing these ugly thoughts from his head. Gunnar's father often said that death was simply part of living, neither better nor worse. He had never shown any fear of dying as his condition worsened. Believing he would join his wife and finally be together with her for eternity with Ymir. Saying that, when he died, he knew he would be missed here and that alone was enough to make him feel good about his life. Gunnar crossed his arms on the table and laid his head down. Closing his eyes, he thought back on the countless lessons his father had taught him. Gunnar wondered if he would be missed when his time came. He supposed by Sassa and their eventual children... His heart ached both for the loss of his father and his love for Sassa. Tears squeezed out the corners of his eyes as he imagined the lives of the little ones they would soon raise together. The life he would live to honor his father. How he would protect this place along with the children soon to come.

Protect and defend it. No matter the cost.

"Oh! How awful, Sassa!" It was Sigrid who had begun working in the kitchen. Gunnar opened his eyes but did not raise his head. He heard Sassa walk over to where Sigrid was preparing some food. Sigrid said, "That hasn't happened before with our chickens. What a waste."

"Let me see, mother. What is it? Eww!" Now it was Sassa who was clearly disturbed. "Blood in the egg! Oh, and the smell! Mother, give me that and get another egg. I'll take this outside." Gunnar sat up and peered over at both women. Sigrid wiped her hands and then reached for another egg with a frown on her face. Sassa gave Gunnar a quick, small smile and began to make her way to the front door holding the putrid egg. "I'll just get rid of this and wash…"

"No, no, no…Oh no! What has happened here? Ugh!" Sigrid turned away from her work, looking pale. Her face pinched in disgust. "Take these all away, Sassa. They are all bad, I fear." Gunnar rose from the table he occupied, walking over to see. But Sigrid met him halfway, raising her hands to his chest. "No need to see that today, Gunnar. Just some bad eggs. It happens sometimes." Sigrid said this without much conviction and avoided Gunnar's gaze. Ignoring her, he gently swept her arms aside and moved over to the place where she and Sassa had begun to prepare food. Peering over the edge of the simple clay bowl, Gunnar saw what disturbed Sigrid so deeply.

From behind him, he heard Sassa call his name, but he ignored it. In the bowl was a partially formed chick surrounded by thick, dark blood. Gunnar raised a hand to his nose and mouth as the smell hit him. Next to the bowl lay the dull brown egg shell. In one half, it still held what looked like a dark, sticky clot. Gunnar thought he could see two tiny legs sticking out from the red mass. He looked over again at what was once the beginning of a chicken lying in the bowl. It was very small, so very fragile at the beginning of what was a doomed life. Gunnar could see that only the top half had developed. He could make out its beak and the delicate skull attached, tiny bare bones where a wing should be. He felt Sigrid pulling on his arm, "Gunnar, please. Come sit back down."

As Gunnar began to turn away, a hushed whisper called his attention back to the bowl. As he looked down at the tiny deformed chick, he saw fresh blood oozing from the end of the beak.

Then it opened one black eye.

CHAPTER 14
10TH CENTURY

SIGRID AND SASSA had quickly disposed of all the eggs, unwilling to take a chance on eating even one. Sigrid tried to convince Gunnar that he hadn't seen any movement or sound from the aborted chick inside the bowl. Saying she had been beside him the whole time and had witnessed nothing. Gunnar realized what she was trying to do, but he knew what he had seen and heard. The tiny black eye had opened; that disturbing image would not leave Gunnar's head. The black eye, though much smaller, had been a near mirror image of Vidar's odd rock. Both were, it seemed to Gunnar, unnaturally bright yet blacker than a cloud-filled winter's night at the same time. He couldn't help but tie the two things together. The blinding darkness from the twin eyes crowded in on his thoughts.

Only when Erik, his spirit brother since childhood, came to Sigrid's home to check on him was Gunnar able to push the horrid image of the spoiled egg from his thoughts. Erik sat with Gunnar and, after offering his condolences, shared some of his favorite memories of Gunnar's father, doing his best to lift his friend's spirits. During a break in the conversation, Erik reached over and grasped Gunnar's shoulder briefly. "Tor has asked me to travel with two others over to Thorfinn's clan. They are waiting on me now. But I wanted to see you before I left."

"Thorfinn! But why? For what reason?" Gunnar asked, shocked. "Have you not heard of the tale Vidar told last night? There is an evil loose in this land. You and I saw what it did to Nimki's people. Vidar said that…"

"Vidar's tale is why Tor has asked me to leave." Erik looked across the room at Sigrid and Sassa working nearby. He lowered his voice before continuing. "Tor thinks Vidar is a madman. He wants Thorfinn's counsel to see if he vouches for him. Find out what he knows about Vidars village's troubles."

"A madman? But you and I saw what happened at that settlement of the dark-skinned ones…" But Erik cut Gunnar off again. Waving his hand dismissively.

"What we saw was the work of those Skraeling savages warring with each other. Nothing more. I told you as much that day." Erik, his voice still lowered, hissed.

"But what of my father? The spoiled food stores? Vidar's strange rock?" But even as he spoke, Gunnar thought of his father. What would he do if he were here? Gunnar tried to think as his father would. But deep down, he felt more like a little boy than a wizened man of years as he spoke with Erik. Before he could stop himself, he continued on. "Surely, this is the work of sorcery and dark magic. The thing was trying to claw his way back into the world of the living." Gunnar's mind raced as he turned each event over and over in his mind.

"Gunnar, you are rushing to tie the appearance of Vidar and his tale with the events of the day. You yearn to blame Vidar and his silly rock." Erik shook his head once more. "Milk gets spoiled often in the village. No monster beyond man's neglect was ever to blame for that before. What is different now? And a few bad eggs? While disturbing, it, too, is hardly an event of mystery. Those eggs must have been missed when they were first laid and stayed in the nest too long. This morning something in the nest shifted, and those gathering the eggs unknowingly grabbed them." Gunnar listened. He knew his father would have said these things to him…

"And what of your father's death? Deep down, had we not been expecting this all winter? You told me as much yourself when the snows were piled high. He had a big dinner full of drink and smoke in between a long walk back and forth to Tor's home. It was likely the longest he had walked in months, certainly all winter. All this and the excitement of meeting a newcomer on an extra cold night?" When Gunnar did not respond, Erik stood.

"The others are waiting for me. I must leave now if we are to make Thorfinn's village before dark." He reached out once more, this time putting both hands on Gunnar's broad shoulders and looking Gunnar directly in the eye. "When I return, we will speak again. But what I say is all truthful, is it not?" Gunnar nodded his head, but in his heart, the doubts remained. After Erik departed, Gunnar moved to where Sassa bedded at night and laid down. His head hurt, and he longed to fall asleep and forget everything about the day. If even only for a brief time.

Lying where Sassa slept each night, Gunnar struggled to find a comfortable position. But it was very soft, and the blankets smelled like Sassa's hair. He buried his face down in them and inhaled her comforting scent deeply. He drew his knees up to his chest like a newborn babe and closed his eyes, still puzzling over what had happened. His father dead on the floor. Vidar's arrival and Gunnar's vision… The rock Vidar carried with him. Black and blue inside. A kind of black eye. Vidar and his treasure. Tor thought it was treasure… Vidar and his story. The chick's black eye had opened. Vidar and his dark darting eyes. Black eyes, Gunnar thought. Vidar and his black eyes. Gunnar's last thought was of his own shimmering dark brown eyes. Nearly black.

He drifted off to sleep.

When Gunnar woke the second time that day, he did briefly forget the earlier events. Sitting up suddenly, Gunnar felt dizzy and confused. Puzzled that he was fully dressed and even still wore his shoes. Slowly, as he became more aware of his surroundings, the impact of the day's earlier events crashed into him. He shuddered as he remembered the cold touch of his father's hand when he'd had found him.

Looking around, Gunnar recognized he was still at Sigrid and Sassa's home. Judging by the cold air streaming in the window and the evaporating light from outside, it was dusk already. He had slept the entire afternoon. Still groggy, he sighed heavily and briefly laid back down. His head pounded behind his eyes, and he rubbed his temples, trying to soothe himself, attempting to will away the pain. Knowing his father was dead and all that was to come from that tragedy made Gunnar feel like he never wanted to get out of this bed. Closing his eyes, he only opened them again when his stomach began rumbling nonstop.

Glancing across the small home, he saw that someone had laid out a plate of food presumably for him. Staggering to his feet, Gunnar stumbled back over to the same table he had occupied earlier that day. Once he sat down and pulled the cloth off the prepared plate, Gunnar realized he was starving, unable to recall what or if he had eaten anything all day.

Gunnar ripped apart the bread crust left out for him and, adding some of the cured meat from the dish, devoured everything on the table. Thankful for the full meal but confused by the empty house and idly wondering where Sigrid and Sassa could be. Their home was a single room without any separate rooms like his father's house. Gunnar paused, like his house, he now supposed. The thought of the vacant house that waited for him brought back all the misery and heartache from earlier in the day. He filled the clay cup with water a second time and drained it. Refusing to give into his grief again on this wasted day. Looking outside, Gunnar saw the last of the daylight was all but gone now. In the simple house that was like a second home to him, Gunnar was able to easily light a fire and a few candles. Just as he finished, the door opened, and Sigrid entered.

"Hello, Gunnar. I hope you are feeling better now. We wanted to let you sleep." Sigrid glanced at the empty plates and cup on the table. "Ah, I see you found the food we left you. Are you full? There is more here." Sigrid held out an overflowing bag towards him, but Gunnar shook his head no. "Well, if not now, then please take this with you. It is nothing so special, but I did put some of your favorites in here. The dried meats and fruits should all keep. There is some bread inside as well."

Gunnar shook his head no again, but Sigrid insisted. Quietly saying she knows the next few days will be hard for him. Finally, Gunnar took the bulging bag from her and thanked Sigrid for her generosity. "But where is Sassa?" he asked.

"She is at Tor's still. Vidar said he was not feeling well, and she went in my place this time." Hearing this troubled Gunnar, and it showed on his face. Seeing this, Sigrid quickly added, "Tor and his wife are also there. Sassa should be back home soon, I would think."

"I will go there and walk her home then. The fresh air and walk will do me good." Gunnar sheepishly added, "I seem to have slept this day away...." Sigrid nodded at this and seemed to want to say more but did not. An awkward silence filled the room. Neither Gunnar nor Sigrid was sure exactly what to say to break it. It was Gunnar who finally spoke. "I... I want to thank you for letting me stay here today. I am not sure... Not sure otherwise how... Or what..." Sigrid stepped to him then, reaching up to embrace the young man she'd already loved as if he were her own son.

"Oh, Gunnar... I'm so very sorry." She clutched him tightly to her as Gunnar stooped low and buried his face in her neck. She shushed him softly, feeling the silent sobs that racked his body.

Gunnar, unsure of what to say and fearing he likely would be unable to find his voice anyway, merely nodded his head. Finally croaking out, "I... I will go find Sassa now."

Still carrying the bag of food Sigrid had given him, Gunnar wrapped himself in the heavy coat Sassa had made him and walked out into the early nightfall. After closing the door behind him, Gunnar soon found himself taking each step faster than the previous one. Not slowing until he saw the lights from Tor's home at the top of the hill. He paused and gathered his thoughts, readying himself for the condolences and questions he knew Tor would offer as conversation. Shifting the bag of food into his right arm, he knocked on the front door. He was surprised at the enormity of his relief when he heard footsteps and saw Tor's face as he opened the door for him. "Hello, Tor. Please forgive my arrival so late in the day. But I was told Sassa was here. May I see her?"

"Hello, Gunnar. Yes, please, please come in. You can set the bag down over here if you wish." Tor pointed towards a basket on the floor made of intricately woven twigs and vines. As Gunnar put the bag down, Tor continued, "I was so sorry to hear about your father, Gunnar. I always felt like he was a brother to me. You know he and I were very close." Gunnar nodded and accepted Tor's exaggeration, knowing Tor could not help but flatter himself at every opportunity.

"I want you to know you can come to me anytime. You are still a young man, Gunnar. With your father gone, you may find you have questions. Or need the help of someone a little more experienced in life, heh? Maybe when you and Sassa decide to marry, I can offer some counsel or advice?" Gunnar simply stared back at Tor, unsure where this conversation was going. Tor looked around and drew close. "You know, advice on what to do, you see. My wife is not here now if you want to ask questions about... Well, you know. When you get married, men and women get together, and it can be confusing. But I could offer my wisdom on such matters..." Finally, Gunnar saw where Tor was headed with this, and it took every bit of his willpower not to strike the vain old man. He put a stop to this discussion and hastened to put some separation between them.

"Thank you, Tor. Thank you very much. I will remember that. Now, where is Sassa? Back here?" Gunnar gestured but did not wait for Tor's reply before starting towards the room Vidar had occupied since arriving. Glad to be away from the man and his uncomfortable insinuations. Without looking back, Gunnar reached the door, disturbed that Sassa would be alone in the same room with Vidar.

Behind a closed door, no less!

Without bothering to knock, he walked into the bedroom. It was well lit, with several candles burning at either end of the room. The bed itself lay empty, still appearing undisturbed from the morning, thick fur blankets covering the top. Vidar stood by himself in the center of the room, adorned again in some of Tor's clothing. His back to the doorway, he remained motionless even as Gunnar entered. He faced the blank and windowless wall opposite the door that had just opened. Gunnar immediately addressed him, speaking to the back of his head.

"Oh, uh… Greetings, Vidar. I hope you are well this evening." Vidar did not reply. Instead, without turning around, his head slowly drooped to the right. For a brief moment, Gunnar was sure it would tumble completely off his body. But it stopped at the shoulder. Then, in a muffled tone not much above a whisper, Vidar answered.

"He was sure you would come." A pause. "This was where we were meant to be. Now," again, a pause as if Vidar had trouble speaking, "I know all the wonders a man seeks." Yet again, Vidar fell silent. Gunnar strained to hear him and hung on his murmured words and strange cadence. "Wisdom." Pause. "The needs of flesh inside." Again Vidar stopped talking. This time Gunnar could see the muscles in his neck were working as if words were struggling or catching in his throat. "But flesh, you know, is not with us forever." With Gunnar still staring at him, Vidar's head straightened back up, once again squared normally upon his shoulders. At that moment, Gunnar understood Vidar's difficulty in getting his words out. Gunnar could just make out the soft wet crunches, saw his neck muscles move again, and realized Vidar's mouth was full. Biting down and chewing, his mouth working on something tough or thick.

Gunnar, in the stillness of the room, could feel his own heart battering against his ribs. A ringing began to buzz and build in his ears. As Vidar started speaking once again, he began a slow rotation away from the wall. Turning to face Gunnar, who had remained rooted since plunging into the room.

"The soul you see, my brother. It's the soul that is glorious." Vidar now stood facing Gunnar, little more than an arm's length away. His mouth was finishing its busy work. As Gunnar stood mesmerized, Vidar's tongue slid over his bottom lip. He slurped the last of a jelly-like goo that had stuck above his chin, clearly savoring the substance. At the edges of Gunnar's vision, absurdly, he noticed Vidar had a full erection as well. His manhood jutted out forcefully against his pants. Unwavering and just as intense were Vidar's black eyes. Staring and boring into Gunnar as he spoke, "Oh, how the doors of wisdom and knowledge flow when you see with what others once saw." He smiled grotesquely at Gunnar.

Vidar's crooked teeth still showed the remnants of what he had been eating. Gunnar saw it had been both stringy and bloody. Whatever he had been laboring at with his mouth, however, was now completely gone.

Swallowed and consumed.

Gunnar tried to process what he was seeing and hearing. He took an involuntary step back from the bizarre scene in front of him. The small retreat from Vidar widened his vision of the bedroom. For the first time, he noticed Sassa. She was on the floor in a sitting position in the far corner of the room. She had been partially hidden behind the open door Gunnar had entered by. Unmoving, her head was slumped forward on her chest. Gunnar pushed the door wide open and rushed to her side. Keeping one eye on the odd-behaving Vidar, he squatted next to Sassa. Her posture was casual, as if she were merely napping. But the front of her dress was soiled, slick, and shiny. Even as he reached for her, Gunnar knew something was terribly wrong.

He stretched out a shaking hand for her chin, gently tilting it up towards his own face. Under Sassa's jaw, it was warm and wet. Gunnar felt a surge of anger towards Vidar, certain he was feeling Sassa's tears that had run down her face, chin, and neck. It flashed through his mind that somehow Vidar had hurt her. Had he pushed her hard against the wall? But in a moment, his rage turned to horror as he stared down into what was left of Sassa's ruined face.

It had been mutilated almost beyond recognition.

As Gunnar watched, a flap of bloodless skin slid slowly down the side of her face before gravity pulled it the rest of the way off. It fell away from what should have been her cheek. A spot Gunnar had placed many tender kisses and caressed often. Where it had once been very smooth and soft, Gunnar could now see straight through to her teeth. The teeth appeared very white next to the strikingly red flesh and pale pink gums that surrounded them.

Her nose had been severed from her face as well. Looking down, Gunnar saw it had somehow come to lay in one of Sassa's petite hands, which were open in her lap. Unable to comprehend what he was seeing, Gunnar's head began to swim in circles, and his vision blurred. On the verge of a blackout, only a blood-curdling scream from behind pushed him harshly back into this new and terrible reality. Gunnar was too numb to turn or care what the screaming was about, but it briefly cleared his head. He was vaguely aware of footsteps running away from the room as he continued processing the nightmare in front of him.

Though her beauty was devastated, Gunnar did not yet understand she was gone. He took his second hand and lifted her head the rest of the way into the air. Her face was now just inches from his own. Now there was no doubt she was truly gone. Her pretty green eyes were both absent. Hollow orbits were all that stared back unseeing at Gunnar. Sassa's mouth was slack and open as if in one long, silent, accusatory scream. Seeming to say, "How could you, Gunnar, have let this happen to me?" Never would she be the mother she longed to be. Never would the life she and Gunnar had planned together happen.

Gunnar trembled all over.

He carefully placed the head back down on her chest as it had been. When he let go of her face, her body seemed to crumble as if in acknowledgment that her spirit was truly gone. The hollow vessel slumped forward first, then pitched over on its side. Gunnar helped gently lay her body down on the stained floor. When he pulled his hands back from Sassa's body, they, too, were blood-soaked. After a moment, Gunnar rose shakily to his feet. Behind him, he heard the running footsteps return, followed by more hollering. He turned to face the non-stop screaming.

Vidar appeared still frozen in one place. Standing as he had been when Gunnar first saw Sassa's dead body. Vidar remained as a statue despite the screaming and the blubbering that echoed all around the small bedroom. Tor, who had entered the room at some point, stood just inside the doorway. The diminutive leader was red-faced and hollering at Vidar with all he had. Clearly unhinged by the scene of carnage harbored within his own home. His grand-father's sword hung limply at his side in his right hand. Either forgotten or the strength to use it is long gone from the old man's body. Spit flew from his mouth, and Gunnar saw tears streaming down Tor's face as well. He was frantically looking from Vidar to Sassa's body and back again. As if his own eyes were betraying him with each glance. Finally, Tor advanced a single step towards Vidar, but his knee buckled slightly, and he sagged down to the floor.

The movement, however, seemed to break the trance Gunnar had fallen under. Gunnar opened his eyes wide, the dawning real-ization of the evil and unspeakable act carried out against his beloved Sassa. Her grace and love of life were extinguished forever, butchered by the man who stood before him. A man who still bore the taste of her on his lips! Gunnar, rising swiftly and silently, snatched the sword from Tor's weak grasp. In one stride, he stood directly before the still smiling Vidar. His teeth were splattered by the feast of gore he had made of Sassa.

Gunnar reached one hand out and grabbed the top of Vidar's head, clenching his hair tightly in the grasp of his left hand. He then lifted and pointed the end of the sword at Vidar's face. He paused only to line the sharp end of the ancient weapon with the smirking, red-stained mouth of the monster before him.

Vidar neither struggled nor uttered a sound as Gunnar ran him through.

The strength and force of the sword were so great that it snapped out the front teeth on both the top and bottom of his mouth. The sharp blade plunged so violently that it exited the back of Vidar's skull like a hot knife through butter. The handle of the steel brutally crushed his lips and nose with a satisfying crunch. Gunnar withdrew the sword abruptly and not gently. The arc of the retreating blade severed the top half of the skull completely from the bottom half. Vidar was left shattered on the floor. Head split open and swimming in the carnage, quivering among his broken teeth and skull fragments. As Gunnar stood over the collapsed murderer, the right leg of Vidar began to spasm. Tor, who had been rendered silent by the swiftness of the execution, saw it first. Terrified, he let out a wail and pointed it out to Gunnar when he turned. Gunnar raised the sword and amputated the twitching right leg at the knee with one decisive swing.

Nothing of Vidar would ever move again…

CHAPTER 15

10TH CENTURY

GUNNAR DROPPED the heavy sword he'd used to take Vidar's life. It clattered loudly on the wooden bedroom floor. A noise that made Gunnar wince and Tor jump. Both men looked at each other in stunned disbelief. The coppery taste of blood and death swirled in the air around them. The smell and scene before them overloading their senses, leaving little room for any rational thoughts. Gunnar was amazed they were still alone. Tor's neighbors were far enough away that they did not hear the screaming or sense the swirl of madness that had engulfed his home. It was Tor that broke the silence first.

"I...I didn't believe him or the story..." he said, pointing at what was left of Vidar. "But, but it had him. He was turning, or almost. He brought this evil to our doorstep. To MY doorstep! And now... It was going to use Vidar to get back in this world. Just like he told us it would. But... But now what? It will try again, surely. It won't rest. Oh, we are all cursed now, Gunnar! It will take its revenge on all of us for killing its disciple." Tor struggled to gain his feet, trying to avoid the blood creeping slowly across the floor from the two bodies. "The bag, Gunnar! Where is the bag Vidar carried the cursed object in? WE MUST FIND IT!"

Tor moved towards the bed in search of what he was now sure contained the very essence of evil. He stopped above the prone body of Vidar that lay at the foot of the bed. "Here. Here it is!" He gestured at the pouch hanging off the side of what was left of Vidar. "Gunnar! You must take it. Otherwise, it will destroy us all. You must take it far away, Gunnar. You can be the savior of the people." Tor moved close, grabbing the taller man's arm as he spoke directly to him. "Gunnar, you must take this away, don't you see? This is surely what killed your father. This happened to Sassa because of it. Oh, poor, dear, sweet Sassa… You must do this to avenge her, don't you see? Her death can assure life for the rest of our clan. And your dad? You must avenge his death as well. They died so we could see what was happening. They must not have died in vain…"

"Gunnar!"

Tor was speaking very fast now, the words tumbling from his mouth. Spittle sprayed as he spoke, barely stopping to draw a breath. He rambled on, "Terrible as it was, Ymir has saved us. It was a sign and a warning, Gunnar. We must take heed. You must take this far away from us. That is the only way to be sure. CAN'T YOU SEE! This was our destiny. Yours and mine. I must lead and save my people now. Yes! Just as my fathers before me. I was born for this, you see. But Gunnar, you must go now. No time must be wasted. Take my sword, my horse, anything you need. Save our clan, Gunnar. Pray to Ymir, and he will show you the way. But you must leave with this. Now!" Gunnar stood mute and unresponsive to Tor's ranting speech. He felt lightheaded, and the room swam before his eyes. Tor shot his arm out and shook violently at Gunnar's arm.

"NOW, GUNNAR, NOW!!" Gunnar blinked and nodded slowly. Nothing was making sense to him. He had trouble under-standing what had just happened. But he heard Tor. As if in a trance, he automatically began to move over to retrieve the cursed object. Bending over the still body, Gunnar untied the pouch from Vidar's remains. When he straightened up, Tor retreated to the far side of the room, away from Gunnar. He lowered his eyes and would not look at the bag Gunnar now held in his hand.

"You must take this from here. Go now. Return this back from whence it came. Find the Skraelings where this must have come from. Surely such a thing was born out of those dark savages' ways. Go to Nimki and his tribe. Speak with him. Make him take this back! Your deeds today will be spoken of by our people for ages. Gunnar the Brave, you will be! Ymir will show you, but you must have faith. Go now over the mountains and far, far away from where any Norsemen reside. That is the only way, Gunnar. Ymir will bless you. For this," Tor pointed at the pouch without looking up, "was not meant for this time or place."

Gunnar slowly tied the pouch containing the strange object Vidar had brought with him to his side. He then bent over to retrieve Tor's grandfather's sword. Gunnar absently wiped the blood from the blade off on the side of the bed. Without a word, he then turned on his heel to leave. At the doorway, he stopped and looked back one last time at what was left of Sassa. As if just recalling she had been in the room, he sagged and barely caught himself by placing a hand on the wall to stop himself from collapsing completely. His strength seemed to have run out of his body, and tears filled his eyes once again. He was ashamed that he had been unable to save Sassa or his father. How could he face Sassa's mother ever again? Or his father's friends and neighbors… He felt like a failure. If he stayed, what would he be staying for?

Gunnar straightened and stood tall again, feeling the weight of the pouch on his hip. It was nothing compared to the weight of his responsibility for the village and clan. He felt a vague sense of redemption within his grasp. Tor must be right, Gunnar decided. He gripped the heavy sword tightly and made his way out of the bedroom and towards Tor's front door. He stopped to scoop up the bag of food Sigrid's mother had given him earlier before stepping out into the night. He found Tor's horse in the small stable next to the house. He spoke low and soothingly to the large and heavily muscled beast. Gaining the horse's confidence, he then readied the horse for riding. After securing some blankets across its back side, he gently slid the sword between them to both safely carry and hide the long weapon. His motions were automatic. Gunnar slowly untied the dark brown steed and led him out. Moments later, he mounted Tor's horse in the darkness and prepared to ride. Gunnar looked out across the tiny lights that dotted the village. A heavy sadness descended upon him. He nudged the horse towards the trail that led up into the nearby mountains. The bright moon was either a blessing or a curse as he rode into the night.

CHAPTER 16
PRESENT DAY

RON BARNES FELT his patience wearing thin. "I am telling you, this old GPR unit is total crap." He was already tired, dirty, and sweaty from the hike. Ron usually loved getting out into the field every chance he could. But now, working with this archaic unit the university had stuck Ethan with, he began to regret getting roped into this. Frowning, he tried manually adjusting the screen once more to improve the clarity of the images in the bright sunlight. "You know, there are way more advanced versions of these out there. Ones with bigger color screens and with wider bases for larger scans. The technology in the last few years has really advanced compared to what you have here."

"I know, but this was all Danforth said was available." Ethan could feel the fellow university undergrad student's patience waning. But he was far too excited himself to let that hinder his high hopes for the day. Ron Barnes, like Ethan, was an undergraduate in Ann Arbor working on his Ph.D. Ron's degree of study was Geology, while Ethan's was in Native American Studies. Ron was not really a close friend of Ethan's, but they bonded in the library one afternoon over their mutual disgust of the lazy librarians who worked at the undergraduate library at the University of Michigan.

Ethan admitted to himself he only kept their meager friendship going on the off chance he might need Ron's expertise for his project at some point this summer.

"That is one of the reasons I needed your help, Ron. No one else could help decipher the data out of that old unit better than you." Ethan groveled a bit for Ron's benefit, hoping to raise the geologist's flagging enthusiasm both with praise and the few cold beers he brought along in his cooler. They each had downed one together when they first reached the top of Skull Rock. "Everyone says you are the best in the program."

As Ethan knew he would, Ron ate the compliments up and stayed on task. He flipped his long, braided, black ponytail back over his shoulder, getting it up and away from his face so it wouldn't block his view of the digital device's meager screen. The tall and skinny 23-year-old muttered to the GPR unit as he worked. A steady stream of profanity flowed from his mouth, and it sounded to Ethan like the rolling red radar cart had now been officially renamed "bitch." The harsh language apparently worked, however, because, within minutes, Ron began rolling the device back and forth with a satisfied grin.

"There you go, you little bitch, thought you would see things my way." Ron smiled smugly as he looked over at Ethan, "So we are just seeing what is under here, right? See if there is a void below? Hoping for a cave of sorts, huh?" Before Ethan could answer, Ron turned back and once again began pacing behind the GPR unit, methodically canvassing the flat, small cliff above Skull Rock.

As Ron worked the equipment back and forth across the area, Ethan found himself quivering with excitement. He clenched his teeth together tightly to stop himself from calling out and trying to hurry the lanky geologist's answer as the minutes crept slowly along one by one. Impatiently waiting for Ron's assessment of the ground directly below their feet, Ethan knew he was moments away from what could be a landmark find.

Or a horrible disappointment.

"Well, that settles it," Ron abruptly stopped walking and turned the power switch off at the top of the GPR unit. "There is indeed a huge void under us. Tough to say for sure with this piece of crap," Ron slapped the top of the small read-out screen, "but I would estimate it to be about 15 feet from top to bottom." Ron smiled and nodded his head up and down. "You may have been right, after all, Ethan. There is no question about the void. And in my opinion, knowing there are other caves close by in the area, it is likely to be a cave. No telling what rock type is inside yet. The cave itself could have been carved out by man or caused by any of the differing geological processes. It could be a single room, or it could have interconnecting passages many miles long. But anyway, it sure seems like your classic cave. Probably pretty much like all the others around these mountains and lake areas close by."

Ethan was elated! "And from what you said when we first got to the site, you think the boulder below us, this Skull Rock, was manually manipulated by man as well so...."

Ron interjected. "Whoa, whoa, whoa. I said I can't say anything for sure right now. My best guess is this boulder started taking its shape naturally, at least at first. Might have rolled down here from somewhere above us after it was carved by some fast running water currents." Ron pointed over to the stream running down the side of the mountain near them. "That may look small now, but at one time, it could have been a rushing river that dominated the entire side of this mountain. If so, the eyes and the mouth of that boulder may have first formed naturally. What we call rock-cut basins. Those are formed by the action of fast-running water currents that cause smaller boulders to move in a circular motion. The friction created by these small boulders going round and round can erode the natural rock substrate to create concavities."

Ethan threw his hands up to let Ron know he was losing him. Ron continued, "Sorry. Concavities are basically just another word for basins. The more time the smaller rocks gyrate and move, it increases the depth and circumference of these concavities... I mean basins over the years. It is pretty much a physical abrasion effect, and it is really pretty common."

"And you think that boulder was in a river, got carved up like that, and then just happened to roll down the hill and land here?" Ethan's incredulous face betrayed that he found this theory hard to believe.

"I am just saying there are unusual depressions in big rocks all over the world that have led to various folktales becoming associated with them. People start calling them footprints, knee prints, or hell, even elbow prints of saints, heroes, kings, supernatural beings, or whatever." Ron still could see the doubt etched in Ethan's face.

"Probably what happened here is just like King Arthur's Footprint in the UK. That supposed footprint is a concav... er, basin in a rock found at the highest point of a mountain. It is not entirely natural anymore and was clearly shaped by human hands at some point. But local people at one time believed it was divine or something, even using the spot for their inaugurations of kings, chieftains, and whatnot. My point is that it started out naturally. So here we have this Skull Rock that, I guarantee you, started out being shaped naturally. Eventually, it got a reputation because it resembles a face or a skull." Ron walked over the edge and looked down once more on the face of the rock below them. "But like I also said, there are very recent cut marks as well that have made the face more pronounced."

Ethan jumped at the analogy. "That is what I am saying. The rock had an unusual shape, so they moved it here to block the cave. Local tribes in the past carved it to resemble a skull."

"The only problem with that theory is some of those cut marks on the surface are super recent. Like this year recent, not hundreds of years ago," countered Ron.

Ethan dismissed the young geologist. "Well, who knows? And it doesn't really matter until we get a look inside anyway. Come on!" Ethan started down from the ledge above the boulder in question and waved Ron after him. Soon both men stood facing the huge rock. Ethan showed Ron the crack along the side of the boulder he spied the other day with Stander. "This is what made me think this had been placed. See how this is curved here? Isn't that a seam we could dig or pry into? If we could get behind it a bit, maybe we could see inside." Ethan felt like a kid with an unopened Christmas present in his lap. He just had to know what was inside.

"Not sure we are really supposed to be excavating in a state park, Ethan," Ron began.

"Oh, come on! It's not excavating. Just a little digging. What is the harm, and who would even know?"

"Are you kidding? If we damage the face of this rock, everyone will know. And if by chance you ARE right..."

"If I am right, no one will even care!" Ethan knew he was digging. There was no way he was going to be denied. Ethan took a deep breath and appealed once more to Ron's reason. "We are not going to be invasive at all. With your help and guidance, we can carefully get just enough of an opening to shine a light inside. If it is empty, we walk away. No harm and no foul. If there is something inside, I'll take responsibility for anything that happens." Ethan hated that he sounded like he was begging. "I am just asking for a hand here. We are already all the way up here, and I don't want to make that drive back and forth again later to get you onsite once more. Let's just do all we can now. Fair enough?"

Ron relented at last. "Fine, let me get started a bit at the bottom. I'll see if that fissure really is part of the opening from what was once the mouth of a cave or not. If it is, we'll get you a spot where you can eyeball the insides. But if it isn't, I am not going to dig out here in this heat with these hand tools all afternoon. Deal?"

Ethan readily agreed, and in less than 30 minutes, the moment of truth arrived. As unobtrusively as possible, Ron had created a small opening near the ground along the side of Skull Rock. The gap hewn was roughly one foot in height, four inches across, and Ethan had to get down on his hands and knees to see into the cavity. The loose gravel Ron had created from widening the breach dug into the bare knees of Ethan, and crumbled chunks of dry and loose sand filled in the spaces between each of his fingers as well.

Pressing his face to the side of the mountain to see inside, Ethan could taste dirt in his mouth. All of this barely registered as he powered on and lifted a long tubular flashlight to the widened crack.

Angling the bright halogen light, Ethan pierced the black void. Initially, he began to pull back, believing Ron hadn't cut the opening deep enough. However, as he moved the light up and down with his wrist, a flash winked back at him from inside. Ethan stopped and tried to duplicate the illusion once more. As he anxiously peered into the small gap, Ethan could feel the sweat dripping down the sides of his face, mixing with the grit and dust floating all around him. His heart raced, and, for a moment, the heat, the strain, and his excitement got the better of him. Still crouched on his hands and knees, his eyesight suddenly darkened and filled with spots as a wave of dizziness washed over him. The sudden lightheadedness hit him like a freight train, and Ethan felt his consciousness ebb and his body sag. Confused, he no longer understood what he was doing or why his face was pinched painfully against the rough rock on the side of the boulder.

A blinding white light suddenly flashed across his face once more from inside the opening. Startling Ethan and breaking him out of the brief trance he found himself in. Ethan focused once more and tried to establish where the bright flash originated from. He swept the halogen beam back and forth across the ground of the cave, trying to duplicate the effect.

Despite holding it tightly, all his breath was stolen by the dawning realization.

Clamoring for his wits, Ethan quickly inhaled to keep at bay another episode of lightheadedness before it took him down. The sharp intake stabbed his lungs with the swirling particles of dirt floating all around him. Ethan leaned back, away from the opening, coughing violently enough to raise Ron's concern.

"Take it easy, man. You OK?" Ron slapped Ethan on the back and quickly snatched up a nearby water bottle, and offered it to Ethan. Ethan's eyes were tearing, but he smiled as he flooded his dirt-encrusted lips and dry throat with the lukewarm liquid. He took three gulps before stopping and taking several shaking breaths. "Well, what did you see? Anything interesting?" queried Ron.

Ethan beamed up at Ron from his squatted position on the ground. "Interesting?" Ethan glanced once more at the crack in the rock. "Depends on if you consider the badly decomposed remains of a body buried with what I think may be a sword inside a mountain in Michigan interesting or not." Ethan started laughing as the tension flooded out of his body. "I was right. This is a cave! But even better than that, at some point in the distant past, it was turned into a tomb." Ethan got to his feet, suddenly feeling energized by the vindication. Without thinking, he reached out and briefly grasped Ron by his shoulders. "I knew it! I knew it! I knew it!" Releasing the young geologist, he turned to the valley below and yelled at the top of his lungs, "I knew it!!!"

"Well, congratulations, I guess, Ethan," Ron began. "But did you say a body?" Ron turned and, with an incredulous look on his face, pointed to Skull Rock. "There is a body entombed behind this rock? No way," he grabbed the flashlight out of Ethan's hand. "Let me take a look."

After Ron finished confirming that he also saw the remains and a badly corroded metal object - Ron stopped short of calling it a sword - the two men plotted their next move. Eating the lunch they brought along and washing it down with the last of the beers, they sat huddled together under the sullen eyes of the grave's giant rock marker.

As they talked, Ethan became visibly agitated when Ron suggested they immediately call the local police. Ron lived in Ann Arbor, and the local news in Marquette regarding Sherry Stander's recovered remains barely registered in a college town some seven hours away. Ethan had not, and today still did not share with Ron the grisly discovery he and Professor Danforth had made several weeks before. Instead, Ethan lobbied that the two of them examine the location further, arguing there was no way the body inside was recently deceased or interred. He pushed that they confirm what they'd seen and look for evidence of the time period it was from. Then he'd confer with Dr. Danforth on what the next steps should be.

Eventually, Ethan won Ron over and persuaded him to help widen the opening he had fashioned. Making it just big enough for one of them to slip inside and verify what they both now believed was locked in behind Skull Rock. Together they mapped out a plan to quickly obtain a small sample or two, if possible, and the necessary photos Ethan would need to show Danforth. Although deeply disappointed, Ethan accepted that Ron, being long and lanky, would be the sole visitor inside the cave this day. Together, the two men dug out the loose dirt and rocks along the ground and under the crack that they had created and expanded earlier. Soon the gap was large enough for Ron to gain access. He pushed the lit flashlight ahead of him and then squeezed in after.

Inside the cave, the stagnant air was foul but not unbearable. Ron stood slowly and pulled the neck of his t-shirt up to cover his nose and mouth as he breathed. He initially worried about the presence of natural underground gasses that could be dangerous when inhaled. But although the air was stuffy and dense, there was not the telltale rotten egg smell that betrayed the presence of hydrogen sulfide gas. Ron even felt a slight breeze escaping as the opening of the cavern was being widened, so he was reasonably confident there were other openings somewhere along this cavity's chain. He stood upright and motionless while he became accustomed to both the smell and darkness. The immediate area of the cave Ron stood in was overwhelmingly still, not a sliver of light shown beyond his own piercing flashlight.

The absence of color was dizzying.

Moving the flashlight to break the visual monotony, Ron ran it first across the ceiling and walls. The cavity was nearly ten feet high where he was standing and even wider across. Focusing on the area closest to him, Ron could clearly see that this cavern had been formed naturally. He pointed the beam of light towards the back of the cave and away from what was once the opening. Here the cavern's ceiling tapered off slowly as it descended deeper. From his vantage point, he was unable to tell how far the cavity extended into the mountain. Ron felt along the sides of the wall with his hand as his interest in geology briefly overtook him, appreciating the extreme amount of time needed for a cave this size to develop and wondering if the deep cuts were glacial or made by water. His reverie was broken, however by Ethan.

"What are you seeing, Ron? Is there more than one body?" The urgency of Ethan's tone spurred Ron to action. Ethan's voice echoed around the inside of the cavern. "Was that a sword or not?"

Ron began to move the flashlight down toward the floor of the cavern. Not ten feet away lay the remains both he and Ethan had seen from the opening. What was left of the body was only bones. Ron noted the skull was slightly off to the side and separated from the rest of the remains. But he had no idea if that sometimes occurred naturally during decomposition or not. He found it even odder that he could see no remnants of clothing, material, or trinkets anywhere on the skeleton. Next to it, however, partially hidden on layers of accumulated earthen cave dust that had fallen over the centuries, Ron could see Ethan was correct about the oxidized metal object lying next to the soul laid to rest in the cavity. Pulling out the digital camera Ethan had provided him with, Ron took quick photos of everything he saw. Then Ron answered Ethan, his voice booming and, despite it originating from himself, the loud noise startled him.

"Only the one body that I can see. You were right about the sword. I mean, yeah, that does look like a long sword, and it looks super old, like something maybe medieval even." The absurdity of the find didn't strike Ron until Ethan replied from outside.

"How can there be a medieval sword in a cave in Michigan? Was it the weapon used to kill the cave's inhabitants? Or is this some kind of European explorer or something? Nordic or Viking, maybe? This is crazy…" Ethan's voice trailed off, which suited Ron just fine. The hollow sound their voices made in the enclosed space was creepy as hell. Careful not to move and disturb the site in any way, Ron caught himself looking around at the shadows his light played against the wall. "See if there is anything that makes sense to bring out with you. Not the remains or sword, though! Don't touch any of that." Ethan's voice bounced around the cave and then echoed back at Ron again.

Ron didn't answer Ethan immediately as the beam of his flashlight landed on a disintegrating pouch near the cave's wall. It was deeper inside the cavern, maybe another five or six feet beyond the sword owner's body. As the artificial light played across the ground near the pouch, the earth around it suddenly seemed to swell like waves in an ocean. Ron shook his head and felt disoriented by the movement he witnessed.

Or at least thought he had witnessed.

He re-focused and peered closer at the rotted bag. He could see that some of the contents had begun to slip out of the cracks in the shriveled animal skin pouch it was made from. Ron carefully moved a single step forward and brought himself closer to the side of the cave that the bag was nestled against. He began to lift his other foot for a second step when he was suddenly gripped by intense and almost overwhelming anxiety. Ron, briefly forgetting the delicate nature of the site, whirled around and choked back the scream threatening to erupt. Although clearly alone in a long deserted, and empty cave, Ron could have sworn he had felt someone directly behind him. He nearly jumped out of his skin when he heard, "Did you hear me?" It was Ethan again from outside.

"I know. What do you think I am? Stupid?" Ron decided he no longer wanted to be in this enclosed space. He glanced once more at the body and the cave floor surrounding the fleshless remains, hoping to spy a small trinket easily removed from the site. But once more behind him, his back now facing the rear of the cave, Ron felt a sensation like a slight tug at the bottom of his long ponytail. He spun once more, trying to identify the recurring fright, but again, nothing was visible.

However, the panicked shuffling of his feet had kicked up dust that now floated nonchalantly in the artificial light. The dancing particles, like incandescent snow, slowly swirled around him. Ron felt briefly as if he were merely a decorative figure alone and rooted to a spot in a twisted snow globe. One where an omniscient presence was overlooking his every action and periodically tilting the world under and around him. His twirling motions, coupled with the blueish beam of his flashlight among the otherwise utter darkness enveloping him, created a sense of vertigo. Ron lifted his eyes, searching the deep and seeming eternal blackness the cave was home to.

Compelled by the utter void.

The oblivion of the blank space where he now stood somehow called to him. Standing wholly alone, deep in this hole in the earth, felt like peering over the side of a tall skyscraper or cliff. That inexplicable pull and danger that feels tangible, almost physical, despite knowing your feet are safely secured. Often needing to tear yourself away for fear you may inexplicably topple over. At this moment, it was like that for Ron. Metaphorically, he nearly tumbled over to run mindlessly into the deep abyss of the cavern.

Ron's head swam. Out of the obscurity of long-forgotten childhood fears, an unpleasant memory reared itself from the depths of his subconscious. Jarring him to his core.

He'd been twelve years old. It had been late afternoon at a garish local carnival. After begging his mom to take them into the spook house, Ron's little sister suddenly refused to go inside the haunted mansion. His mom wouldn't leave his sister alone outside, so undaunted, Ron had entered the eerie haunted house all alone.

The sun had still been up, and there were not any other patrons waiting in line. He could remember striding confidently into the very first room after the entryway by himself. He was excited to see in-person what he had only seen in Scooby Doo cartoons thus far. But it had been oh so very dark in the manmade haunt. Screams, rattling chains, and tortured moans reverberated loudly around him. A strobe light flickered in a corner where a giant spider dropped back and forth from the ceiling. A towering grandfather clock chimed loudly next to him, and a crow burst from under the clock face to cackle obscenely. Then something (he knew now it was just a costumed character) had crept up behind Ron and whispered "boo" in his ear.

That was all it had taken.

He had run blindly and flailed throughout the rest of the haunted house. His forward momentum stopped only when he would hit an unseen black-painted wall. Rebounding off the obstruction, he would turn and run until he hit another solid barrier. Literally bouncing off the walls until eventually (and mercifully) bursting out the exit. Terrified and sobbing, snot running down his chin and gasping for breath, his sister with a self-righteous smile telling him that she had "told him so."

Ron had never admitted what happened to any of his friends, and he swore his mother and sister to secrecy as well. To this day, Ron could not recall ever having replayed in such graphic detail that unpleasant experience or relived the blind terror that engulfed him in the haunted house.

Until now.

Where the inside of this cave somehow got into his head and dredged up the single most terrifying childhood memory of his life. That surging recollection finally broke the grip the surrounding gloom had weaved so tightly around him. Ron shuddered, and his legs quivered in weakness. Coming back to his senses, Ron knew he was teetering perilously close to bolting. No longer tempted by the black labyrinth in the side of the mountain, but instead, as fast as he could get out of this cavern. His educated and adult mind knew it was completely irrational, and yet, his current fear was the most real emotion he had ever experienced.

Ron walked spaghetti-legged and started back to the bright opening before remembering Ethan wanted him to grab an item for possible dating and proof. But he didn't trust himself to look once more into the recesses of the black cave. Or even across it at the bag rotting on the opposite wall, much less walk back to retrieve an item from that ancient carrier. Ron decided he would simply tell Ethan he had forgotten and that Ethan would just have to live with the pictures. But as he bent down to crawl back out the way he entered, his flashlight illuminated a crumbling item on the floor next to the opening. Ron barely glanced at what he grabbed as he bent down to escape the suddenly claustrophobic cave. Wiggling back out, his shoulders caught awkwardly in the opening, and irrational fear gripped him one more time before he was finally released back into the daylight.

Looking down at his find, Ethan slapped Ron across his back as he emerged from the crack. "Perfect, Ron. That is excellent. It looks like the remnants of a burned-out cane torch used by many Native American tribes. Looks like maybe a bark cane torch. You can even still see bits of cordage here." Ethan was pointing out and complimenting Ron on his choice, but he was already walking towards the equipment and away from the opening in the mountain.

"Great. Yeah. It should help your case for sure, Ethan. Now let's head back before it gets dark…"

CHAPTER 17
PRESENT DAY

STANDER ALWAYS ENJOYED BRINGING FRAZIER DOWN to the bar with him. He didn't do it often, and when he did, it was usually only for a few hours in the late afternoon or early evening. But the regulars loved the friendly canine, and Frazier ate up all the attention, as well as anything he could beg off of a plate or two. The steady thrum of his tail on the barstool legs imploring their generosity with a hard-to-resist syncopated rhythm. Stander just had to keep an eye on what the boxer/pit mix got fed by the customers. The dog's fart could make a Billy goat gag, and there was nothing worse than waking up to that late at night. Talk about night terrors…

"Didn't you have mushrooms on that burger, Matt?" Stander asked the visiting construction worker. "I don't think you have eaten here once yet where you didn't have those added."

"Well yeah, so what? I love them on just about everything I eat," the dark-haired patron in his steel-toed boots and single-pocketed t-shirt responded. "Unless you're allergic to them, I don't know how everyone doesn't…"

"I am not arguing that. Just don't give any of your hamburger to Frazier. His ass will smell like a dead man's shit all night if he eats that." Stander smiled while chastising the man but the intent in his voice was clear. The burly foreman, in town temporarily while overseeing the renovation of a hotel four blocks down from Stander's bar, sheepishly withdrew the piece of burger he had begun to offer Frazier. He popped the last bite in his own mouth instead and let the dog lick his fingers clean.

"Sorry, big guy," he spoke to the dog earnestly. "I'm not disobeying the one dude in town who keeps a decent scotch in stock." Matt tipped the last of his drink back and nodded towards Stander. Frazier looked over at his owner as well, but with a look that conveyed, he knew Stander had just betrayed him. Hannah walked between the dog and Matt at that moment with three orders of French fries. Frazier eyed the bar girl as she passed and turned to follow, hoping to charm the three patrons in the corner booth out of a few fries before Stander ruined his chances once again. Matt watched the dog retreat and then began to pester the bar owner about offering fried mushrooms on his menu.

The corner jukebox came to life as one of the customers pumped credits and their favorite songs into it. The thumping bassline that started was easily recognized as "Some Kind of Wonderful" by Grand Funk Railroad. Both Stander's and Matt's heads began to bob up and down in unison like two bobble head dolls touched on the head. Or, as Hannah liked to tease them, touched in the head.

Matt grinned up at Stander, and then both men cast their eyes around the other 15 or so patrons of "In This Corner." Both men were wondering who was trying to set a bit of a party mood with the crowd this early on a Thursday evening. Phil, at the far end of the bar, lifted his half-full beer and nodded towards the other two men in acknowledgment of the deed. Then turned a sly eye towards where Hannah stood, taking an order at a nearby table. Stander returned his conspiratorial grin with a noncommittal shrug. Matt just laughed out loud at the older divorcee's intentions. Phil had been seriously trying to get in Hannah's pants for the last several weeks despite being almost twice her age. Looked like tonight he was planning another run at her. Stander was pretty sure it would be a "dry run" again, but he admired the man's tenacity and optimism, if nothing else.

The entrance to the tavern cracked wide, and, looking up from behind the bar, Stander saw Ethan entering. His glasses hung slightly askew across his face as he walked directly over with his hand outstretched. Though it had been several months since Stander had last seen him, he was shocked by the unkempt, wilted appearance of the man. His clothes looked as if they'd been slept in, and Ethan's hairline had receded greatly since they'd hiked up Mt. Arvon together. His balding head shined brightly under the pendant lights that were strung above the bar. The few remaining strands of hair plastered awkwardly across the top of his head as if unsure of their place and embarrassed to still be there. As the two men finished shaking hands, Ethan turned to acknowledge the woman who trailed behind him.

"Let me introduce you to Dr. Elizabeth Drexler. She is the Professor of Medieval History at the University of Michigan in Ann Arbor." Although clearly older than Ethan, she was younger than Stander, maybe mid-forties, and with deep green eyes that sparkled and even outshone Ethan's prematurely balding head. Though undeniably pretty, she had a slightly intimidating, no-nonsense look about her.

"Please, call me Stander. Everyone does." As they shook hands, Stander noted her unpolished fingernails were trimmed short, her hands were slightly rough, and she wore no rings.

"Fair enough then, Stander. I'm Liz. That is, unless you are a student like Ethan here, then I'm Dr. Drexler. Pleased to meet you." Her handshake was short and perfunctory. She looked quickly around the tavern. "Can you point me in the direction of the ladies' room?" She turned back with a small but pretty smile, "I am dying to get some of this dust and dirt off of me." Stander pointed, and she made her way through the customers seated around them without a second glance. As she retreated towards the back of the bar, Ethan asked Stander if he could join them at a table while they ate, explaining he had some news to share.

Within a few minutes, Ethan, Stander, and Liz were seated together in a booth on the opposite side of the bar from where the music was streaming. The jukebox cranked out song after song from Phil's playlist. Bob Seger kept telling everyone that what he really wanted to do was go to Katmandu while Hannah took their food and drink orders. Waiting for her to return, Stander gave Liz his usual spiel about how long he had owned the bar, his apartment upstairs, and the unused gym below their feet in the basement. He was wrapping up as Hannah returned and served the table drinks. Liz had ordered ice tea, as did Ethan, who gulped his first one down so fast that he was on his second before Stander had barely taken two sips of his own beer.

Ethan wiped at his mouth with the back of his hand and then started the conversation. For Stander's benefit, he recounted his discovery of the void near the top of Mt. Arvon behind Skull Rock. How he and a geologist graduate student friend were able to identify the cavity and some ancient remains inside. Ethan then summarized all the contacts with the county coroner, local tribe leaders, the University of Michigan, and the subsequent activity it had spurred. By the time he finished the synopsis, both Ethan's and Liz's food had arrived. As they started to eat, Stander digested the information Ethan provided and began to ask questions.

"So let me get this straight," Stander began. "All these years behind Skull Rock, there was a burial inside an unknown cave that was sealed up for centuries?"

Liz interjected at this point between bites of her salad. "What makes the site so extraordinary is not the age, which is believed to be as much as a thousand years old, but the fact that the lone interment was not a Native American or Indian in the traditional sense. Which at least would have fit with the known occupants of upper Michigan around the 10th century. There is more testing needed to be 100% scientifically certain, but, based on the evidence recovered from the site, the single body inside is almost assuredly of Eastern European descent."

"What the fuck does that mean? Like a Viking who got blown

way off course or something?" Now that Stander was seated directly across from Liz, he realized she was an extremely attractive woman. She had pulled the bun on top of her head down while in the bathroom, and her light blonde hair now hung shoulder length, thin but slightly wavy. Her eyes were animated, and her expression softened as she laughed at Stander's crude analogy.

"I suppose he could turn out to be of Norse heritage, yes," Liz answered.

"You said he. So there was only one body found, and it was a dude?" Stander sat forward and put his thick arms on the table. He liked showing off his well-defined arms and brightly colored tattoos adorning them top to bottom. Stander hoped Liz would take notice and comment or question the inked images he'd chosen over the years. But, for her part, she at least pretended not to notice or be impressed. Holding his gaze while she replied.

"Yes and yes. One body, and you can tell the sex by the bones of the pelvic area." Stander noticed she blushed slightly when she said this. He cocked an eyebrow wondering why she hadn't used the word gender instead of sex... Maybe it was his imagination, but she seemed to rush and cover herself. Quickly adding, "I only saw the initial report and photos. The remains were already removed by the time I got down here for my part in the process. But now, having been at the site, I am sure no one else was buried there or in another cavity of the cave or anything like that."

Stander, unabashedly flirting now, lowered his head and moved a couple inches closer as if about to impart a secret. "So tell me, Liz, was this one of those ancient giants like they found over in Minnesota a few years back?" Stander delivered this question in a mock-serious tone. Then he broke into a wide grin. "Or maybe a merman fished out of Lake Superior? I saw a documentary on mermaids and mermen one time that was very compelling..." Stander now sat back and spread his arms out. "You can trust me." He winked across the table at her. "I can keep a secret." A not-so-subtle innuendo.

Liz, her face re-shading with color, laughed, "Don't believe everything you see on TV. And no, there were not any fins or fish-tail bones. But the guy was big. Not a giant, but," she turned to Ethan, who had remained silent and picking at his food during the exchange, "what was he measured at again?"

"The pathologist said he would have been close to seven feet tall. Like maybe six foot nine or something like that. Which for back then, around this part of the world, would have seemed like a giant."

"You kidding? That is a big guy even now," commented Stander. "So, are you disappointed in what was found, Ethan? You wanted old Indians, not old Vikings. You bummed out about this or what?" Stander was genuinely curious.

"No, not at all. In fact, I think it could be kind of a one in a million find." Ethan perked up again and became more animated. "My original interest in the area was from all the old legends and tales handed down that surround that mountain. Remember I told you about the Anishinaabeg people who originally populated the area?"

Stander nodded. "Not that I remember how to pronounce it, but yeah…"

Ethan went on, "The thing is their legend of the Wendigo basically boils down to a lost, lone hunter from a faraway land who is more monster than man. One that inspired fear in the people that was so dramatic it was never forgotten and became legend." Ethan looked at both Stander and Liz. "Don't you see? What if the guy we just found was that monster?"

Liz was shaking her head doubtfully but undeterred. Ethan continued, "Now, I am not saying he was actually supernatural or anything like that. But he must have seemed completely alien to those tribes. Different sizes, the color of skin, iron weapons, and tools. It was a completely foreign culture and way of doing things. Maybe he looked down on the simplistic tribes of the area. Thought they were beneath him and tried to rule or even enslave the locals."

Liz spoke up now, "That is some huge leaps and suppositions there, Ethan. It's way too early to predict what we will find about his ancestry or the time he lived in. We may find he was from a time much earlier than we initially thought. Or a later time closer to the present day just carrying older artifacts."

Stander cut in again, "Well, I guess you answered my question. Sounds like you are not disappointed then, huh?" Ethan shook his head emphatically no. Stander turned the conversation back to Liz. Hoping to find out more about her, "So why are you up here, Liz? You said you never even saw the skeleton, and it was gone before you arrived. What is your role in all this?"

"As Ethan mentioned, there were some artifacts found in the cave that appeared to be from the medieval time period. The university asked me to consult with the other departments involved to document and authenticate what was recovered. So basically, I am here trying to verify what those items actually are and bag and tag anything of note."

Ethan excitedly cut in once again, "Dr. Drexler confirmed the sword we found was from Eastern Europe and likely, based on the design and craftsmanship, of Norse origins. She said it is unquestionably well over 1,000 years old! And once it was confirmed the remains found were not Native American, we got the greenlight to scour the site. We've spent the last couple of weeks working with colleagues going over the entire cave looking for more artifacts or any other evidence linking that time period to the find."

To Stander, this sounded like she may be in town for an extended period of time. He tried to sound nonchalant as he asked more questions. "Was a lot found then? A pretty big job ahead of you then, Liz?"

Her answer doused his climbing hopes in cold water. "Actually, no, the sword was significant for sure. But, outside of a few other really odd artifacts that don't exactly fit with everything else and require more testing, nothing of significance was found this week. I plan to stay one more day to finish up and then head back to Ann Arbor." Stander sat back in the booth, a bit crestfallen despite having just met the doctor. As if on cue, Frazier jumped into the booth and sat next to Stander, helping shield his disappointment.

"Frazier!" Stander exclaimed. "What have I told you about climbing on the booth seats? Your nails punch holes in the fucking plastic. Are you gonna pay for new cushions? Huh?" Stander was scratching the dog behind his ears as he pretended to scold his best friend. The dog panted and appeared to smile at Liz. Just like Stander, trying to make a good first impression that might result in a treat or two later. Liz obliged him and leaned across the table to pet him. Her hand brushed against Stander's as they both petted Frazier together. Stander noted her full breasts straining against the shapeless field work shirt she'd worn. He thought to himself, damn, if this dog isn't the best wingman ever…

"Oh, what a pretty dog!" Liz obviously liked dogs, another good sign, thought Stander. "Is he yours?" She kept petting the dog. "Frasier? Did you name him after Kelsey Grammer? My mom used to love that show."

Stander groaned and shook his head while rolling his eyes. He was used to this assumption when he introduced his dog. "No, he wasn't named after the TV show. There was a boxer, a heavyweight champ named Joe Frazier, in the seventies. I named him after that guy, not the wimpy therapist from TV." Liz sat back and began to finish the last of her meal. Frazier turned towards Ethan expecting equal attention, but, at that moment, Ethan excused himself without acknowledging the dog at all. He headed towards the restroom, leaving the other three seated at the table. Frazier whined softly and then turned back to Stander.

"Don't sweat it, Frazier. Maybe Ethan doesn't like dogs? In which case, fuck that guy…"

Liz laughed and offered, "Maybe he's allergic to dogs." She seemed to be more relaxed, and though it may have been Stander's imagination, he thought he caught her looking more intently at him. In the brief silence, Frazier, still seated in the booth beside Stander, laid his head down on the top of the table and started to slowly close his eyes as if the lull in conversation bored him. Liz smiled down at the dog, exhibiting such very human-like behavior. "Well, look at that. What's the matter, Frazier? We just not exciting enough for you?" Frazier only moved his eyes to look over at Liz as she spoke, not his head. The perfect picture of relaxation and human indifference.

Stander tried to take advantage of Ethan's absence by learning a little more about the visitor from the U of M, "So you live in Ann Arbor then?" Liz nodded while wiping a dab of salad dressing from the side of her mouth. "Are you originally from there? Family around town?"

Liz smiled back at Stander, and he thought to himself that, as smart as she obviously was, she likely understood exactly what he was asking. "No, I'm not even from Michigan. Just moved here for the job a few years back. Needed a fresh start. The only family I have are two boys. One enlisted in the army last year, and the other just started high school. He still lives with his dad in Indiana." She seemed to study the look on Stander's face for a few beats before continuing. "I got divorced a few years back, and when this opportunity at the University of Michigan came up, it was too good to say no. But we all agreed it would be better if my youngest stayed in the school where he was."

"Yeah, tough for kids to move at that age. Must have been hard leaving him, though." Stander was surprised by her reply. Her honesty and blunt admission were refreshing.

"It wasn't as bad as most people would think," she paused. "I really was not very good at being a mother. It just never came natural to me for some reason…" Liz shrugged, seeming comfortable with a truth most women would deny. She was watching Stander's reaction and appeared pleasantly surprised by the absence of judgment. He didn't press her for more. Intuitively understanding things of that nature are rarely able to be explained.

"Better to be honest than live a life where you have to pretend or act every single day." Stander looked around his bar and then focused back on Liz, "In this place, I hear everything. Miserable married guys and gals venting about each other. Or people coming around just to avoid their fucked up home life. I always wonder why they stay together or live a life full of falsehoods." Stander reached over and petted Frazier, who only briefly opened his eyes. "But what the fuck do I know? This four-legged guy here is just about the only roommate I ever had to stay with me longer than a few months."

"Hmmm… Any ideas why that is, Mr. Stander?" Liz was clearly enjoying the company and conversation of the straightforward man so at ease with himself. He was the exact opposite of her male peers at the university, who all clamored to flaunt their degrees, titles, and self-important trivialities. Each defensive of their own little fiefdom on campus.

"You know, from time to time, I have contemplated thinking about thinking about that." Liz laughed at his deft avoidance and spin on words. Stander was smiling again, his grin adorably pushing the full, white whiskers of his mustache up on his cheeks. "But usually, I can drown that idea by getting another drink or two in." He lifted and drained the last of his beer. "Which I think I am due for about now. How about you, Liz? Can I buy you a drink?" Stander leaned forward like a spy in some old black and white movie concerned with eavesdroppers. "I hear the owner conceals a bottle or two of really good stuff back in the kitchen. But," Stander looked over his shoulder dramatically, "he is willing to unveil it on tragic nights."

"And what about this night has been tragic, Stander?" Liz shook her head confusedly, though, still smiling and enjoying herself.

"Well," he started slowly, his voice playful, flirtatious, and silly. "This is the night I met a beautiful, intelligent woman living seven hours away from me that I most likely will never, ever see again." Stander slumped his shoulders forward as if defeated. "And that is just fucking tragic…"

Liz let out a throaty laugh. "Oh my, Mr. Stander. You must be deadly around these parts." She giggled slightly. Flattered at being hit on by the handsome and slightly more mature man. Generally, Liz found she intimidated most men even if they were interested in her. Rarely had any member of the opposite sex been so straightfor-ward or sincere in their approach. "Maybe there should be a warning sign on the door that says 'Beware of Owner.'" But she was snickering good-naturedly.

Stander winked, turned, and pointed to a plastic novelty sign hanging behind the bar that read,

-CAUTION-
Never Mind The Dog
-BEWARE-
Of The Owner

Both Liz and Stander burst out laughing together. Stander shrugged, "Hey, I do OK, I guess." Then he gave her his most radiant smile and reached across the table and lightly touched the top of her hand. An obvious mock seriousness reflected in the tone of his voice. "You know, I would give anything to be your tragedy, though." Liz did not withdraw her hand until she saw Ethan approaching the table.

Oblivious, Ethan did not rejoin the table but instead stood a few feet away. Frazier raised his head and stared at him, no longer relaxed but rigid. Ethan announced, "Well, we should be heading out of here, I suppose. We have an early start to the day in the morning. I am sure Dr. Drexler wants to finish up and head back to Ann Arbor as soon as possible tomorrow."

Stander sighed deeply and wryly shook his head, two motions only Liz understood. Frazier jumped down and went directly over to the bar and then sat behind it. Stander and Liz stood, and all three shook hands once more. Stander said, "So why did you guys come over here tonight anyway? Just to tell me what you found?"

"I told Dr. Drexler I wanted to introduce her to the man who showed me Skull Rock. This could really turn into something big. We could rewrite history with this find!"

Liz nodded. Then impulsively added, "What are you doing tomorrow, Mr. Stander? Would you like to see the inside of the cave you helped discover? The artifacts, I mean. They are all being shipped out very soon, so this may be your last chance. I am not saying the items will rewrite history as Ethan suggests - still a little early to say that - but it is significant and, in a lot of ways, the academic community owes you for that."

Liz was a little surprised to hear herself asking this. It was not exactly professional protocol to allow some bar owner to trudge onto the site, even if all the work was nearly complete. Yet something seemed to be egging her on... Looking slightly embarrassed, she told the two men to work out the time if Stander could make it. Then excused herself to use the bathroom again, telling Ethan she would be right out to the car.

A few minutes later, as Liz walked past the bar, she waved at Stander, who, leaning against the counter, called out he would see her tomorrow. Frazier sat attentively next to his owner, watching her walk out as well. Music still played, and the tavern was busy. As Liz was about to hit the door, she paused and listened, briefly puzzled by what had caught her ear before recognizing it was something in the song playing overhead. The Bee Gees were singing "Tragedy." She turned her head back once more where Stander stood, her hand on the door handle of the entrance. She nodded her head and pointed one finger in the air acknowledging the song. Liz was rewarded by the handsome man's smile and another wink. She was delighted by his attention, and Liz caught herself smiling and laughing softly as she walked towards Ethan's truck and climbed in.

CHAPTER 18
PRESENT DAY

SECRIST PULLED open the door to his old office. He greeted and fist-bumped Craig, his partner for the last eight years before he'd retired, then sat down across from him. This was only his second trip back to the state police office he'd worked out of before he'd begun collecting his pension last year. It had been odd walking in and seeing a few new officers he didn't recognize. Especially considering Craig had said he wanted to talk over the Sherry Stander case with him. But he knew even if a few of the newbies whispered amongst themselves or questioned his presence, the veteran cops he'd served with would shut down any unwanted or stray conversations. Over the years, he'd earned their respect and trust.

And a bit of leeway…

After some catching up and small talk, Craig started in. "I appreciate you driving over. I know we could have talked some place less conspicuous, but I wanted you to see something with your own eyes. And as much coverage as this case is likely going to get by the media, I couldn't exactly lug the stuff around without raising a few eyebrows." Craig, his generic blue JC Penney suit wrinkled and stained, smiled wryly from across the desk. "No one spent more time investigating this case than you. Thought something might jump out at you."

"What is there to solve, Craig? There's no question Tathum got Sherry Stander." Secrist had puzzled over Craig's cryptic invite since receiving it early yesterday. "Did the coroner find something that was overlooked previously?"

"No, no, nothing like that. There's just been a new development that's about to hit the news. Before it does, I wanted to get your thoughts." Craig, handsome and eternally optimistic, frowned. Secrist could count on one hand how many times he'd seen Craig frown before. "A few things just feel off about all this. I can't shake it… Anyway, let me start by bringing you up to speed first. Fair enough?"

Secrist shrugged and sat back in his chair. "Sure. Shoot."

"So when the news outlets first reported the recovery of Sherry Stander's remains, both state and local police departments received a few phone calls. As you can imagine, some of them were well-intentioned and genuinely concerned citizens trying to help out. The usual, yada, yada, yada… At that point, we hadn't said publicly that Sherry Stander's murder had been solved. Or that her murderer was none other than our own resident bogeyman James Tathum. Of course, as always, a certain percentage of the calls were the usual crackpots with false claims and conspiracy theories of, uh… shall we say dubious origins?"

"Par for the course," Secrist commented dryly.

"Exactly. But then came a call about a hole in the ground." Craig picked up a pen from his desk and started twirling it in his hand. Secrist recognized his old partner's habit. He knew it meant Craig was bothered by something.

"Why would a call about a hole in the ground be transferred to the Homicide Division?" Secrist asked.

"Exactly. I almost dismissed the report when it came across. That is until I saw the dimensions and the location. The hole was reported as being almost six feet in length, three feet across, and nearly four feet deep. I guess some hikers stumbled upon it near

Mt. Arvon the month before Sherry's remains were found and had initially not thought much of it. One of the two hikers even stated they'd joked at the time that it looked like a freshly dug grave. Only weeks later, when he'd read about the recovery of a long-missing local girl and saw a picture of where she was found, did he report it." Craig was frowning again. The pen was still twirling in his hand as he continued.

"The hiker pinpointed the location in the Huron Mountains, near the base of Mt. Arvon and off an old, seldom used gravel access road. All traits, as you well know, shared by the spot Sherry's body was found." Secrist sat up in his chair. Immediately thinking about the five other girls still missing from the same time period as Sherry. All were thought to be potential victims of Jimmy Tathum. Each disappearing in the vicinity of Marquette and its surrounding communities in the late seventies when Tathum had been on the prowl.

Craig, reading Secrist's mind, said out loud what he was thinking. "Exactly. Any chance to help those families with closure trumped my doubts about the relevance of the new find. So out into the woods to see the hole in the ground me and my new partner went."

"And?" Secrist could feel his anticipation grow. After decades of nothing, had another of Tathum's victim's been recovered already? Part of him almost wished he'd put off his retirement for another year.

Almost.

"The scene," Craig continued, "was nearly identical to the site where Sherry's remains were discovered. Not far from where a vehicle would have access and surrounded by a bevy of tree cover. The dirt surrounding the empty hole had recently been turned, but how recent was not easy to determine right off." Craig pulled a few pictures out of a file folder and tossed them on top of his desk. Secrist eyed the photos as his old partner went on. "But it appeared to have happened within the last several months. Certainly after the previous winter season and spring thaw anyway."

Secrist picked up each photo and scrutinized them one by one. In close proximity to the hole, there were no obvious clues as to why it might have been dug. It was not a place where any type of building or foundation would have been started. Nor was there any evidence it was the beginning of a trench or a ditch being laid. Nothing about the hole resembled any digging or burrowing normally associated with the wildlife of upper Michigan. Secrist handed the pictures back to Craig and motioned for him to go on.

"After some exploratory probing of the crater, we found items of interest. Visually there were signs that pointed to the patch of ground being a place of the previous interment. So we called in the forensic team to try and verify our suspicions. It didn't take long for them to find enough physical evidence to definitively say the dirt hole once held human remains."

"Evidence, huh? But no body? Had scavengers gotten to it?" Secrist could feel his stomach tensing. Was this the break he'd hoped for decades to have?

"No, the team figured that out right away." Craig shook his head, pen still spinning in his hand. "What they found were several human teeth, other bits of bone, and particles of clothing, metal, and leather. They were able to determine the remains had likely been buried and undisturbed for more than thirty years before the recent desecration and that the body had been exhumed sometime in the last sixty days by means of human activity, not animal. Everything seemed to point to another victim of Jimmy Tathum being found."

"Right. Makes sense..." Secrist paused, both men silent for several seconds before Secrist continued, thinking out loud. "But if someone found what would likely only be bones, how had they done that after all this time? Why had they not reported it and, more importantly, where had the remains been moved to?"

"Exactly!" Craig sat up straighter in his chair. "We debated several possible scenarios. At first, thinking it may have been some local campers, hikers, or hunters who frequented the woods and somehow stumbled upon a clue to the location. But, since the body was clearly removed methodically and with some care, this didn't seem likely unless they had been kids or teenagers that had unwittingly discovered the burial site. Maybe dug it up before they realized what it was and then panicked at the gruesome discovery. Tried covering their tracks."

"Or perhaps cooler heads prevailed and decided they didn't want any attention drawn to themselves. So they just high-tailed it out of there." But even as Secrist spoke, he realized there had to be more to it than that.

"Possibly. I mean, you could even entertain the notion that someone with a morbid obsession might have hung onto something like the skull as a memento." Craig was shaking his head now. "But not the entirety of the remains, right? That doesn't make sense. So what then? Could they have possibly moved and reburied what they didn't want? I mean maybe... I figured it was a long shot, but we ended up deciding to scour the immediate vicinity just to see. So we called in the cadaver sniffing dogs and brought them up to the area."

"I take it they found something?"

"Within an hour of the assembled search team's arrival onsite, our hunch paid off. The hunt produced human remains which had, of course, been the goal." Secrist started to congratulate Craig but stopped when he saw another frown contorting his face. "But that discovery solved nothing and only deepened the enigma. The skeletal body the dogs had sniffed out had been undisturbed where it was buried for the last three decades. It had not been, as we'd hoped, the reburied remains from the empty crater first reported by the hikers, but rather a new previously undiscovered murder victim of Tathum's."

"My god, are you serious?" Secrist was feeling overwhelmed. Had they really found the remains of three of the five missing girls who'd been missing all these years? And found them all only months apart?

Craig was nodding yes as he spoke. "Like Sherry Stander, the recovered bones were from a young female and told the same story of violence inflicted upon them as hers. Both before and after death. The all too familiar narrative detailing her likely end at the hands of James Tathum. His gruesome trademark, the orbital damage, and markings, easily identified this as the handiwork of the serial killer. But, at least we were able to identify and notify the victim's family."

"But what about the missing body? The one that would have come from the empty hole that started the whole search? Where did that end up at?" Secrist was beginning to understand why Craig had wanted to talk. Everything about this was slightly off…

"The cadaver sniffing dogs and the search party combed the area for three additional days in hopes of finding more remains before we finally called them off. That early success was never duplicated over the course of the days that followed. So the original mystery of the empty hole and the missing body was still just that: a mystery. But the search team produced several bags worth of potential evidence from the area. Random objects picked up adjacent to where the two murder victims were unceremoniously discarded by their killer." Craig stood now and walked behind where Secrist sat. He drew down the blinds on his office door. "Doubt anyone on this floor would question why or if I should show you this. But I had a partner once who told me you can never be too careful…" Craig smiled as he quoted a line Secrist had repeated often when they'd still worked together.

After handing Secrist a pair of gloves, Craig reached under his desk and pulled out several smallish bags labeled as evidence. He dumped the first bag and, though he'd already done so several times himself, he and Secrist painstakingly sifted through the various items recovered. Both men looked and hoped for something that could point to where the missing body may have been redeposited. Each piece a potential clue that could lead them to this modern-day grave robber. Secrist wanted to recover the victim and see another cold case brought to an end. While Craig was also hoping for something to identify the body snatcher so he could bring the person in and understand how they'd located those long-lost remains. See if there was any possible connection all these years later to Tathum.

Doubtful. But answers are only ever gleaned from doubts.

After going through the first two bags without much comment, Secrist spread the meager contents of the last evidence bag across Craig's desk with his hand. Something sharp poked through the thin plastic glove he wore, pricking the sensitive skin between his forefinger and thumb. The offender was a thin, rusted, bent wire that was just meaningless junk by itself. However, Secrist recognized there had been another wire very similar to it in the previous bag he'd rifled through. The retired detective went back to the items from that last bag and pulled the first steel or aluminum wire out to compare it to the second. It was identical in length and circumference, and both seemed to be equally weathered. Although non-descript, the matching wires struck him as somehow familiar. As Craig watched from the other side of the desk, Secrist paired them together and set them aside before resuming his examination of the remaining articles.

Secrist scrutinized scraps from the last bag for another minute before discovering a third matching wire. This one must have been pulled directly from the ground for the bottom three inches or so were still caked in dried mud. But it was the top of the wire that immediately drew his attention. Attached to that end was a dirty, torn, white plastic flag. He was sure each of the matching wires at one time would have had the same style of flag if not the same color.

"Yeah, I noticed those also." Craig picked one wire up and turned it over a few times in his hand. "They're modern stake flags used for surveying and marking spots on the ground. They're typically used by engineers, utility company employees, and construction workers. Just junk…"

But their familiarity with Secrist, however, was because they were also identical to the ones Ethan Glaser was currently using in his search for Native American artifacts. While, as Craig had pointed out, these types of stake flags were common and could be purchased for pennies, Secrist did not believe in coincidences. At the very least, Ethan must have been working near the area, and his tool of choice for that work was a GPR unit that identified disturbances in the soil. Ethan had found and reported one body. Could he have somehow actually found two and dug one of them up? Again, Secrist did not believe in coincidences. Maybe it was time they did a little digging of their own and find out who Ethan Glaser was.

Except for the three wires - one with a white flag at the end - Secrist and Craig bagged up the rest of the finds they'd been reviewing. After sharing his suspicions with Craig, the two men decided to dial up the college professor Ethan was working with when he'd found Sherry Stander's remains. Craig pulled the report filed the day of the macabre find and familiarized himself with the details before ringing the contact number listed for Professor Danforth. Activating the speaker function on the desk phone so Secrist was able to listen in on the conversation as well.

After a brief introduction, Craig began to hone in on some of the specifics they were now questioning. He explained his inquiries were simply standard background information missed initially but still needed to fully complete and file a report on the discovery. The older educator seemed at ease on the phone and remained friendly and forthcoming over the entirety of the call. Each answer itself was fairly ambiguous, but combined, they filled in missing blanks and helped clarify some of the vagueness in the official report. The educator reiterated he was present when Ethan had discovered the half-buried body of Sherry Stander. That it had been found not by use of the GPR unit but rather during a break in the work they had been engaged in that day. He also vouched for the authenticity of their quick reporting of the find to the local authorities.

With some additional friendly prodding and casual conversation, the professor also shared what he knew of Ethan's past. That he had attended Florida State University some years before, where he obtained his bachelor's degree from. Also, he'd only moved to Ann Arbor a short time ago from Seattle, Washington, where he had lived for the past several years while working a poorly compensated retail job before finally deciding to return to school and continue his education in hopes of bettering himself. Over several years, the two men learned, Ethan had dutifully taken classes at a local community college to meet the educational requirements to be considered for the graduate program at MU.

Danforth went on to say Ethan had been accepted by the university last fall, and he was currently pursuing his Doctorate in Native American Studies under the tutelage of the professor. He also shared that, as Ethan's chair and sponsor of his paper, the educator initially had doubts about the Mt. Arvon sites Ethan had wanted to focus on. The professor said, as the coauthor of a paper they both expected to be published, that he'd felt there were other geographic areas that held more promise. But, in the end, he had relented and now been proven wrong.

Secrist raised his eyebrows at the last comment, and Craig nodded silently in agreement. He pushed the professor for an explanation for what he meant by being "proven wrong." The older educator seemed genuinely shocked the detective hadn't heard the latest news. Saying he assumed part of the reason for his call was the more recent discovery at Mt. Arvon. Professor Danforth went on to provide some background on the excavation already underway of the ancient tomb that Ethan uncovered in the Huron Mountains. One that, the professor breathlessly explained, could turn out to be a monumental find once everything was verified.

Secrist sat stunned as he learned Ethan, who, when the detectives placed the call to the college professor they'd suspected of discovering two gravesites and only reporting one, turned out to have perhaps found three previously undiscovered bodies. One of which had been housed behind the local landmark known as Skull Rock of all places! The retired detective tried to hide his astonishment as Craig artfully ended the call, thanking the Michigan University professor for his time before hanging up.

The two men, armed with this latest information, quickly turned their attention to the details and information about Ethan the professor had shared: the timeline and previous places Ethan Glaser had lived were the perfect starting point. Together, just as they'd done countless times over the past eight years, they spent the afternoon pulling records, making phone calls, cross-referencing, and slowly connecting dots. Certainly less exciting than the drama-filled side of fictional police work you see on TV or at the movies. But often, when done right, the most revealing.

The detectives learned that Ethan Glaser had been born in Wisconsin near the small town of Plainfield. Here he'd spent his entire childhood before becoming nomadic as an adult. While he was still in Wisconsin, the record showed Ethan had been charged with assault. However, at the time, he had not yet been of age and was still considered a juvenile in the eyes of the court system. So the records were sealed and not easily accessed without going through the proper channels, which would take some time.

After high school, Ethan attended college at Florida State University, as Professor Danforth had shared, graduating with a degree in English Literature. But interestingly, while living in Tallahassee and going to school, he was picked up and questioned by the police during a murder investigation. Once again, official details were scarce, so Craig had made several phone calls before finally tracking down and getting a call back from one of the detectives who'd worked the case. Craig learned the case had still never been solved, and the Florida cop had considered Ethan Glaser a suspect.

The victim turned out to be a female student found bludgeoned to death in her apartment while she slept. She had been a classmate of Ethan's and last seen with him earlier that same evening. However, there had not actually been any evidence or witnesses that linked him to her murder. The fellow detective admitted that his interview with Ethan and follow-up investigation had not yielded any clues or further suspicions either. He also shared that the girl's death on the campus of FSU had sent shock waves through the entire community. The killing was very reminiscent of the slaughter notorious serial killer Ted Bundy had done at the same university town in the late seventies. At that time, Bundy had killed several young female students by beating them to death and assaulting them while they slept.

Like Craig and Secrist, the police in Florida had learned of Ethan's previous assault charge from his hometown in Wisconsin. The detective in Florida had seen those case files during his investigation, and he shared what he recalled with Craig. The assault charge had been filed by a female student. Also underage, who testified Ethan choked her briefly and threatened to hurt her if she ever told anyone. Ethan's family must have some sway in their local community because, although found guilty, his punishment was pretty minimal and basically amounted to probation. The detective in Florida seemed disappointed to hear that Craig was only inquiring about Ethan in relation to some missing bones. Both men hung up after the Michigan detective promised to keep his peer in Florida informed if anything enlightening came of his investigation.

While Craig was making his phone calls, Secrist spent his time confirming what professor Danforth had shared regarding Ethan's movements as an adult. Using Ethan's various online social media profiles and posts over the years, he was able to verify his work history. Discovering, just as Danforth had said, that after college, he'd moved across the country to Seattle, Washington. There he had worked at a couple Bed Bath & Beyond stores in and around the city and suburbs. Living in Washington until recently and, as a citizen of Seattle, he had zero reported interactions with police. Not even so much as a speeding or parking ticket. Neither he nor Craig could find anything of consequence in the seven years Ethan made his home in the Pacific Northwest. They did note, however, not that it necessarily meant anything, that there were several unsolved murders and missing women over that time span. But realistically, that would be true of any major metropolis.

Ethan had moved to Ann Arbor just last fall and was enrolled, just as reported, at the University of Michigan. The phone call with Professor Danforth verified his current study plan and that he truly was writing a paper on the Native Americans who once populated the upper part of Michigan. Yet, despite the apparent bland existence Ethan lived the past eight years or so, something wouldn't let go of the two veteran detectives. But, as the day came to an end, neither could yet put their finger on exactly what felt so off.

"Thanks again for coming in and looking over all this," said Craig as the men made their way towards the building's exit. "I really just wanted to talk everything over and get your two cents on the items collected from the site. That was a great catch matching those wires to Ethan's work. We may not have found anything definitive today, but at least it gives me something to keep following up on." Craig smiled as he shook Secrist's hand. Pulling him in close, he whispered conspiratorially, "Sorry I blew your whole afternoon. It wasn't my intent, and thank god no one seemed to really notice. But man, it was good working beside you again…"

"Invite me over to the house sometime soon for some steaks on the grill, and we'll call it even. Otherwise, I'm charging you by the hour." Secrist laughed before adding, "And don't sweat it. I'm happy you contacted me. Felt good using that part of my brain again. I just wish we'd nailed something down."

"Glad you agreed with me that something wasn't smelling right about all this, and I wasn't just wasting your time." Craig pulled his car keys out of his pocket. "I'm out of here. You want to go grab a beer or something?"

"Nah, maybe some other time." Secrist gestured towards the public restroom near the entrance. "You go on. I need to step in here for a bit." Craig waved once before disappearing out the front door.

Walking into the restroom, Secrist passed the empty urinals and pushed aside a grey metal door on one stall. Closing it behind him, Secrist undid his khakis and sat down to empty his bowels of the heart-attack-in-a-sack he'd downed for lunch earlier. He pondered what he'd seen and learned today, feeling like he'd just spent half a day peeling onions. Each layer pulled back more shocking and offensive than the last. Craig may not yet have enough to cook-a-goose, he thought to himself, but their work today certainly added flavor to what Secrist felt sure was going to be a full meal once they stuck a fork in it.

As he sat hunched forward, chin resting on his hands, another cop entered the bathroom as well. The fellow officer was on his cell phone and talking as he peed in a neighboring urinal. Secrist couldn't help but overhear parts of the dialogue. This anonymous lawman was commenting to whoever was on the other end of the conversation about the recent report of a second missing girl in Ann Arbor. Saying he hoped they didn't have another psycho on their hands down there.

Secrist bolted straight up, squeaking the toilet seat loudly as his weight shifted. If he had not literally been sitting on a toilet, his analogy would have been that he'd "shit his pants" when he learned there were now two missing women from the University of Michigan. Secrist hurried to finish the crap he was halfway through and then bolted out to his car. Racing home, he pulled out his laptop and consulted with all-knowing Google to verify if his memory was correct.

The detective in Florida had reminded Secrist that Ted Bundy killed at FSU. Ethan perhaps had only coincidentally ended up in school at FSU. But after that, he moved to the northwest, where again Bundy had killed. Perhaps more striking, though, Ethan's residence was Seattle, where Gary Ridgeway, the Green River Killer, had done his killing. Now for the last year, Ethan had lived in Ann Arbor, Michigan, where yet another serial killer operated in the past. John Norman Chapman murdered several women in the late sixties and was nicknamed the Ypsilanti Killer after the neighboring community of Ann Arbor -Ypsilanti, Michigan. And right now, Ethan was doing field work in the area right where James Tathum most likely slaughtered and then buried his victims in upper Michigan.

Secrist did not believe in coincidences.

The retired detective hit the keyboard with the only two fingers he had ever learned to type with. Google verified his question about Plainfield, Wisconsin. That small Midwestern town was the place where the godfather of American serial killers had operated and ultimately been caught. He'd inspired moviemakers and writers who created Psycho, The Texas Chainsaw Massacre, and countless others. Ethan Glaser grew up under the dark shadow and echoing memory of a town that birthed and gave rise to perhaps the most infamous of all serial killers: Ed Gein.

Secrist sat back in his chair contemplatively. Was Ethan some weird serial killer groupie or a sick devotee of some sort? Or was he in some way emulating these monstrous men's deeds?

CHAPTER 19
10TH CENTURY

GUNNAR SPENT the first several days riding deep into the mountains along trails he was familiar with. He knew well the way to Nimki's homelands from previous journeys. Accompanying his father when some of the first truces between their clan and Nimki's tribes were agreed upon and on later trading trips between the two groups. The natives' leader was well respected by his father and the Norsemen's leader Thorfinn. Both had visited with him many times in the past, and Nimki's knowledge of the land and the peaceful ways of his people had been a blessing for the Norse clans when they'd first arrived at Vinland. Gunnar only hoped Nimki would remember him and be able to explain what had happened to Vidar and his clan. But, more importantly, help Gunnar, and his village destroy the stone and lift the curse seeping into their lands.

Traveling well-trodden paths and hunting trails along the range overlooking the valley of his clan's village, Gunnar tried to push from his mind the nightmare of the last several days. Instead, focusing on and remembering childhood adventures with his father in these wooded areas. Calling to mind the lessons he was taught about the cautious balance between man, nature, and the gods. For in these same woods was where Gunnar had first learned of the mystical beings that lived within the forest. The fairies, the skin-walking shapeshifters, the witches and mares. Their clan had no shortage of tales and warnings of people who had gone missing in these same hills. Surely befallen by things best left unsaid but always said in hushed whispers anyway. For Gunnar, it was an eerie coincidence that he was now looking to distance himself from one such creature in this very same timbered area. He wrestled with his wariness and strained to hear or see anything out of the ordinary as he rode.

Fears first learned as a child kept pace with him.

Gunnar was able to keep the horse on a steady clip with his knowledge of the area, sweeping along ridges and down into deep ravines. Walking the horse around felled trees, rotted logs, and across small mountain streams they came across. Avoiding the patches of snow and ice that remained in the higher summits of the mountain range. Thankful for his warm coat, thick clothes, and the blankets and food he grabbed before leaving Tor's home. The temperatures fluctuated wildly as the warmer spring air pushed out the lingering chills of the areas he rode through.

Gunnar told himself it was the favorable weather and familiar terrain that kept him moving so swiftly and not his fear of the barely known thing he felt hunted by. Before the events of the last several days, he had never personally seen anything he didn't later come to understand or could be explained to him by his father. Nor had he witnessed a tragedy connected with these dark mountains or the beings who made them their home. But now, Gunnar was unsure what to believe anymore. The world he had come to know had shifted under him. His entire being had been his father, his home, and his future with Sassa. Now all that was swept away and stolen from him.

At times, as he plunged deeper into the mountains, hot tears clouded his vision and streaked down the sides of his face. He alternately sobbed and raged, cursed, and prayed. Day and night blurred, but Gunnar pressed on as much as he dared. He did his best to push the fantastic events he witnessed from his mind. Instead, he focused on the trails and paid close attention to Tor's horse. Gaining its confidence and learning its habits, often stopping so as not to exhaust his travel companion. Gunnar felt fortunate that in the early spring, there was plenty of vegetation and water available for them both. Together, he and the horse fell into a familiar pattern of riding during the day and finding or making shelter each night.

Despite feeling bone weary and sore at the end of each day's riding, Gunnar gained no solace or comfort in sleep. It now came rarely and never deeply; his dreams were full of disturbing images and foreign conversations. Haunted by a singular being stepping out of the shadows in Gunnar's mind.

Often it came as a man, dark-skinned and with long flowing black hair. Usually bare and unclothed, hideously ugly, and difficult to look upon. But at other times, his tormentor came to him in other forms. A large, snorting, black, barebacked horse with eyes glowing red like hot embers from a fire. Galloping full force towards a numb and paralyzed Gunnar, overtaking and crushing him under hoof in a thundering rush. Sometimes it appeared as a whirlwind or tornado bearing relentlessly down upon him, destroying everything in its path as it rushed forward. Splintering homes and tossing aside anything lying between itself and Gunnar. Swooping him up with a force that hurtled him across trees, water, and land. Gunnar was helpless within the grip of the roaring winds as it moved onward.

Another reoccurring appearance was that of a duck. It peacefully paddled across a small lake or still stream towards the place where Gunnar stood rooted until it finally reached the soft mud of the bank and waddled onto land. In this dream, Gunnar pounced upon it even as the duck began to flee from him. He would chase it deep into the high reeds that lined the sides of the water. The reeds snapped back on Gunnar as he clutched desperately for it, slapping his face, arms, and legs as he ran, struggling to keep the duck in sight in the foggy gloom. Eventually, Gunnar would find what he knew was its home nestled in among the toadstools and ferns of the marshy shore. The soft nest of feathers surrounded by muck and embracing a single egg. Within that brown egg shell, he knew, was the spirit of his tormentor. Gunnar would gleefully crush the egg under his heel only to find it held a grey rabbit. The rabbit would run away, darting in and out of the underbrush far faster than Gunnar could chase in the dim light of his dreamland. Soon exhausted, Gunnar would eventually collapse onto the ground and watch the white tail of the rabbit bob up and down until even that was out of sight.

During these nightly visions, Gunnar could hear a voice taunting him over and over, dream after dark dream. "I am immortal. Existing before time was counted. I am known by many names: Koschei, Draugr, Ithaqua, Haugbui, Lich, Wendigo…" Continuing to name itself on and on and often in languages Gunnar could not comprehend. The repeating cycle eventually became a disturbing buzz so close and loud it would wake him. The sound dry as fall leaves crackling in a fire.

Each morning Gunnar woke early and watched the sun burst across the land as he readied for the day. Anxious to avoid the lurid thing hunting him, hoping in a small way he was tormenting the monstrous thing a little more with every step forward. Though often engulfed by the thick undergrowth of the tangled forest floors, Gunnar and his horse kept moving steadily. Where possible, finding trampled game trails and natural tunnels within the ungroomed woodlands to help ease their way. Several times barely avoiding huge, water-logged, and diseased branches that splintered and crashed nearby. Dead wood snapped and dropped to the ground so endlessly that, when the forest remained still for long, it made Gunnar very nervous. He tried not to think of the strange cargo he carried with him or of what may be following to reclaim ownership.

He pressed on day after day, sometimes having to walk the horse around deep ravines full of mist-filled timber. Twigs whipped across his hands and face, sharp thorns reaching out desperately for his attention. Endless wooden spears extended from the virgin forests he traversed, each threatening to impale him should he lose focus. Wading into oceans of slippery wet leaves hiding gnarled roots that threatened his every step. Often traveling in almost perpetual darkness and shadows. The sun glimpsed only briefly through the treetops among the thinnest band of trees or tiny clearings of the mighty forests before finally emerging in a trampled field or meadow to bathe once more in the rejuvenating rays of the sun. During these times, he was always on guard and fearful he would be caught from behind. Certain he could feel a dark presence creeping ever closer.

Gunnar climbed over impossibly high rock formations covered in slick moss and green ivy. At times, only to find they led him to the edge of a deep gorge that was impassible without the gift of flight. Having to then backtrack until he could find a place where the dense foliage was thin enough for him to find a new path forward. He crossed countless streams and rivers and circled around lakes and bodies of water that stretched as far as his eyes could see. Gunnar passed over flat fields and others full of hills that rolled like the waves on water. He made his way through weeds as tall as his horse, seemingly waving him forward in the breeze, and pushed his way into the undergrowth as high as his waist. He trampled over saplings and small green grass that, when he laid on it, was soft as the finest of silk cloth.

Eventually, despite the recurring dreams and seemingly endless riding, Gunnar found the great body of water that he knew bordered Nimki's homelands. Gunnar sighed wearily as he took in the enormous breadth and size of the lake. He knew Nimki's village and home were close now, but he still had two more days of hard riding to reach his final destination. He dismounted and kneeled to replenish his water skins while the horse drank deeply. As he rested, Gunnar watched as a series of dark and ominous clouds rolled across the lake towards him. He felt the wind pick up and the temperature drop as the waves lapping the shore grew larger and more urgent.

A storm was coming.

Gunnar stretched and arched his back as he warily watched the gathering clouds. He refastened his water supply and tightened his pack on the horse before looking once more across the waters at the troubled sky above him. In the distance, far out across the lake, lightning streaked menacingly. Gunnar understood he needed to find shelter. Fast. Just ahead of him, down the shore of the gigantic lake, was a mountain range. With any luck, he'd be able to find cover among the cliffs until morning. It was close enough to dark now that continuing, especially if the rains fell hard, would be foolish. He remounted and took off for the base of the tallest peak. Finding the incline on the side closest to him was gradual. Starting up it, he remained on his horse, crisscrossing some of the natural switchbacks and animal trails. Making his way higher and higher.

As he continued his ascent of the summit, Gunnar could see small wisps of smoke rising lazily in the air nearby. The white smoke starkly outlined against the backdrop of the dark trees and forest. He knew he was not alone along the base of this range. Perhaps a village or group of travelers were nearby. Gunnar continued carefully, making his way upwards, opposite the side where the smoke was visible, uninterested in meeting up with any of the local dark-skinned people until he'd met with Nimki.

He climbed the slope of the mountain by following a barely visible game trail among the green pine trees and loose rocks. It was slow going, and the horse seemed unsure of its footing, so before he could reach the top of the summit, the rain began. Gunnar began looking for quick shelter.

Soon his efforts were rewarded by the discovery of a small cave. It's opening next to a stream running down the side of the mountain. The yawning cavity was carved naturally into the side of the summit. Gunnar inspected the surrounding area and judged it to be secure; the cave itself shallow and unoccupied. He quickly set up inside for the evening and unpacked the horse, tethering it outside where it was able to reach the water source. In short order, he had a fire lit just inside the mouth of the cavern. As the rains fell, Gunnar decided he would stay the night inside the shelter before continuing on towards Nimki's village in the morning. Satisfied he had a good plan for the next day, and thanking Ymir for the blessing of the safety of the cave, he ate and soon fell fast asleep.

CHAPTER 20
10TH CENTURY

THE STENCH of death filled the air.

Gunnar woke to a presence very near him, dominating the cavern. Opening his eyes, he could not see even a sliver of light. He lay in complete darkness. The entrance to the cave and the night-time sky of stars had somehow vanished, leaving Gunnar alone and blind with this intruder. The panicked whinnying of his horse filled the chamber with ethereal sounds that bounced around the small enclosure. As the noise reached a crescendo, Gunnar understood the horse's audible terror was what woke him. Moments later, the desperation of the horse rose to a fever pitch. In a burst that Gunnar could only imagine in his mind's eye, he heard the horse break free from where it had been hitched. In a rush, it sprinted away, and Gunnar followed its thundering hoof beats with his ears as they pounded farther and farther away. Tor's horse escaping and abandoning him to his own fate.

Still utterly unseeing, Gunnar began to focus on new sounds near him. Very near. A deep and heavy breathing accompanied rustling movements that echoed around him. Ears straining, eyes wide and bulging out of his head, Gunnar's mind screamed at him to run, but his body refused to listen. Though blind, he searched the blackness with his eyes for any hint of light, desperately trying to make sense of his surroundings but having little success.

He lay motionless, barely daring to breathe.

Gunnar was flat on his back, his heart pounding furiously within his chest. Exposed and defenseless. He cautiously reached for where he thought he laid Tor's sword, urgently sweeping his hand silently across the dirt floor of the cave without success. With each inhale more unpleasant and repugnant than the next, Gunnar had no doubt the monstrous thing from his vision of Vidar's clan's battle had finally closed the gap, coming to reclaim what Gunnar had taken. More movement came from his left, and Gunnar felt something hot as fever advancing towards him.

Gunnar inhaled a dank breeze that teased his face, a hot and foul breath that made his eyes water. The horror above him was sniffing him intently, inhaling his fear and savoring the tension and anxiety pouring out of him. Gunnar hated himself for his cowardice, allowing pleasure to be drawn out from him this way. He began to tremble uncontrollably and could hear his own teeth chattering inside his head. Gunnar desperately wanted to cry out, but all that he could manage was a small whimper. No sooner had the sound escaped him when he felt the drip of something wet and hot upon his cheek.

It was looming over him.

In his blindness, every other sense was raised to high alert. Gunnar could feel what had dripped down on him was heavy and warm as it slowly slithered its way down to the crook of his neck. No sooner had the thick drop settled when a second came down upon his face. Gunnar imagined the blood of the creature's latest kill was steadily dripping down upon him. Leaking out of an opened and gore-smeared mouth. Gunnar idly wondered if the blood was from a man or a woman running down his neck when a third drop splattered across his mouth. He gritted his teeth together so tightly that it parted his lips slightly. Gunnar felt the slimy content of the vile fluid enter his mouth, and he gagged involuntarily.

A deafening roar exploded all around him.

Instantly his face, open eyes, and clenched teeth were coated with a thick nauseous spray. Gunnar's bowels let loose, and terror overwhelmed every other command he once had of his body. He shot up from the ground, screaming and flailing against the fiend in the cave. The bulk was covered in hair, dense and unmoving despite Gunnar's best efforts to gain his feet. As he tried to push himself forward off the ground, Gunnar was abruptly thrust backward. Landing hard against the rough and rocky ground of the cave, the breath was crushed out of him by the force of the blow and the ground beneath him. The searing pain, hot as fire detonated across his left shoulder and arm. Without breath and unable to scream, Gunnar could hear the distinctive wet snap of his own bones being crushed. The extreme agony caused him to briefly lose consciousness, only to wake moments later as the thing pushed down hard against his leg on that same side of his body, the leg instantly torn to shreds.

Gunnar finally regained a breath, only to scream it out until he was breathless once more. He tried to pray to Ymir but could no longer form words. Opening his tear-filled eyes briefly, Gunnar was amazed to once again see the entrance to the cave and the twinkling stars of the nighttime sky. He fleetingly decided it was the scenery for his last voyage up to meet Ymir in the heavens above. Then the pain overwhelmed him once and for all, and Gunnar fell mercifully unconscious.

When Gunnar next opened his eyes, it was under radiant sunlight that streamed in from the mouth of the cave. Briefly, he believed the events of the night before were nothing but yet another nightmare. However, the smallest of movements attempted soon brought into clear focus just how real the attack had been. A throbbing pain of unimaginable intensity flowed from both his shoulder and his leg. Movement of either soon proved futile, and the accompanying waves of agony convinced him to stop trying. Instead, lying motionless, Gunnar let his eyes adjust slowly to the harsh sunlight and tried to piece together the remaining traces of his attack in and around the cave. Had his life been spared, or was it merely playing with him? Turning his head slightly, it appeared as if all of his belongings were still with him. Although some were now strewn around the insides of the cave. Gunnar croaked out a sound like a dying dog's last bark when he saw that Tor's sword proved to be mere inches from where his hand lay. Next to it the weathered brown bag of Vidar was still bulging with its lone content.

Untouched.

His pouch of remaining dried meats and foods, however had been torn asunder. Much of what was left was now tossed across the ground and appeared crushed. Gunnar could also just make out a paw print stamped deep into the soft earth of the cave next to him. There was no question now about what had attacked him. Gunnar knew that print from some of the earliest travels and hunts he had taken with his father when they'd first arrived here at Vinland. It was a bear print. Much larger than anything he'd ever seen before, but unmistakably that of a very large bear of some sort.

Perhaps the cave was the bear's home, but Gunnar didn't think so. Yesterday he'd carefully searched for tracks in and around the cave as well as in the soft clay next to the stream and seen none. As Gunnar struggled to pull himself up from the ground, he pondered if the bear was somehow sent by the creature. He doubted it. Gunnar knew he had been very lucky to have traveled so long and so far without having encountered the fiercest side of nature. The bear was most likely just curious or smelled the dried meats Gunnar foolishly left unburied. That bad decision he would now have to live with.

If he lived…

Gunnar groaned loudly as he finally got himself upright and into a seated position in the cave. He propped himself against the nearest rock wall for support and took stock of his injuries. He could see his leg was cut deeply in several places. The bear's claws had ripped him open and left his leg with deep, red gashes in the flesh along the top. It was completely caked in dried blood, and although it hurt terribly, Gunnar did not think it was broken. His shoulder, however, he knew was a different story. He could see the bone itself when he looked down at his arm. Or what was left of it. Gunnar's head swam at the sight of his ruined shoulder and the pain throbbing deep within it.

Turning his head, Gunnar threw up next to himself on the cave's floor. His heaving chest racked his shoulder in unimaginable pain, and the agonized scream that followed only brought more pain. Gunnar somehow managed to regain a measure of control and finally stopped himself. Now silent tears streamed down his grimy face as he looked upon the ruined limb. The bear had bitten down on him and crushed both his shoulder and upper arm. It was a miracle the blood had stopped flowing, but Gunnar could not see how he would ever be able to use that arm again. He knew his injuries would take a very long time to heal. If at all. There was no way he could continue on to Nimki's village until he tended them. Although, at this point, he wasn't sure he could even make it out of the cave. Tired, torn, and exhausted from the loss of blood, Gunnar soon fell unconscious once more. But terrible visions and thoughts invaded his mind.

Sights of blood-soaked lands and ripped and torn bodies.

Gunnar slept on and off. For how long, he had no idea. Occasionally moving just enough to reach his water skins and the remains of the food scattered on the floor of the cave. It was days before Gunnar was finally able to drag himself out of the entrance of the cave. Desperation gave him the strength to reach the cold-water stream pouring down from the mountaintop. Cupping his one good hand, he greedily drank in the fresh, bubbling water as it flowed along the side of the cave.

In the warming sun, he pulled the blood-caked clothes off his body. The cloth tore his wounds open once more. The pain was almost unbearable and caused him to grow faint. But he had learned from Sassa and her mother the importance of cleaning wounds thoroughly. He tried to apply their knowledge of healing to himself, speaking to both in his delirium as if they were there to provide guidance. Eventually, he gained the courage to pull himself over to the shallow side of the stream. He found a piece of wood along the riverbank that was soft and wet but still solid enough for what he needed it for. He placed the short stick in his mouth, tasting the remaining bits of green moss covering it. Biting down with all his strength, he then dipped his broken body into the cascading water. He screamed through his teeth as the rushing water cleansed the dried dirt and blood from his wounds and body. The icy water and pain caused him to shake violently.

When he could take it no longer, Gunnar managed to drag himself back out of the rushing stream with his one good arm and leg. His wounds were bleeding again, and the torment was almost more than he could have imagined. But as his angry wounds calmed down and he lay naked in the sun, Gunnar felt a bit of hope for the first time since the attack. He had made it to the river, and he was confident he could make it back to the cave once more. He had water and what he needed to make traps for small game and the fish in the stream. Gunnar knew he could survive on his own.

The only question was if he was truly alone out here or not...

CHAPTER 21
PRESENT DAY

KNOWING that he was meeting Ethan and Liz up at Skull Rock today, Stander woke much earlier than usual. Without opening his eyes, he rubbed fervently at the end of his nose to snuff out the sneeze a rogue mustache hair was trying to coax out of him. Then pawed groggily for the cup of water at his bedside. Grasping the glass, Stander gulped it down greedily before finally pulling himself out of bed.

After eating breakfast, he takes a quick walk around the block with Frazier before filling his dog food bowl and refilling his water dish. He then grabs his wallet and car keys, fills his Jeep with fuel at a gas station near the edge of town, and heads towards the Huron Mountains, specifically Mt. Arvon. His three-year-old, four-wheel drive black Jeep Wrangler had a manual transmission, and as he shifted through the gears, Stander cranked his favorite satellite radio station. Ozzy's Boneyard pumping out tunes that made it hard to keep his speed close to the posted limit as he drove.

Stander wasn't kidding himself that, deep down, his interest in the previously hidden cave was not the real reason he had gotten an early start this morning, nor why he was looking forward so much to the day ahead. While it was cool he had a hand in its discovery, Stander knew any number of local people could have taken Ethan up the mountain to see the big, skull-shaped rock. If his efforts ended up helping Ethan get his name etched in some scientific journal somewhere, he was happy for the grad student. Stander owed the guy for finding Sherry and bringing her back home. In some ways, Ethan's discovery helped Stander remember his older half-sister in a way he otherwise may never have done. For that, he was grateful.

But Stander knew he was most excited by the prospect of spending more time with Liz. He doubted anything much would come from today, but he had felt an undeniable connection to the attractive U of M professor. Even though Liz said she would be heading back home to Ann Arbor tonight, Stander let his staff at the bar know not to expect him at all today or this evening. He was cautiously optimistic that, since it was a Friday, he might be able to convince her to stay one more night in town.

As he drove along the two-lane blacktop highway of hills and curves, Stander alternately sang along with the hard rock anthems from his youth while also rehearsing ways he might be able to entice Liz to stay. "Detroit Rock City" from the face-painted group Kiss came across the Jeep speakers, and Stander cranked the volume up, shifting up and down through gears as he approached the base of the mountain range.

Pulling into the empty gravel parking lot, he spun the steering wheel hard and kicked up dust and rocks as he slid to a stop. It wasn't often Stander was able to take his Jeep off of paved streets. So over the last mile of his journey, he splashed directly into and across any mud puddles he could find, accelerating and spewing dirt from his wide and knobby tires. He knew it was juvenile, but Stander also knew he didn't care. Besides, he had beaten Ethan and Liz up here, and there was no one else around to judge his adolescent endeavor. For good measure, he spun a doughnut and watched gleefully as dirt and dust filled the air, grinning from ear to ear.

He turned off the Wrangler's engine and got out, gauging the temperature for the day at the elevated altitude of the summit and re-checking his hair in the side mirror. Within ten minutes of his arrival, the pair from Ann Arbor pulled up in Ethan's truck as well. Stander thought Liz looked amazing and felt it was a good sign she'd taken the time to apply a bit of make-up that morning before heading out. Stander couldn't help but notice her legs and arms were tan, smooth, and shapely. He fell in behind her as all three made their way together up the side of the mountain using a now well-traveled path. Admiring the swing of her hips as she ascended along the dirt trail.

Ethan's own appearance, on the other hand, apparently was of no concern to the grad student that morning. The half-empty backpack slung over his shoulder was splashed with old and dried mud. Wrinkled clothes hung limply from his body, and within minutes of walking, he was both panting and sweating. While still overweight and pudgy looking, it seemed to Stander that Ethan had begun to shed some pounds while doing all the physical fieldwork over the last couple of months for his upcoming paper. At least his face seemed leaner. But instead of it helping Ethan look healthier or in better shape, the weight loss seemed to have had the opposite effect. Ethan looked sickly. The skin on the back of his neck had several bright pink spots where he must have missed applying sunblock the day before. On his elbow was a poorly applied bandage, partially covering a raw-looking rash.

However, despite the apparent lack of concern over his appearance that morning, Ethan remained talkative as he climbed up the smallish mountain. Recounting his ideas again that the find may eventually bring a greater understanding of the ancient ways man traversed the globe and populated this part of the planet. Ethan did not seem to notice or care that neither Stander nor Liz was able to get much of a word in as he rambled on. All three marched in line ever higher along the path.

Arriving at the base of what was now a cave, Stander was happy to see the locally iconic Skull Rock was still settled in place and largely intact, just as before. Numerous "No trespassing" signs and various other warnings and memorandums had been added since he'd first shown Ethan Skull Rock earlier that summer. Stapled to hastily erected wooden sign holders, the official-looking documents and memos were either in clear plastic sheet protectors or laminated to help protect them from the weather. But, after months in the outdoors, most were now faded and waterlogged. Alongside the boulder, a man-sized opening looked like it had been hand dug into the side of the mountain. A temporary gate of grey metal bars had been placed over the doorway, and its frame was bolted directly into the rock on the outer wall of the cave.

The metal gate was unlocked and opened. The swing of the heavy door screeched like a seldom used ironing board in an old hotel. The sound reverberated across the mountain and down the hillside, startling a brown hawk in a pine tree high above them that audibly complained as it heaved itself skyward. Stander watched the large bird as it floated effortlessly across the bright morning sky, tilting its long outstretched wings and banking to the left and out of sight. Ethan pulled several hardhats, each with the U of M emblem painted on the back, out from inside the cave where they had been stored behind the locked entrance. All three placed the helmets on their heads, and Stander fiddled with the small light attached to the front of his.

"Shall we?" Ethan gestured, and Liz ducked through the opening first, followed closely by Stander and Ethan. Battery-operated lights, still in place from all the previous work at the site, sat five feet high off the ground on several yellow aluminum steel stands. Each was lit one by one, and the cave was soon illuminated nearly as brightly as the outdoors. Ethan remained talkative as he gave a brief tour of the small enclosure and explained to Stander exactly where the skeletal body had lain and where the few artifacts were discovered. Stander was also shown several digital pictures of the cavern's lone occupier over the last several centuries. Plus, other photos taken by the university's contingent when they first arrived onsite. Many of the images were close-ups of the large and beautifully crafted sword found alongside him. It had been meticulously cleaned and, though still badly corroded, you could just make out a few of the symbols and odd script the metal blade was adorned with.

As the three looked at the images, Ethan and Liz shared that at some point, whether still alive or already dead, the head of the man found in the cavern had been separated from the body by a sharp implement. Further testing would determine if that blow happened in the cave and whether it was what killed him or not. Liz also pointed out the man had sustained older and significant injuries to his shoulder and leg that had partially healed. She speculated, with the severity of those wounds, he may possibly have even been put out of his misery.

A mercy killing.

Stander wanted to be impressed, but the tiny cavern was hardly a cave of wonders, small compared to the few caves he had ever visited in the past as a tourist. The rocky interior appeared almost antiseptic in the artificial light, and, like the ledge directly outside, the ground seemed unnaturally even and free of debris, as if Mother Nature had known they were coming and tidied up.

Liz waved Stander over to a small crate not yet sealed but labeled and ready to ship. It was lying on the ground beside one of the interior walls of the cave, away from the entrance. "These are the two artifacts we found that I mentioned don't really fit with anything else."

Stander could see that nestled inside the container were two faded and shriveled animal skin bags. Both were incredibly aged and fragile to the touch. Cautiously and methodically, Liz partially emptied one out. Inside the first one was smallish stones and dried bits of what may have at one time been plants or flowers that were braided together. But, more interestingly, were the remains of what appeared to be bits of intricately carved bone. One piece clearly was meant to represent a wolf, and another one had been shaped into a bird-point or arrowhead. Some were individual pieces, and others were strung together by a material that Stander didn't recognize. The bones appeared brilliantly white in the artificial light. In the same bag were also several other small statues that might have been animals, human figures, or deities of some sort. Liz added, "There is more down deeper inside the pouch, but we won't investigate more thoroughly until we get this back to the lab. The local tribe normally would have already claimed and removed these. But because of the frailty of the pouch and contents, they are allowing us to have them analyzed back at the U of M first."

Gesturing to the entire first pouch, Stander asked, "What do you think that is?"

"A medicine bundle." It was Ethan, who had somehow crept up behind Stander unnoticed, speaking. The close proximity of his voice made Stander jump. "Of a sort anyway, I am sure of it. It's unusual to find one abandoned in this way. Every medicine bundle or bag is unique and contains items that tell the owner's tribe and story. I have seen others, but none of this age that are still so well preserved. The shaman who would have carried one this large must have been considered very powerful. "

Stander glanced back at Ethan as he spoke. The grad student clearly relished the finds Liz was showing. His grin appeared extra wide, obviously accentuated by shadows created in the artificial lighting he was bathed in. The halogen bulb's close proximity to his face dramatically bleached out his already pallid skin tone. Stander decided Ethan was too close to him, and he took a half step closer to Liz and away from Ethan.

"This other bag just had a single, I guess, kind of medium-sized, black rock in it." Liz was talking again and held up the second, slightly larger bag also made of decaying animal skin. It was empty, and Liz gingerly opened the top of the artifact and let Stander briefly peer inside. Liz placed the second bag back inside the shipping container before pulling out a softball-sized, shiny black stone.

"Again, we will have to get this analyzed when we get it shipped back to the lab at the university to be sure. But we think it may be obsidian." Seeing the confused look on Stander's face, Liz continued. "Obsidian is basically lava from a volcano after it cools down. It's black volcanic glass that sometimes forms when erupting lava from a volcano cools rapidly under the right conditions. In ancient times it was often used by local tribes to make tools out of."

"But there aren't any volcanos here in Michigan..." Stander moved closer to Liz to get a better look at the rock she held in her hand. "Where did it come from?" As he spoke, the odd black rock seemed to pulse with light once, a timid blueish flash at the center. Stander looked up at Liz, but she seemed not to notice. Perhaps it was just the artificial light reflecting off it or his imagination.

Stander kept quiet.

Liz shook her head noncommittally as she replied. "Hard to say. But certainly, volcanos were present all across this land in the far distant past. So if it was local and not brought here by trade, it would be almost immeasurably old. But none of us who have seen this so far are geologists, so I suppose it may turn out to just be, literally, a rock." She shrugged and, surprising Stander, suddenly held it out and placed it in his hands. "Feel how heavy this is? Whatever it is, it sure is dense and..."

But Stander lost track of her voice and himself as he cradled the smooth black stone in his hands. Abruptly lightheaded, he felt his feet give way under him. The sensation reminded him of a trip he'd once taken with friends to the top of the old Sears Tower in downtown Chicago. After they'd looked out over the city and Lake Michigan, they'd all piled back into the elevator. The swift descent had been startling, the floor falling fast under their feet. Stander had never felt such an odd sensation before or since. Until now... As he felt himself falling, a blinding bright flash robbed him of his sight at the same time. Closing and covering his eyes, he didn't raise his eyelids again until the sinking sensation ended.

As the extreme light faded and his sight returned, Stander found himself staring into the blank face of a young woman he didn't recognize. She was slack, and Stander was peering directly into the whites of her eyes as they rolled up in her head. Feeling his hands aching as they gripped tightly, he glanced down to see a pair of smaller hands at the ends of his suddenly skinny arms. The unknown hands, somehow he knew they were meant to be his, were wrapped tightly around the throat of the unknown woman. She'd collapsed, her weight still held by the hands as they throttled the last of the life out of her. Stander, or the body he suddenly found himself occupying, continued choking the young woman before callously dropping her dead body onto the dirt ground at his feet.

Stander's head swam. Where was he? How was he here? He instinctively knew he'd just murdered the woman at his feet. In the same way he knew her death was merely the beginning of far worse things to come. Mortified by what he witnessed, Stander tried to speak and cry out but found himself unable. He was paralyzed, the body he was in refusing to obey his commands. Stander merely a puppet, controlled as if by a mad marionette gleefully pulling the strings. As his mind raced to understand what was happening, he became aware of the churning darkness inside this body. An unquenchable hunger was rising up from within. The body he was in quivered with excitement as the black gloom slowly consumed his thoughts. Contaminated, Stander felt himself longing for what would come next. Though blasphemous, he knew it was... He tried to stop what he knew was coming. Frantic to end it. He wasn't sure if it was his desperate efforts, but the body he was traveling inside of stopped. But it was thinking horrible thoughts. Remembering...

Ghastly memories came then, not from Stander's life, but unspeakable acts committed in the past by this person Stander had somehow fused with. Stander shuddered at everything the eyes he was looking through had seen. Woman after woman slaughtered before him. There were terrified screams like daggers in his ears. He saw the same hands he now wore digging into flesh, pulling out wet things that splashed sloppily on the floor. Stander tried to stop the onslaught of these thoughts, but another memory slammed into his mind. It was an unknown young woman making inhuman gibbering and hissing sounds as soft parts were wrenched out of her. Stander couldn't handle the whirlwind of memories this body he found himself trapped inside of was recalling. His eyes burned with hot tears against the screaming insanity he was forced to witness.

There were so many terrible things…

Without his own mouth, he couldn't even cry out…

Without his own mind, he couldn't stop witnessing the horrid deeds…

Plunged into an impenetrable blackness swirling like liquid madness all around him…

He watched the hands fracture finger bones with glee. The sound of snapping twigs as the victim whimpered like a small trapped animal. Stander fought hard to pull himself out of whatever he'd somehow fallen into. Was it a vision? Was he hallucinating? How could one person do so many horrible things! Stander's mind reeled as he desperately tried to claw his consciousness out of this and back to his own body and life. But something seemed to be holding him tight. Like the undertow of the ocean, his struggles against this tide of misery seemed hopeless. He was forced to witness the atrocities one after another. The macabre scenes began to run together, separated by flashes of white light that began to come faster and faster like a slowly quickening strobe light. Soon the horrid thoughts became brief flashes themselves. Personal snapshots from the devil's own camera.

A ruined face. A headless torso. A severed and sightless head. Blonde hair turned pink as it was mired in gore. The blond hair was so much like Sherry's… Stander felt his agonized roar explode out of him. He would take this no more! He could not see Sherry fall under these hands! At the next flash of light, Stander instinctively leaped for it, howling as he clambered for the lit void. Imagining himself running to the light until he was blinded by it. Balling and refusing to accept the lunacy engulfing him. Now blind, he held his arms out in front of him as he fell once more.

"…really makes you wonder how it arrived here. But anyway," Liz continued, "we'll know more when we get all the results back." She pulled the polished black stone back out of Stander's hands, smiling. "Until then, it is all just guesses." Stander looked at her dumbly. He was back in the cave once more with Liz and Ethan. When he glanced at both, it was clear they'd not seen or experienced what he had. In fact, the conversation they'd been having was not even interrupted.

Though to Stander it had felt like an eternity trapped in a hell spawned by Satan himself. The vision, or out-of-body experience he'd had, took no time. The terrible things he'd experienced were already fading. Like a morbid nightmare that leaves you clutching for what you'd seen, the worst of it was slowly leaking from his thoughts. What had he seen? He could still feel the throat in those hands, the whites of the victim's eyes, the red crimson blood... And the blonde, the strawberry blonde hair tinged with red blood. The strawberry blonde. He'd seen a strawberry blonde and... And what else again? Stander shook his head.

What just happened? He could only remember the hair...

Stander stood rooted as Liz meticulously placed both bags back inside the small, deeply padded protective shipping crate before placing the top back on. Stander turned groggily and saw Ethan was already retreating back outside, presumably to escape the barely circulating stale cave air. Seeing a clear path to the exit and feeling confused and less comfortable in the small enclosure by the minute, Stander quickly followed. Once outside, he greedily sucked in the fresh mountain air. A few minutes later, Liz joined him, also pulling off her helmet, smiling in the late morning sun.

She pulled her phone out, "That's right, no signal up here. I keep forgetting," Liz pocketed the useless device. She said to both Stander and Ethan, "I was going to try and call one of my peers and see if there was any preliminary word back on the sword. I sent those digital images to a colleague in Europe to get his initial opinion, and I'm anxious to hear his take on the weapon and symbols it's adorned with." She turned and pointed back to the cave. "Since we didn't find anything else yesterday to add to our collection, Ethan and I will ship the sword and that last crate straight to the university before we leave town. They'll go there first for some basic analysis before being shipped directly to a lab specializing in ancient recovered works."

Liz paused, still smiling at Stander. Her green eyes open wide, almost as if she'd been startled, glittered in the bright sun of the near cloudless day. Stander felt suddenly mesmerized by them and by her. She broke his brief trance by announcing, "I am going to rinse my hands off in the stream. Be right back!" After a moment, Stander decided he should take this opportunity to speak with her privately now that the tour of the cavern was over. He left Ethan standing alone and walked after her.

Stander caught up with Liz as she hit the bank of the running water. "Good idea. Maybe I should wash some of that old cave dust off of me as well. I've seen Poltergeist, and, for all we know, there might be some old Indian burial ground curse or something. I don't want to bring that shit back home with me." Smiling, they both crouched down side by side and dipped their hands in the cool running creek. A large leaf twisted and twirled across the surface of the water close by, briefly catching on a protruding stick that poked out from the bank. It spun in a circle three times before it broke free and continued making its way farther down the mountain in a rush. As if the small waterside branch had made it late for an important engagement downstream.

Their backs to the cave and faces turned from Ethan, Stander reached for Liz's hand under the chilly water. She turned to look at him, and Stander decided he had better hurry up and find out if she would consider sticking around Marquette another night or so. Figuring it would be better to start in on her early and leave himself some extra time this afternoon to change her mind if needed. Stander was unsure if Ethan would remain by her side for the rest of this little field trip.

"I wanted to tell you," Stander started, "that I really enjoyed meeting you last night. I hope you don't think I was being too forward or anything." Stander suddenly became tongue-tied and was briefly at a loss for words. A sensation he rarely experienced anymore. He felt like he was back in junior high, trying to work up the nerve to ask the prettiest girl in class to dance with him. To buy time and collect his thoughts, Stander looked back at where Ethan was standing. But the cliff directly in front of the cave opening was abandoned, and Ethan was nowhere to be seen. Relieved that he wasn't about to be interrupted, Stander turned back to a smiling Liz.

"I just, well, I really thought… You know, that maybe I would really like to maybe…I mean you, maybe you and I could spend some more time together before you leave." Stander heard the words and was horrified at the nonsense sputtering out of his mouth. He looked down at the stream, and then, releasing Liz's hand, he pooled some of the rushing stream in both his hands and splashed the cold water on his face. Mortified, he hoped the water would bring him back to his senses. He turned back to her, "Jesus, what the fuck am I saying…." He rolled his eyes. "What I mean is, how about you stay the night with me?" Liz, who had still been smiling, started to laugh, and Stander's chest lurched. Then, realizing for the second time what an ass he'd sounded like, he burst out laughing as well. "Listen to me, my god!"

Embarrassed, Stander scrambled to his feet and then reached down to help Liz up as well. He shook his head at how ignorant he sounded, sure he just blew any chance he might have had with the pretty educator. Once they were both on their feet, Liz and Stander each started to say something at the same time. Both stopped and chuckled while Stander, feeling very embarrassed, started on an apology but didn't get the chance. Out of the corner of his eye, he saw Ethan retreating from the cave entrance for the second time that morning. Ethan, thankfully unaware of the awkward exchange between them, quickly strode over to where both stood together.

"I am really not feeling well, Dr. Drexler. Would it be possible for you to take the crate and maybe let Stander drive you back?" Ethan turned and looked at Stander hopefully.

Stander admitted he'd thought Ethan looked a little weary and disheveled during that morning's hike and tour of the site. But he was surprised to hear him beg off so early in the day. Not to mention boldly asking one of his college professor's peers to essentially finish the last of the work on Ethan's behalf. But, Stander was also smart enough not to look a gift horse in the mouth, either. He certainly didn't wish the man ill will, but inside, Stander was turning cartwheels over the timing of the sickness. Hopefully, on the drive back, he would get a do-over with Liz.

"Of course, no problem, Ethan." It was Liz who answered first. "Are you OK to make your way down from here and drive yourself back to town?"

Ethan nodded and then added, "Please don't tell Dr. Danforth I bailed on you today…" Liz shook her head no with an expression that conveyed Ethan had nothing to worry about. Turning to Stander, Ethan asked, "You don't mind?"

Trying to sound calm and convey concern he didn't really feel for the grad student, Stander said simply, "No problem. You go and take care of yourself. I just hope Liz can tolerate my singing, or she may end up sick by the time we get back to town." He was beginning to feel slightly recovered from their disastrous earlier conversation, more like himself again. Stander shrugged at Liz, who was looking questionably at him. "What? My car, my tunes." She just rolled her big, beautiful green eyes in a playful way that buoyed his hopes further. But he still remained bewildered by his fumbled first attempt.

Both Liz and Stander watched as Ethan made his way back down the trail. She turned to Stander, "Well, there is your answer," Liz was smiling up at the still sheepish feeling bar owner. "Since you now have to babysit and chauffer me around, I guess you are stuck. I'm not saying where I'll spend the night just yet. But that," she pointed after where Ethan had just disappeared down the trail, "just gave me an excuse to stick around. I mean, now I have to do all the work by myself!" Her voice inflected the last five words with an overly dramatic tinge. "How about if you, my smooth-talking, silver-tongued friend, go grab that crate from inside the cavern for me." Liz was snickering, and Stander felt hugely relieved. His hopes for the day soared, and he practically pranced over to the yawning opening of the cave.

Ducking inside, he bent down and reached for the unsealed crate. The top of the shipping container was off and leaning beside the open box. Stander looked inside, a fleeting and gnawing feeling that something was different or off. Hadn't Liz put the lid back on when they were inside the cave earlier? Stander, hunched over, stayed transfixed and studied the outside and inside of the box. Running things back and forth in his mind. Over and over again.

"Earth to Stander. Hello!" Startled, now with the sealed crate in his arms, Stander stood swiftly and focused on the woman... Liz, Liz was her name... calling to him. Feeling slightly confused but not exactly sure why he smiled broadly across the cave floor at her. "What took you so long? Are you practicing more of those oh-so-subtle and coy lines?" Stander laughed along with her playful teasing. She waved him over to the door. "Come on, you were in here so long. I already have everything else packed and finished up. Let me turn off those lights and lock this gate."

Within five minutes, they both headed back down the trail to where Stander's Jeep was parked. Stander carried the crate, and Liz commented several times about the gorgeous Michigan day and countryside as they walked. Once they arrived at the gravel lot, Stander loaded the box onto the floorboards of his backseat.

He drove Liz back to Marquette and her hotel, alternately talking and, as promised, singing loudly whenever his favorite songs came across the radio. Pulling into the parking lot, Stander was impressed the university had put her up in the nicest chain hotel in town. It was a far cry from the dumpy, locally owned motel room Ethan was staying in all summer. After turning the engine off, Stander transferred the crate into the back of Liz's black SUV. One backseat was already laid down inside, and a long slender shipping crate was nestled on top of it - obviously the container the sword was transferred inside of - but the rest of the backend was empty. The lack of luggage surprised him, and he commented on it as he slammed the back of the Buick Enclave shut.

"Oh, that," Liz responded, "I never checked out this morning." She stepped in close to Stander, putting her forefinger under his jaw, which had involuntarily dropped open at the revelation. She pushed up and shut Stander's mouth for him. "I was hoping we could uh.... Well, I really thought... You know, that maybe we could like maybe...I mean you, and maybe I and you could spend some more time together before I left." Liz mocked him softly, giggling as she mimicked the blabbering nonsense Stander had uttered earlier in the day beside the stream. Stander opened his mouth a second time to defend himself, but he never got a word out. She covered his mouth briefly with a small kiss. Stander, once again completely out of character, was speechless. Liz, with a devilish grin, filled the silence. "Maybe I can even stay the night with you?"

Liz then spun on her heel and started for the lobby door of the hotel. She was halfway there before Stander found the breath she had robbed him of. "Wait! What time do I pick you up?"

Without turning back around, she answered, "I'll meet you at your bar around 5:00. And I like my wine red and my steak well done." Stander stood next to her SUV in the afternoon sun with what he knew was a huge and stupid grin plastered across his face. He finally turned and made his way back to his Jeep only when a family of five pulled into the mostly empty parking lot. Three kids, all under ten, spilled out of the side of the minivan, screeching and sprinting ahead of two exhausted-looking parents. Stander pulled his car door shut and cranked the radio up before putting the Jeep Wrangler in gear. Joe Elliot of Def Leppard asked Stander if he wanted "To Get Rocked."

CHAPTER 22

PRESENT DAY

LIZ PULLED up to the curb and parked one block down from the bar Stander owned. The drive from her hotel to the small downtown area had taken less than ten minutes. But feeling nervous, she still pulled down the grey sun visor and mirror to check her hair and makeup. Debating with herself whether she had done the smoky eyeshadow and black eyeliner above and around her eyes too thickly. Or perhaps used coloring that was too dark. She noted her lips still shined but added another quick layer of the shimmering pink color anyway.

As she inspected herself in the mirror, Liz wondered if she wasn't too old for the look she was putting out tonight. The summer dress she wore was held up with thin spaghetti straps and barely made it to her knee even when she was standing. It was bright yellow and flowered; one she was talked into purchasing by her niece last year that, until tonight, she had never actually worn. She wasn't even sure why she'd impulsively tossed it into her suitcase at the last minute while packing for this business trip. It showed a lot of skin and was not a style that fit her personality or profession and was atypical of the kinds of outfits she picked out for herself.

Grasping the padded black leather steering wheel with both hands, she looked down at her lap. Panic leaped up her throat. What was she doing? During the last few years of her marriage and since the divorce, Liz rarely even bothered to put makeup on anymore. This was not how she normally dressed, looked, or even acted. After such a disappointing marriage, men barely registered with her anymore.

Liz knew she was attractive. She still got hit on by guys that were either ignorant of or not intimidated by the set, stony, and serious expression she usually wore. The guarded and disinterested vibe and responses she returned in those instances usually made their advances mercifully short. Even her girlfriends at work or in the condo where she had lived since moving to Ann Arbor gave up trying to match her with their unattached male friends. She stayed busy at work, went home each night, cooked and ate solitarily, read books, and then went to sleep. Alone. Usually, spending a weekend day every other week or two with her youngest son. At nearly forty, she had no time or desire for the company of men. Besides, she had her trusty and reliable vibrator. So why was she here?

Liz thought again of her impulsive kiss and what she'd said to Stander earlier in the day. She blushed as she recalled how she'd acted. It had been so completely out of character for her... Liz had always been very even-keeled and kept a measured pace in her life. The closest thing to being wild in the past was when she got her one, and still only, tattoo. But that had been back when she was just a kid of barely 18 during her high school senior class trip to France. And she had been so drunk on local wine that she didn't even remember getting it done! Luckily, it had turned out to be a beautifully drawn, celestial sun between her two shoulder blades that she never regretted. Of course, compared to Stander's full sleeves of inked color, that hardly would qualify as out-of-control behavior to him. She idly wondered if she was going to start menopause soon. Was it her raging hormones going crazy on her? Shaking her head, she placed the key back in the ignition and restarted the motor. What had she been thinking coming over here?

Earlier in the day, Stander had taken Frazier down the street to a neighbor's house. The nearby acquaintance was a regular customer and owned a couple of dogs Frazier was friendly with. Both Stander and his neighbor helped each other out with dog sitting from time to time. A mutually beneficial arrangement of the most innocent kind. Although, Stander suspected if Frazier still had his balls, he'd likely be banging that crazy female dog of his neighbor's named Aerie like a screen door caught in a tornado. Every time they got together, they wrestled aggressively, chewed dog toys together, and took turns doing the old bump and grind on the same couch pillow. It was frantic, adorable, and slightly disturbing at the same time. He hoped Liz wouldn't be disappointed since she had obviously taken to Frazier.

Stander sat on the concrete steps that led up to the front door of his tavern at exactly 4:40 PM. As a rule, he never brought an actual date into his place of business. Maybe he was old-fashioned, but hanging out where you work - no matter how much you liked the place or even owned it - was not his idea of a date. Stander intended to keep Liz all for himself tonight. That was why Frazier was having a doggie sleepover and why he was looking to head her off at the pass. He didn't want to be interrupted by friends or customers who thought they were his friends all night. Plus, Stander knew on a Friday night, there was apt to be a female patron or two showing up that he had a not-so-innocent mutually beneficial arrangement with.

When he first spied Liz walking down the street towards him, Stander literally did a double take. At first glance, half a block away with his fifty-plus-year-old eyes, he didn't think it was her. Her colorful and cute little sundress and tiny white sandals called attention to a body he hadn't dreamt was under the stiff khaki clothes he had so far seen her wear. Watching her approach, Stander felt underdressed in his scuffed boots, faded jeans, and button-down

Jimmy Buffet Hawaiian-style shirt. As Liz drew closer, Stander also realized part of what had thrown him was the makeup she now wore. To him, those efforts accentuated her natural beauty and only added to her allure. By the time Stander got to his feet to greet her, more than just his legs were standing up straight.

After an awkward greeting that included a simultaneous hand-shake, brief hug, and small kiss, Stander led Liz around the side of the building. He took her up to his loft apartment, gave her a small tour, made sure she knew where the bathroom was and apologized for Frazier being indisposed for the evening. Grabbing the bottle of merlot he'd left breathing earlier and two wine glasses, he handed them over to Liz for safekeeping. Stander then opened his stainless-steel fridge and pulled out the seasoned steaks he had already prepared that afternoon. With both their hands full, they made their way back down the stairs to the outdoor patio below.

Stander grilled the steaks until Liz agreed the cuts of meat were cooked to her liking. He then retrieved the twice-baked potatoes and salad he had made earlier in the day for them. They ate together outside in the warm breeze and, under a slowly setting sun, they started to get to know each other a bit better.

Liz was already aware of how Ethan came to know Stander and how the grad student helped recover his sister's remains earlier that summer. Stander talked briefly about both his sister's and mother's untimely deaths when he was just a boy. Sharing that he was born and then raised in Illinois by his widowed father, a doctor who never remarried after his mom died. He talked about the summer home his father had owned on Lake Superior in Marquette and how Stander grew to love the times he spent there as a child. So much so that he ended up moving here as an adult after his own wife had died. Perhaps because of, or perhaps in spite of, his sister's disappearance from the area.

Liz listened more than she talked, finding herself extremely at ease in Stander's presence. She shared her oldest son had been born when she was just barely nineteen to a guy from her hometown who never really matured. Later turning into enough of a drug addict that he'd overdosed and left her a young widow at barely 21. How her family had stepped in to help so she could enroll and focus on college. That she discovered her love of history there and found her niche in that, as well as the man she later married. Her second marriage lasted twelve years before ending in divorce three years ago. Her youngest son, as she'd mentioned before to Stander, was still living with his father.

As they shared their history, even the trauma life threw them, the conversation stayed comfortable and easy on the near cloudless summer evening. When the dinner was over, both she and Stander thought the second bottle of wine would make the best dessert. Back upstairs in the apartment, the next bottle was opened, and they settled in together on the living room couch to share it. Liz downed half of her first glass in one swallow, kicked off her sandals, and tucked her pink toenail-painted feet under her while they talked.

During a lull in the conversation, Liz changed the topic back to their field trip from earlier in the day. "So I have to ask you something," she started. "When I got back to the hotel, I discovered that spectacular black rock that was found in the cavern was missing. You don't know anything about that, do you, Mr. Stander?" Liz asked the question in a very direct manner, and her change in tone caught Stander by surprise. With a mouthful of wine, Stander shook his head back and forth "no" in reply. Thinking to himself that, as he did so, Liz seemed to cast her eyes about the apartment as if looking for possible hiding places. He felt briefly offended before she turned to face him once more with a slightly knowing grin on her face. Stander said out loud what he suspected they both were actually thinking.

"Why the fuck would Ethan have taken one of his 'finds?'" Stander made quotation marks with his hands in the air when he said the word "find." "Wouldn't it be pretty obvious later when it comes up missing?"

"Yes, I was wondering the same thing. I also thought it was odd how he suddenly said he was sick and bailed on us today." Liz had already given this topic some thought earlier in the day. "I don't get it because pretty much everyone agreed the rock is probably just obsidian. No real monetary value unless Ethan finds something out about it that no one else knows. But I guess by leaving when he did today, he just created his own "plausible deniability" when it comes up missing. Now he can say maybe one of us "stole" it." Liz mocked Stander's air quotes by over-exaggerating her own when she uttered *plausible deniability* and *stole*.

"Did you just make fun of my air quotes?"

"Yes, don't do that. It's lame…" Liz, relaxed and giddy from the wine, was feeling playful. "I bet you play "air guitar" when no one is looking too!" Again she made her own wildly exaggerated air quotes around *air guitar* and then burst out laughing.

Stander tossed a couch pillow at her head. "I will have you know I do not play air guitar. But I do play air drums!" Stander play-acted pounding on drums while making a pouting face. "You should see me when 'In the Air Tonight' comes on from Phil Collins."

Liz was still laughing. "I bet…. I bet you… I bet you had a big mullet at one time. Like… Billy Ray Cyrus-sized mullet." She covered her mouth, giggling uncontrollably now.

Stander stood and pulled his thick grey hair back away from the sides of his head, exaggerating the length down the back. Mimicking the music video for the song, he started line dancing in front of the couch, singing over and over again, "Don't break my heart, my achy breaky heart…"

Liz soon slid down off the couch and sat on her knees in front of Stander and his gyrating hips. Her head was eye level with his crotch, and she looked up at him, no longer laughing but still smiling with two of the most beautiful green eyes Stander thought he had ever seen in his life. He decided he could spend all night looking into them. Unexpectedly, Liz reached under the bottom of his untucked shirt and popped open the top button of his jeans. She cooed, "Or it might 'blow' up this man?" Again, she used air quotes snickering, then tugged at his fly once more until it was wide open.

Stander reached down to her hair and softly stopped her, "Wait. I mean, don't stop but let me go grab some protection." He jerked a thumb back towards his bed in the corner of the apartment.

"Right now, I just want you inside my mouth. And I really prefer that it not be inside a condom." Stander, eyes wide, took his hand away from the side of Liz's head and helped her tug his jeans down farther.

His breath quickened while he unbuttoned his shirt, feeling Liz's hot mouth on him and watching the rise and fall of the blonde hair on the top of her head. Liz pulled the straps down from her dress, and Stander reached down, running his fingers through her hair and massaging her full breasts, alternately rolling each hardened nipple between his fingers. Moments later, when he helped her to her feet, Liz wiggled completely free of the dress.

Stander tasted himself on her lips as his fingers traced the curvature of her breasts. He let one hand drop slowly past her stomach before pulling her panties to one side and reaching between her thighs. Liz moaned as he stroked the wet folds, her tongue demanding in his mouth as they kissed. Falling backward softly onto the couch, Liz pulled Stander after her and greedily helped guide him into her. Wincing and grunting loudly when Stander entered her for the first time. They took turns with each other, their bodies finding a comfortable rhythm as they rode one another. The initial patience and tenderness gradually became more heated and desperate as the loud slaps of their bodies echoed through Stander's living room.

After, Stander collapsed on top of the equally sweaty and panting college professor. In the frenzy just ended, one side of the couch had moved several feet across the hardwood floor. The piece of furniture sat diagonally away from the still perfectly square area rug it normally bordered. The new empty space between the carpet and the sofa was filled with scattered clothes and two pairs of shoes.

Stander's face was buried in Liz's hair, and he inhaled deeply while he tried to catch the runaway train that had just hauled all his breath away. Stander's chest thumped, and he felt the muscle in one of his calves quivering slightly. After a few minutes, he rolled his bare chest off the top of Liz's slick back, stopping briefly to admire the brightly colored tattoo of the sun up near her neck before settling over to the side. The air around him suddenly felt like it was coming from the open door of a refrigerator, cool and refreshing. He sat back on the couch they'd just abused and felt a line of beaded sweat crawl out of his hair and trickle down the side of his face.

After another minute, Liz sat up as well. She smiled at Stander and kissed him once before regaining her feet. She swayed slightly and tilted to the left before righting herself and walking wobbly-legged to the bathroom. When she came back out a few minutes later, Stander had not moved an inch, still waiting for the full return of all the senses he'd lost while inside of her. Liz dabbed at the streaked black eyeliner on her face with a tissue. Then ran both hands through her damp hair as she announced, "I know, I'm a mess. Look what you did to me, hot stuff…" She gestured at her head while standing nude in front of Stander.

"What I did to you?" Stander feigned incredulity but was relieved he could actually still speak. "I doubt I can even walk." He pointed down to his still-twitching leg muscle.

"Oh, I think you'll walk again, you big baby. I'm the one who is going to be walking funny for the next couple of days." Liz was smiling and laughing as she collapsed on the couch next to him. Stander opened his arm, and she squeezed under it. Her breast covered his, and their bare thighs pressed tightly together.

Liz reached over and ran her hand along the back of Stander's arm. Stopping when her fingers encountered a raised patch of skin along his shoulder, she leaned over and pulled his thick arm towards her. "I thought I felt something on your arm earlier. Is this a scar underneath all these tattoos?" Liz peered closer as her fingers traced the circular mark. "How did you get this?"

"That?" Stander turned his shoulder towards Liz so she could get a better look. "That's just a birthmark I've had my whole life. Like Lady Gaga says, baby, I was born that way…" Smiling, he took one of her fingers and traced the circular raised patch of inked skin with it. "One of the first tats I ever got was this wolf's head covering my birthmark. Growing up, I hardly ever wore tank tops or took my shirt off unless I had to. You know how kids are, and I was really embarrassed by it. Took a fair amount of teasing about it when I was a little guy."

"Birthmark? Well, didn't your dad or mom have the same thing? It would be normal for one of them to pass that on to you. When you were little, didn't they explain that to you?" Liz moved her head slightly to get a better look. "That sure looks like a pattern. Like a perfect circle with odd little marks in the middle of it…"

"Nah, neither of my parents had one. My Great Aunt Madeleine did, though. She showed it to me once. Told me it meant we were special. But I think that was just to make me feel better about it." Stander laughed as they both settled back in the couch cushions. "My dad practically refused to even acknowledge it was there. It's hard to see now with the ink covering it, but those little raised bumps you felt in the middle of it actually look like little off-kilter swastikas. I think the likeness embarrassed him." Stander shrugged.

"Well, he shouldn't have been. The swastika was only appropriated by the Nazis. The symbol itself goes way back through the ages. I recently read they even discovered a swastika symbol carved onto a figurine they think is over 15,000 years old. And get this, the bird-like figurine it was carved on was made from ivory that came from a wooly mammoth tusk! Incredible, huh?" Stander nodded and whistled appreciatively. "And there have been versions of that symbol found in ancient cultures all around the world. Hinduism, Buddhism, in ancient Asiatic culture, and even on Greek currency. All the way up through my area of expertise: Medieval and the Renaissance. If I remember right, I think it was supposed to stand for peace and well-being before the Germans corrupted it."

"Hmmm… Interesting. I don't know about all that. I guess unless you and I get married and start having kids, this weird ass birthmark ends with me." Stander chuckled, but as he did so, Liz's face darkened slightly. "Oh! Sorry, just a bad joke. I didn't mean to imply we should go get married and start popping out kids. Although I got to say, after the amazing time we just had together, it's hard to imagine how any guy would ever let you get away from them." Stander was still smiling, hoping he hadn't just said the wrong thing.

After a moment, Liz smiled back and replied. "You know, I was married for a very long time. But however cliché or comical it may sound, I really was stuck in a repressed marriage all that time. So you should know this experience and time with you is not my normal." She paused. "I just realized we didn't even use a condom. I… I usually am extremely reserved and very practical about these kinds of things." She was shaking her slightly as she added, "Frankly, this doesn't even seem like me here with you right now."

Stander looked down at the gorgeous woman under his arm. She was stunning and didn't even know it. Her eyes drew him in close, and he bent down and kissed her deeply on the lips. He whispered in her ear, "What happens in Marquette, stays in Marquette." Stander winked and gave her a sly smile. "There is nothing you need to worry about with me as far as saying anything to anyone or judging you in any way if that is what you are worried about. There is nothing to justify here…"

She interrupted him, "But what we… I mean, what I did… How I acted and what I was saying. That just isn't me. Or who I have been. Or who I think I am?" Liz was struggling to explain something she didn't understand herself.

It was Stander's turn to shake his head as he added, "There is nothing wrong with being a woman desiring to be touched. How long has it been since you have had sex?"

After a long pause, Liz answered, "Four years give or take…"

"Four years! No fucking way!" But Stander's face showed he was just pretending to be shocked. "If that is true, I think you have some long overdue fucking coming your way. How about we grab some more drinks and head over to the bed? My turn to taste you this time." Liz blushed at his blunt language and straightforward manner, but the thought of spending the night as they just had also stirred something deep down inside her. The feeling in the pit of her stomach reminded her of when, as a little girl, she would swing as high as she could on the playground swings and look up at the bar above her head as she passed below it. Being pressed in close to Stander, hearing his voice in her ear and the expectation of being with him again, that excited rush moved down between her thighs. Liz squeezed her legs together tightly.

Stander stood and, after using the bathroom himself, grabbed two bottles of water and also opened their third bottle of wine that evening. He retreated to the bed and beckoned Liz to him. She got up slowly from the couch and savored each step she took towards the large bed. Pushing aside her usual modesty and concerns over her body's imperfections, Liz liked seeing Stander's blue eyes raking her naked body up and down as she lithely made her way over. She stared back at him and his body, enjoying the growing effect she obviously was having. Liz straddled him, and they spent the evening locked together, consuming each other's energy until both finally fell wearily into a deep sleep.

———

Dreams and nightmares, or at least the remembrance of them, were a rarity for Stander. They never woke him as they did many others and what little images he ever recalled upon waking were fleeting at best. Stander always believed this was because he'd already lived his worst fears. The disappearance of Sherry and the awful understanding that came with it at that young of an age. Knowing that something was terribly wrong for her to be absent from his life, and baring that very adult acceptance all alone. What could a nightmare offer Russell Stander that could eclipse the perpetually long shadow that stretched from his childhood?

But he dreamt now.

In the dream, Stander is walking for what feels like a century. It was a hike in a disturbing wilderness under a moon, so bright Stander dared not look directly into it. Yet despite this, the path he strode in the dream never broke out of a dreary, dull, all-encompassing thick grey that surrounded him on all sides. Impenetrable thickets lined the trail, and Stander could see nothing beyond a few feet or so on either side of him. The trees around him were bare and appeared prehistoric in size and age, dropping their dead things in this forest. Stander was forever stepping over rotted branches, both big and small. Maintaining his footing was next to impossible, but somehow he never once fell.

Stander could hear the movement of leaves. The sound was like the tearing of old, yellowed papers. Yet the ancient timbered wood and branches surrounding him were utterly bare. The ground filled only with discarded twigs and thick sticks he continuously stumbled across the top of. A riot of lifeless tree limbs that Stander saw slowly gave way to piles of rounded bones. They snapped underfoot, dry and dusty, completely devoid of flesh, and heaped in a pile as if by a small child with no regard for order. Stander felt fearful about continuing the journey he was somehow engaged in. Yet stopping, or worse yet, looking over his shoulder at what may be at his heel, was unimaginable. He seemed unable to stop advancing. A terrific pressure filled his innards. Like a spring wound tight inside, each step released the tiniest bit of tension. Momentarily allowing him to sniff progress before despair at his next step. He felt like a windup toy soldier set to go with no will of its own.

Stander withdrew the step he almost placed; the first conscious action he had taken. The rustling sound of the forest's unseen ghost leaves heightened, creating panic, but Stander stood still. "Go," he thought, in quotation marks, quotation marks in the air... The spectral buzzing of invisible leaves abated, and Stander raised his eyes, not looking down as he had with each previous step. It was Liz standing barely a yard from him. Her eyes were almost translucent. Stander, stupefied, realized the green in her eyes was the only color he had yet encountered in this timbered world of endless, dry wooded death.

The eyes shimmered and floated inside her head. Stander reached for them. Slowly and almost tenderly as a mother longs for her child. Liz became his mother then. Still impossibly reaching on, Stander sobbed when he understood how close she was. His fingers just brushed the hair that fell gently forward from her.

As he touched the first strand, Stander stopped himself. Something was wrong. His mother had blue eyes like he did... Like Sherry did too... The eyes melted, and the green spread all around her like ink dumped in water. The two holes left hollow, void of anything, and the skin around them ripened as if rotten. His mother's entire face then blackened, spoiled, and corrupted. A rot that comes from the inside like bruised fruit.

Sherry, Stander realized. It was not his mother, but Sherry. He lurched for the last remnants of his sister's face as it decayed and faded. He put his hand through the apparition and was left with nothing in his grasp. The entire episode was an intangible vision leaving only hot tears welling within his own eyes. He raised both hands to his burning eyes to rub away the pain and tears but stopped mid-reach. His sight riveted at the scene ten feet ahead.

Liz lay across the ground on her back, held in the arms of another man. Only her feet and the backs of her legs touched the dirt-covered ground of the cave. Stander understood that he was now outside the mouth of the cavity once hidden near the top of Mt. Arvon. He was on the outside of it and looking in at the scene developing within the earthen walls of the cavern.

This other man cradled Liz's upper body and head, the pose not unlike a mother about to breastfeed her baby. Stander could see Liz and though she never looked up at him, he was relieved to see her magnificent green eyes were open and intact. Stander tried calling her, but his voice made no sound. Or his sound made no difference. Like the flailing of an innocent toddler dropped in water of oceanic depth. Wasted energy with no impact on the destiny about to unfold.

Stander stopped shouting and instead focused his attention on the man possessing Liz. His face was turned, and no matter which way Stander twisted his neck, he was unable to see him clearly. But something about the man was profoundly disturbing. His body was undefinable and cloaked in a long, colorless robe. The man's head was the only part of his body visible; the flesh stretched tight across the skull beneath it. The skin was translucent like the surface of a featherless, cold, and barely thawed chicken you might buy at a supermarket for a holiday meal. A few long black strands of hair stood out and contrasted wildly with the otherwise bald head. Stander tried screaming at the man again, asking over and over what had happened to Liz. The man, unlike Liz, addressed Stander without turning.

"What happened to her? I happened to her." Movement caught Stander's attention for the first time. The man's hand appeared from under his robe and moved methodically to Liz's face. The object in his hand touched her mouth. She parted her lips like a lover about to be kissed. Or a believer about to receive communion. The round, paper-thin, dark brown patch disappeared down her throat silently. Seemingly swallowed whole. The man reached under his robe again and repeated the act, feeding Liz again and again. Over and over. Stander strained to see where each mouthful was coming from.

The veil lifted.

Stander saw the man pulling at his own elbow on the opposite side of his body. Slender fingers with impossibly long fingernails slid under a poorly applied, dirty bandage barely sticking to the joint. Stander watched in horror as the soiled dressing fell away and revealed a badly infected rash that ran the length of the man's arm. The worst of it was seeping at the bend of the elbow. Dirty yellow fingernails scratched furtively at the wound until a piece of wet scab came loose. The man moved the dripping layer of flesh higher and higher to Liz's opened and wanting mouth, ecstasy and hunger etched upon her features. The long bony fingers stopped an inch from her mouth. Transfixed, Stander watched Liz's tongue extend out from her lips. The man turned finally and faced Stander as she licked at the piece of scabby skin before he dropped it into her mouth.

It was Ethan that held Liz as she chewed, and his ensuing laughter encompassed the whole of Stander's nightmare.

Stander woke early with a thundering heart in the filtered light of a cloudy morning. Confused at even the occurrence of a dream or nightmare-filled night, the sickening and horrific images toyed with his start to the day. In a panic, still slightly drunk, mightily hungover, and confused, he called for Frazier. The pattering sound of rain outside was the only response to his plea. As the events of the early evening and night with Liz echoed in his head, he called for her as well. Disturbed by the already evaporating dream and images. But, like Frazier, Liz was also no longer with him.

Stumbling to his feet, Stander searched for any sign of her. The bathroom was unoccupied, and the kitchen table was empty as well. Her clothes were nowhere to be seen, so he wandered to his second-floor window to see if her SUV was still parked on the street where she had left it. But all he found was an empty parking space where the black auto had sat the night before. He scoured his apartment for a note she may have written before she left but found nothing. Scrolling through his phone, he finds no texts, missed calls, or messages from her either.

Groggy and moving slowly, Stander brew a pot of strong coffee. The action helped to put some space between himself and the bizarre dream he experienced. He starts to punch in Liz's number to call her and stops. Instead, he decides to send her a simple text but then struggles with what would be an appropriate message. Finally, resolving to wait until a little later in the morning to catch up with her. Stander waits on his steaming cup of Joe to cool and focuses on the pleasure-filled part of the night before he fell asleep and entered his fucked up dream.

Smiling, he blows a raspberry, "Repressed, my ass...."

CHAPTER 23

10TH CENTURY

TIME PASSED SLOWLY for Gunnar as he attempted to nurse himself back to health. Each day he struggled to simply remain alive as he dealt with the devastating wounds the rogue bear had inflicted on him. He understood clearly the peril he was in from the near-fatal encounter. He was badly injured, vulnerable, and in an unfamiliar land. Though he knew there were others close by, locals that may or may not have been part of Nimki's tribe, Gunnar did his best to stay hidden from them and alone.

He did not really fear whomever these neighbors might be. In fact, in the dark, agonizing time immediately after the bear left him mangled, he sometimes wept for them. A desperate longing inside for some measure of relief from his torment and the simple kindness of his fellow man. During these pain-filled early days, he often found himself thinking of his own village. He thought bitterly of how Vidar wrecked that place by bringing the damned object Gunnar was now burdened with. He feared he was doing the same to the innocent people living among these mountains, and he yearned to finish his quest and reach Nimki's village before a similar fate befell them. But travel, at this moment, was completely out of the question. His injuries were severe enough that he was no longer able to continue any semblance of the journey that drove him to this place. He felt powerless. Trapped and caged within the tall, slim trees surrounding the cave.

Gunnar rarely ventured far from the cavern now serving as his new home. Each day marked only by the constant struggle to eat, heal, and survive. Despite the freshwater that flowed nearby, there was very little forest game to be found. The absence of creatures he would expect to find in the surrounding wilderness worried Gunnar greatly. He couldn't help but recall what Vidar described in his tale. How animals, and even nature itself, seemed to scatter when the monstrous thing had drawn close to his people. He feared the creature was closing fast, certain it still tracked him.

Now sedentary, Gunnar was forced to sustain himself almost exclusively on the small fish, tadpoles, and various water creatures found in the nearby stream. Fortunately, there were also several trees and bushes close by bearing fruit at this time of year. Yet despite this blessed bounty, Gunnar at times had to resort to eating the worms and bugs burrowed within the soft soil near the water's edge. Squishing their soft bodies between his weakened fingers as they tried to squirm from his feeble grasp. Gagging as he swallowed them, sometimes whole and still alive, feeling the desperate scurrying of their legs and pinching mouths as he consumed them.

When night fell, Gunnar remained plagued by fitful dreams and nightmares, often waking to his own screams bellowing inside the echo chamber that was his shelter. Haunted by the specter of what was coming to invade his body, possess his mind, and use him as its dark tool. Though at first, Gunnar had still prayed to Ymir, asking for his blessings and protection, as time crept on, he found himself cursing his fate more than praying. Frustrated by the useless and ruined left side of his body. The outer wounds had finally begun to heal for the most part. Leaving behind jagged red lines that he would trace with the tips of his fingers back and forth, repeatedly. But it was the internal damage, Gunnar began to realize, that was not going away.

One arm was left crooked, and it now hung at an unnatural

angle from his mangled shoulder. Useless and unmoving beyond a bit of flexibility that remained in his wrist and fingers. Gunnar could still hold and grip things slightly with his left hand, but that was the extent of its remaining usefulness. Similarly, the leg he first thought escaped real damage proved to be more of a liability than expected. It bore his weight well enough, and most of the pain had slowly subsided, but something deep inside the joint was stopping him from being able to flex that leg at the knee anymore. Crouching was nearly impossible for him. Even the simple act of rising from a laying position on the ground was a slow undertaking. With his hunched-over shoulder, dangling arm, and abnormally straightened leg, Gunnar was now a shuffling cripple.

Even the most basic of tasks were compromised and a chore. He gave up trying to cut the locks on his head with Tor's sword or shave his facial hair anymore. Bathing was forgotten, and mending his torn clothing, and worn belongings soon fell by the wayside as well. What little energy and movement remained were used almost exclusively in capturing and collecting food in a daily race for survival. Gunnar avoided looking at himself in the cool running waters of the stream when they pooled or slowed. He no longer recognized the gaunt and hairy thing he had become. Once proud, intimidating, bright-eyed, and filled with purpose, Gunnar had been reduced to a shambling thing closer to an animal than man.

Isolated and alone on the mountain.

Some evenings, as the sun dropped low and darkness descended, Gunnar could pick up a steady and rhythmic beating of drums in the distance. When first heard, the sound terrified him, and Gunnar hid. The pulse was low and monotonous. He would feel it in his chest and bones as much as he actually heard it. Seeming to start without warning and coming from all around him. Eyes wide, he would watch closely for any movement and strain to hear if the strange sound was coming closer. But as more evenings came and went without any intrusion or danger, the sound gradually became a comfort for him. At least reminding him that he was not alone in this foreign place. Eventually, Gunnar found himself looking forward to the strange music being made, disappointed on the nights it was absent.

As more time passed, Gunnar slowly became aware the local people living near the bottom of the mountain were much closer than he'd originally thought. Perhaps even feeding off and sharing the very same clear mountain spring waters that he used. Whether it was the thoughts of this communal stream, the early evening sounds, or the occasional sights and smell of their fires, Gunnar was unsure. But soon, a gnawing feeling began to reshape his thoughts about the locals so close to him. He found himself inexplicably being drawn to them more and more. It started first as a curiosity, an imagining of these people living life below him. Gunnar wondered what they looked like, their ways and beliefs, and how they lived. Within a few short days, these random thoughts grew into an obsession, the musings building on top of one another. Pressure grew like flowing water against a dam struggling to contain it.

Gunnar soon began to wonder if he might possibly learn from these strangers. Convincing himself of the value in actually seeing them and how they lived. That it could help him survive the upcoming winter months. Gunnar found himself, almost subconsciously, scouting around for any sign of trails leading down the side of the mountain. He began to daydream of routes that would lead him unseen directly to their dwellings below. Pondering how far away the tribes at the base of the mountain actually were from him. Calculating how to best work his way up and down the side of this gently sloping mountain in his current state. Gunnar's earlier anger and fear at anyone ever finding him and his secret cargo were now somehow dismissed.

Early one evening, Gunnar found he could no longer avoid the constant barrage of thoughts about his neighbors. In the settling dusk, he daringly moved the farthest away from the cave since first ascending the side of the mountain months before. He crept forward and downward, following what appeared to be a recent trail, long weeds - still green even - pressed hard to the ground. After several missed turns and dead ends, he was able to identify what were obvious manmade footprints. The thrill at this discovery filled him with a joy he could not ever remember feeling so strongly before.

Gunnar was elated.

Risking everything, he gradually picked his way down the mountain and slinked along barely visible trails. When he was sure of the direction and that it indeed led down towards where he often saw smoke rise, Gunnar doubled back up the mountain. His body, racked by pain and the exertion from the small hike, was completely spent. As the last of the daylight left the sky, he finally pushed himself back into the clearing at the base of the mouth of the cave. After gulping mouthfuls of water directly from the stream, he collapsed just inside the entrance of the cavern. He smiled to himself despite the waves of discomfort and weariness spreading across his body. Even with the soreness and aches that settled in his joints, Gunnar was amazed at how good he felt. He was proud of his accomplishment that evening and felt invigorated with a new sense of purpose.

As he drifted towards sleep, he replayed his path into the woods and down the mountain. Memorizing the landmarks seen and dreaming of his next attempt, a wide, toothy smile splayed across his filth-caked face. Imagining the settlements and the tall poles each dwelling was wrapped around, puffs of grey smoke escaping out the top of each. He saw deeply tanned people with brightly painted faces as they danced in odd movements around roaring fires. As with all dreams, Gunnar did not question the images or certainty of what he saw. He simply knew how the people below him on the mountain lived and looked. Each vision soon became broken into separate scenes defined by the outline of the sloping trail, and its twists and turns that went up and down, back and forth. Often he would wake briefly, unclear of the length of his sleep, day, or time. Still feeling tired and weak, he would pinch his eyes tightly shut again, revisiting the path and gliding once more up and down the side of the mountain.

Over and over and over again...

CHAPTER 24
PRESENT DAY

SECRIST CALLED Stander's cell number, and after five rings, it went to the automated message. He killed the call without leaving a voicemail since he knew Stander, even if he was awake, rarely bothered to check his phone anyway. He decided to drive over to Stander's place, figuring he would rouse him this Saturday morning so they could grab some breakfast together. Something they did at least a few times each and every month anyway.

During the short drive, Secrist opened the driver's side window and tried to clear his head while the mild summer morning air washed over him. He knew he was anxious to speak with Stander and share some of what he and Craig had pieced together regarding Ethan's odd past. Craig had already communicated what he and Secrist had uncovered about Ethan to colleagues in Ann Arbor investigating the disappearances down there. But, at this point, that was about as much as he could officially do unless something more concrete turned up. They both knew all they really had were unsubstantiated suspicions. It was no crime to have lived in any of the places where Ethan once resided. Even if he had moved each time with the intent of living in cities where some of America's most prolific killers once called home. And without finding the actual remains he and Craig suspected were dug up and missing, they really couldn't even prove a crime had been committed, much less that Ethan was a suspect in that crime. So things were at a standstill. But, since Secrist knew Stander had spent time with Ethan after he'd shown both of them where he'd found Sherry Stander's remains, maybe Stander had seen something that was unusual. Or at least offer his take on the guy. Secrist figured it was worth a shot.

Arriving, Secrist slowly climbed the stairs to Stander's apartment. His surgically repaired foot ached by the time he reached the top step and knocked on the front door. Stander opened it wearing a pair of jeans but otherwise looked like he had just come out of the shower. His thick grey hair was still wet, and he had the bath towel in hand that he'd been drying the longish locks with. He stepped away from the front door and beckoned his longtime friend inside.

"Didn't think I'd see your ugly mug this morning. Aren't you supposed to be retired and sleeping in all the time? It's the fucking weekend, man." Secrist waved his hand as if swatting away a troublesome fly, knowing there was no need to reply. "Help yourself to some coffee. Let me go grab a shirt, and I'll be right back." Stander strode back to his bathroom while Secrist shut the front door. He opened the cupboard above the coffee maker and pulled out a mug that said, "Don't keep calm, listen to metal" and filled it from Stander's half-empty coffee carafe. He sat down heavily on a kitchen chair and propped his sore foot up on the wooden chair next to him.

Stander returned wearing an Iggy Pop shirt and carrying a pair of soiled hiking boots. He sat down next to Secrist's elevated foot, saying, "I saw I missed your call while I was in the shower. Sorry about that..." He bent down and began to lace his footwear up.

"I am stunned you even turned that thing on this early," Secrist replied. "You expecting an important message or something?"

"Not exactly. But I did have someone over last night. When I woke, I was surprised that she was gone already. I keep thinking I'll hear from her." Stander trailed off.

"Jesus, since when have you ever been disappointed to wake up alone?" Secrist loved ribbing his friend about his revolving love life. "I seem to remember a few Saturday or Sunday mornings where you messaged me to come over so you could have an excuse to get away from what you woke up beside." Secrist lifted the coffee cup and took a sip. Then added, "Looks like the worm has turned, huh? Just not as good as you once were…"

"Oh fuck off. At least I get to make choices," Stander paused, "bad or otherwise. You're just jealous."

"Yeah, that's me. Living vicariously through all your sexual conquests and exploits." Both Stander and Secrist enjoyed giving each other a little bit of shit. Generally, the opportunities were endless the way they both lived opposite lives. "So who was this seductive mistress that has you all downtrodden this fine summer morning? Anyone I know?

"Nah, it was a college professor that came down to help Ethan." Stander then added, "Did you know what he found up in the mountains?"

Secrist pulled his foot down and leaned forward, keenly interested. "I just found out, actually. Have you seen Ethan lately? How did you meet the U of M chick? Did he introduce you?"

Stander was surprised by the turn of demeanor from his friend. "Ethan came in the bar the other night and brought along…"

Secrist cut him off. "What night?"

"Thursday night," Stander continued. "He told me what he found. Wanted to thank me for showing him where Skull Rock was on the mountain."

Secrist interrupted once again. "So you were the one that originally took him up there? He'd never seen it until then?"

"Yeah, I had told him about it a few months back when I'd invited him to the bar. It was the night after you and I met him out where Sherry was found." Secrist was nodding, agreeing he remembered. "I went out with him a few days later, and he showed me what he was doing and what he was working on up in the mountains. Since the rock was close, I took him up near the top of

Mt. Arvon and showed it to him." Stander stopped to see if Secrist had any other questions. When he didn't, Stander continued. "Right away, Ethan felt certain something was up there. I guess he got someone to verify what he thought and then convinced the university to come down and check it all out. The other night Ethan brought one of the experts in with him to the bar, and she and I kind of hit it off. Last night, well, she hung around all night." Stander stopped to take a drink of coffee.

Secrist asked, "So the last time you saw Ethan was when? Thursday?"

"No, it was yesterday morning. I met him and the college professor - her name is Liz - up at the site. I wanted to see what he found. Most everything was already packed up and gone, but I did see the inside of the cave itself."

"So yesterday then… Did he meet you at the site?" Stander nodded. "How did Ethan seem?"

Stander gave it some thought before replying, "I guess he was a little ragged looking. Like maybe he had slept in his clothes or something. He only stayed with us for a few hours, then begged off. Said he was sick and headed back to his motel early." Stander could see the wheels in his friend's mind working. He didn't know why he was so interested, but he went ahead and continued.

"One more thing that was a little strange I guess. Liz, the college professor I mentioned, said Ethan must have taken this black rock they found in the cave. It had been there that morning, but after Ethan left, she discovered later that it was missing. She said the rock was worthless, but apparently, he took it anyway for some reason." Stander shrugged, got up from the table, and walked over to the kitchen sink to rinse out his mug. Finishing, he turned back around and faced his friend, still seated at the small table. "So why all the interest in Ethan?"

Secrist knew he could trust Stander. He also knew he would only be speculating with a friend anyway and that bouncing his ideas off someone besides just Craig might prove beneficial. Get a different perspective from a guy who had spent more time with

Ethan than he had. So Secrist recounted what he and Craig discussed that week. The empty hole, potential missing remains, and the white stake flags were recovered near the site where another of Tathum's missing victims was found. He also relayed what their poking into Ethan's past history revealed and the two missing coeds from the University of Michigan.

When he was finished, Secrist leaned back in his chair and drained the last of the coffee from his cup. Stander sat stoically at the other end of the white kitchen table, thinking. He didn't doubt any of what he just heard; there were few men he knew as honest as Secrist. Stander also followed the logic he'd laid out regarding his own personal suspicions. But it was hard to square the awkward, pudgy, slightly nerdy student with the picture Secrist was painting. The guy was, without a doubt, a little goofy and may have taken an artifact he shouldn't have, according to Liz. But Stander had a hard time believing that he personally wouldn't have picked up on something strange about the guy if he really was a serial-killer-groupie of sorts. Or worse yet, as Secrist was insinuating, potentially a murderer himself.

Stander visualized Ethan again as he'd appeared in his nightmare and shook his head disgustedly at the image. Perhaps subconsciously, he had picked up on something not right with the guy. He also felt some anxiety building inside concerning Liz. Stander thought again of their intense night together and her big beautiful green eyes. What if Ethan had contacted her early this morning, feigning an emergency of sorts? Or realized she would report him for taking the stone? Liz lived alone and wouldn't be expected to return to work until Monday. What if he had her now and…

Stander stopped himself, annoyed at how fast and solidly this far-reaching conspiracy theory took root in his thoughts. He needed to get a grip. Stander stood up, pulled out his phone, and dialed the number Liz had put in it last night. There was still no answer. So Stander left an overly relaxed and, what he hoped was a reasonable sounding message, asking her to contact him so they could meet today before she headed back home. He ended the call feeling no better than when he placed it. Returning the phone back to his ear, he then tried the number Ethan had given him when they agreed to meet near his worksite a few months back. Again, no answer. Stander left a similar message just casually saying he was looking for the professor and, if Ethan knew where she was, to please call him back. Ending the second call, he stuck his phone back in his pocket with little faith it would ring any time soon.

Stander turned back to Secrist. "I am going to drive over to Liz's hotel and just be sure everything is fine with her. After that, I'll go over to Ethan's motel because I am so concerned about him being sick. See? A perfectly reasonable reaction to yesterday's happenings in the life of Russell Stander. And there would be zero reasons for you to even know I was doing any of that. But!" Stander pointed at the retired detective, "If I ran into trouble doing these normal, everyday tasks, calling you, my dear old friend, would also make perfect sense to anyone who knows us. Of course, if you just happened to be close by in your car, you might even pick up and reach me faster than if I had called, say, 911." Stander gave Secrist an exaggerated wink.

"And, other than this cup of coffee, nothing passed between us. Understood." Secrist climbed to his feet and pulled a small slip of paper out of his pocket. "Here, this is Ethan's room number at the Starlight. Just promise me you won't do anything stupid. Anything weird, you call me pronto."

"Of course," Stander said, smiling. "Have you ever known me to do anything impulsive?"

Secrist snorted, "Just every other weekend…" Then made his way back outside and down the stairs, Stander following close behind. Both men walked to their cars and soon were on their way to Liz's hotel.

After parking, Stander walked into the hotel entrance to find out what room Liz was staying in. The short visit to the hotel lobby ended minutes later when Stander walked back to Secrist's car instead of his own. He stood next to the driver's side door and talked into the open window.

"They wouldn't give me her room number, but they dialed her room for me. There was no answer, and I don't see her SUV parked anywhere either." Stander felt an uneasy mix of rejection and a deepening concern for Liz in equal parts.

As he made his way back to his own car, questions dominated his thoughts. Why would she have left his apartment so early and not left him a note or called? Was last night something she already regretted? If so, Stander knew his behavior this morning bordered on stalking. Calling her cell phone, driving to her hotel, and having the hotel staff try her room for him. As he got back into his Jeep, Stander looked around sheepishly in case Liz suddenly pulled up. On the one hand, he was dying to look deep into those emerald eyes once again and know she was safe. But would he feel relieved or embarrassed at being caught hunting her down already before lunchtime? Stander knew he was not acting the way he normally did.

Maybe he was the crazy one here…

Stander and Secrist drove their cars to the edge of town where Ethan's motel was, but Ethan's truck was nowhere to be found on the pothole-riddled black pavement that served as the motel's parking lot. Secrist pulled his car into a neighboring Dollar General store on the opposite side of the street in case Ethan unexpectedly showed up. He shut off his car engine, flipped his sun visor down, and slipped down lower in his seat. Across the street, Stander jumped out of his Jeep underneath the motel sign. He walked over first to a newer model, shiny black SUV that looked out of place among the other older, dented, and rusted autos of the other motel's customers and employees.

Stander peered inside the passenger and rear windows of the SUV, cupping his hands around his eyes to shield them from the glare. It only took a few glances to verify it was the same one Liz had been driving. Stander briefly contemplated the significance of the large vehicle being parked at Ethan's motel before walking over to the outside door of the room where Ethan had been staying all summer. He knocked on the ugly brown door and waited. After a second knock, he put his ear to the painted wood and moved in very close to the motel room door, carefully inspecting it. The old motel room door and its frame were soft and pliable with the rot of age and constant use. When Stander got no answer to his third knock, he discretely leaned his bulk and weight into the locked entryway. With a little push, it popped open easily, the old, soft wood bending rather than breaking under the force. The door handle itself was locked, but the inside chain had not been pulled across. As Stander turned to quickly shut the door behind him, he saw why. The screws holding the chain and its hasp had splintered the door jam, and it now hung down untethered and useless on the side of the door.

"So much for not doing anything rash or impulsive," muttered Secrist from across the street.

Stander brushed off the paint chips and brown smudge left on his t-shirt from the door. Turning back around, Stander was pleased to see there was no reason for him to worry about attracting attention to himself by turning on the overhead light. The frayed and olive green curtains, though drawn together, still allowed plenty of sunlight inside the tiny motel room. The bed had been made, and the small metal trash can next to it was empty, so it appeared the motel's maid had already made the rounds earlier that morning as well.

Stander, relaxing slightly, now took in the whole of the room. The walls were painted ivory or, perhaps, were actually once white. It was hard to tell. The small no-smoking sign on the bedside table was mocked by the stale cigarette smell that hung heavy and permeated the entire room. A single picture hung perfectly straight above the covered bed, the image of a cactus alone in a flat desert plain. On the opposite wall was a lone mirror that sat crooked, bending the streaming light from the windows and reflecting it directly onto the screen of the TV in front of the bed.

In the back corner of the small motel room across from the bathroom, a stainless-steel rack was mounted to the wall for guests to hang their clothes. Hanging from it was a shirt Stander had seen

Ethan wear in the past, as well as a few other items of clothing that were obviously his. Below that was a pair of shoes, and an empty U of M duffle bag sat nearby on the floor. A quick tour of the minuscule bathroom revealed only a few unused white towels, basic toiletry items, and a rust-stained tub/shower combo. Within three minutes, Stander had seen everything there was to see in the depressing roadside motel room. There was no Ethan, no Liz, and no pile of bones freshly pulled from the Michigan countryside either. It was the room of someone trying to live as cheaply as possible while finishing his schooling.

Stander was both relieved and disappointed.

Before attempting a clandestine exit back out of the motel room, Stander once more pondered the significance of Liz's SUV parked outside. Clearly, she had driven over here this morning. Perhaps to complete some work or help Ethan with something? Or had she felt the need to confront Ethan over the missing black rock from the cave? Again, Stander thought of Liz's intense Kelly green, emerald-like eyes, and an ugliness came over him. A blaze of jealousy suddenly burned from the inside out, and its intensity surprised him. Was there something between the two of them? After all, she stayed here in Marquette after her peers had returned home. Had she come to Ethan after being with Stander? Perhaps even now sharing what transpired between them?

Stander stared at the perfectly made bed fuming inside. Absurdly he yanked down all the covers as if he might somehow gleam answers from the sheets, pillows, and blankets. In his haste, the thin mattress shifted on the hollow box springs where it rested, exposing a corner of it near the top of the bed. There, hidden and crammed between the old mattress and the sad box spring, was a skinny black book with the single word "Journal" embossed across the cover. A red cloth strap, tight across the front cover, held a yellow pen with the University of Michigan logo printed in blue on it. Stander reached down for the journal he'd sprung from its hiding place. Grabbing the book, he immediately thumbed it open with complete disregard for its personal nature and its owner's out-of-sight placement.

Each of the random pages at the beginning was crammed with scribbled writing. Stander saw the lined pages in the back half of the book were untouched and blank while the first fifty pages or so had been filled from top to bottom by the owner. The handwriting across every page was the same and done by someone with very poor penmanship. It was not easy to decipher the lines written, but with a little patience and a growing familiarity, the scrawl slowly became legible.

Flipping past multiple pages, Stander skimmed over the contents. Keywords jumped out that gave him pause, but it was the lurid, hand-drawn pictures on every fourth or fifth page that caught his eye. Frowning, Stander realized he needed to show Secrist what he held in his hand. He snapped the book shut and tucked it behind his back, halfway down the back of his jeans, then made sure his untucked shirt completely covered it.

Stander knew every minute he stayed inside Ethan's room increased the risk of being caught. He carefully repositioned the mattress and hastily remade the bed so that it resembled, as best he recalled, how it appeared before his arrival. Taking the black-bound journal with him, Stander unlocked the front door of the room, cracked it open, and peered outside. Liz's black SUV remained where it had been, as did his own Jeep. No patrons or motel employees were visible on the walkways around the motel or in the motel's parking lot.

Taking a deep breath, he relocked the door handle as it had been and then moved swiftly outside, silently closing and latching the locked door behind him. Stander then casually made his way back to where he had parked, started the engine, and made his way out of the motel parking lot. Checking his rearview mirror, he decided his little incognito adventure had gone unnoticed.

As he turned onto the highway heading back into town, Stander waved Secrist after him, and both vehicles headed back into Marquette. Stander drove back to his place so both men could peruse the journal away from prying eyes. As Stander drove, his worries of being seen at the Starlight Motel or someone noticing his quick in-and-out of the room evaporated. Realizing an older man's quick foray in and out of a dumpy motel near the edge of town was likely not an unusual or a unique event there.

CHAPTER 25
10TH CENTURY

THE WARM DAYS and humid nights began to cool in tandem with the steady passage of time. The first visible signs of seasonal change were reflected in the nearby trees, their dead leaves and pine needles falling to the ground in droves all around the cave. As if the object still nestled within Vidar's bag inside that dark cavern was causing the trees to give up early on the year. But things such as these were of little concern anymore to Gunnar. Time was blurring now, and the transformation of one season to the next no longer held any significance for him.

Even the simple separation of night and day was no longer clear to Gunnar. Often finding himself at the entrance of the cave, unable to decide how he had even gotten there or why. The bright sunlight hurting his eyes, Gunnar would move listlessly back into the open mouth of the cavern. Safely shrouded once more within shadows where he could remain undisturbed, taking little notice of new gashes and sometimes still bleeding scratches arcing across his unclothed and filthy body. Pulling at wood twigs, he randomly found caught in his wiry, unkempt, and filthy hair.

Before slumbering once more.

At times he would feel more like himself, clear-headed and

awake. But even then, Gunnar found excuses to stay within the confines of the cave itself anyway. He began to relieve himself in the farthest corner of the cave instead of using the stream as before. Though it barely registered with him any longer, he knew the rancid stench within the cave should concern him.

More and more, he rarely wanted nor could find the strength to rouse himself off the ground of the cave. Even after sleeping, his body no longer felt rested, and he remained in constant agony from his earlier injuries. His damaged leg ached, and the wounds he thought had been healing were now oddly colored and badly misshapen in places across his body. Several times he made game attempts to stir himself to action, hunger hollowing out his stomach and begging to be filled. Only to find he barely made it to a sitting position before slumping once more to the ground in exhaustion, rolling painfully over on his side. Bone weary and weak, he could feel himself fading, often burning from the inside out. Other times unable to chase the chill coming from deep within his own body. His teeth chattered uncontrollably, and a sheen of sweat covered his pallid face.

Lurching in and out of consciousness.

Terrible nightmares still plagued him regularly, keeping any sleep he did achieve short and troubled. When he wakes, the half-remembered scenes left stamped in his mind from these dreams horrify Gunnar. Scores of nameless faces recoiled at his presence, running fearfully from him and speaking in tongues Gunnar didn't recognize. He tries to place the flickering images from his night-mares when he wakes but is unable. Some of these visions are of bodies ruined and torn, and of strange places and dwellings he couldn't remember ever visiting before. Regaining consciousness, he sometimes found his cave disturbed while he slept; his meager belongings moved from where he remembers last leaving them.

One time, he wakes to find a single long, brown, and white feather stuck in Vidar's old bag. When he struggles over to examine it, he finds he cannot touch it. Though beautiful and graceful look-ing, Gunnar is repulsed at its presence. He rolls back over so he doesn't have to look at it any longer and vomits violently. The bile burned in his raw and parched throat as it came up. When the heaving passes, he rolls the remains of a small sticky lump across his tongue and spits it into the puddle of his mess. He closes his eyes once more, audibly groaning at the taste still in his mouth and the sickness overpowering him. Trying to will himself towards unconsciousness in an attempt to banish the reality of the sights and smells of his sad existence. Unsure if what was happening to him when he was conscious was better or worse than what he experienced when he was unconscious.

The monster haunting him a permanent resident in his dreams.

Perhaps tunneling in his head like a rabbit burrows underground, but never truly leaving and never resting. Pursuing Gunnar down dark corridors in his mind, each with its own endless twists and turns. Paths barely seen and where he had never trod before. Unsure of how or where he could escape his dogged pursuer.

Gunnar blindly tries to rise once more from the floor of the cave, unsure if he is awake or asleep. He feels his legs moving under him so he decides he must have made it up from the ground. The next thing he is aware of is passing under a now familiar tree. He feels the soft swipe of a low-hanging branch as he makes his way past it. Looking down, he pauses and curls his toes around the soft brown pine needles bedding the forest floor. Wondering how such prickly and hard needles can feel so soft now that they lay dead on the ground. Usually, when things die, that is a bad thing. Isn't it? Gunnar is baffled by both the question and the death of the pine needles covering the ground all around him. Pondering this, he silently continues shambling along a path now worn by his own constant travels up and down the side of the mountain.

Unseeing and barely aware of his own movements, he arrives once more at the edge of a small clearing familiar to him. Ahead he notes the tall, cone-shaped tent dwellings made of stretched animal hides over their skeletons of wooden poles. Gunnar feels both an excited anticipation and a deep shame at his arrival. With considerable effort, he manages to turn away, intending to make his way back the way he had come. Soon he is indeed back along the trail and heading up the mountainside once more.

As he limps forward, Gunnar becomes slowly aware of an uncontrollable trembling and shaking in his hands and arms. Struggling to understand, he looks down at his hands as he hears cries that begin to wake him to full attention. The squirming thing in his grasp moves and shakes, twisting and turning as it shudders in his hands.

An unclothed child bawls up at him.

Defenseless and soft with locks of shiny black hair crowning its head, silent gasps follow each of its terrified screams. The tiny face soaked wet and covered in tears. Each eye pinched tightly shut, and its mouth opened wide. Dimly, Gunnar registers the two lone small teeth barely poking from the pink gums at the bottom of its mouth.

Startled and scared at what he finds in his arms, Gunnar drops the baby in astonishment and confusion. It thumps heavily on the bed of leaves and pine needles that cover the forest floor at his feet. The cries of the infant were instantly silenced. But moments later, the full-throated howl of the child resumes once again. Impulsively, without thinking, Gunnar reaches back down to try and retrieve the wailing infant and comfort it. In the slivers of moonlight that fall between the trees, he sees the baby open its eyes for the first time. Full of tears, each eye is unfocused and wide in fear as it lies on the ground. Both eyes were coal black at their center and rimmed in brilliant white. Gunnar pauses halfway, hunched forward, hovering above the innocent baby.

All sound fades from Gunnar's ears. No longer hearing the cries, no longer feeling any pain, no longer startled at the vulnerable thing just found in his arms. The exposed and open eyes of the screaming infant tugged at something deep within Gunnar. Bringing it up and out of him in a rush. As he creeps lower, his shadow blots out the filtered light of the moon that exposed the child. The baby is pulled from the pile of leaves almost tenderly. Its shrill screams continue reverberating but Gunnar hears nothing.

Enclosing the child's tiny head tightly in his two sticky and grimy hands.

Gunnar is tender no longer.

Pressure builds inside the child's skull as a new fountain of strength flows from deep within Gunnar. He grunts from behind teeth now pulled back menacingly. The emaciated gum line high-lighting peculiarly long and filthy teeth. The echoing cries in the woods crescendo in a high-pitched squeal. Then ceases abruptly and completely.

The absence of sound is deafening.

The small lifeless body slides out of slippery hands covered in fresh blood. The gore shone in the light of the moon that once again peeks between tall, skinny pine trees, exposing the ruined and life-less baby.

Gunnar staggers backward, casting the crumbled child aside on the trail. Empty, hollow orbits where its bright eyes had been just moments before.

CHAPTER 26
10TH CENTURY

THE WARRIORS, long practiced in silent tracking, advance methodically up the mountainside. Each is armed and ready to attack or defend themselves at a moment's notice. Dressed and ready for war, they slip swiftly among the trees of the forest on foot toward their quarry. Only slowing to allow the ancient medicine man to keep pace with them, his long white hair trailing behind him as he follows. The weathered face frowning in deep meditation as he repeats a chant in muted tones, barely whispered but very powerful among those entrusted with the sacred knowledge of their people. Reciting the same words and verses over and over. Reverent in the belief this alone can protect them from the evil spirit that haunts this mountain.

The group of men was badly shaken when they'd found the missing child. Saddened, they were too late and angered the abomination had stolen yet another soul from their close-knit tribe. The once unimaginable desecration left on the infant's face the tell-tale sign of the demon menacing their people. The band of muscled warriors communicated among themselves with small hand movements and facial gestures as they move. A skillful art practiced and mastered by their forefathers and passed down, but among these men, never had it been used against such a formidable enemy. The evil thing they chase has haunted the surrounding area for the entire summer season. Like a dark infection, they believe it is responsible for many unexplained deaths, disappearances, and sickness among their tribe. They carefully choose their footing along the trail they follow. Each somber in the quest, they move quietly higher and higher, up a mountain now feared and believed possessed. This evil spirit, they knew, lived high and deep within the side of the mountain. Its very presence made the place, once serene, now cursed and spoiled. One they had all come to fear greatly. Each step forward takes them higher up the mountainside.

Closer to the monster and its home.

The men stop as one. What they hunt seen just ahead, lumbering slowly up the trail. Instantly the medicine man hushes, lips still moving but silent. His brow furrowed in concentration; he reached into his pouch for the sacred artifacts his father handed down to him before he passed. Just as his father and his father's father had before him. Grasping the objects in his hand, they grant him both comfort and faith. The warriors silently fan out to surround their prey, weapons drawn and in hand. Ready to strike in an instant, they push beyond their fear. Channeling their collective anger, they focus on what they have been told must be done. Behind them, the medicine man uses his magic to sway the spirit before them. Freezing it in one place and distracting it with his powerful talismans. His chants begin to rise once more in his throat. Verbalizing the verses out loud once more.

Unsure why, Gunnar pauses along the trail, knowing he's nearly reached the shelter of the cave. He is surprised to find himself bathed in the light of the full moon above him, uncertain how he came to be there. He listens intently to the sounds of the forest. He hears nothing, and the air around him feels thick. Gunnar begins to shuffle forward again, suddenly fearful, but soon stops abruptly once more. His eyes lose focus, and his head begins a slow and tortured spin. An urgent and longing need in his loins suddenly consumes him. These two feelings combined, not unlike in a happier and distant past when he drank too much wine. He is unsteady, confused, and desperately needs to relieve himself.

He reaches down and is surprised to feel his manhood has grown long and hard. It aches, and Gunnar groans as he works it up and down in his still wet and slippery hand. Looking down at his engorged member, he is shocked by his nakedness. His body is so covered in grit, grime, and gore that it is dark and caked on like a second layer of skin. In places, the carnage is so old it is peeling and cracking yet splashed bright red.

Wet with bits of torn flesh.

He staggers back against the rough bark of a nearby tree as he tries to steady himself. Settled for the moment, he relaxes, dimly aware that he has just lost control of his bladder. The relief this brings him borders on pleasure. Gunnar can feel his face cracking wide with joy, and he tries to remember the last time he ever felt this wonderful. He feels no pain and a comforting warmth spreads across his chest and upper thighs. Still uncomprehending and groggy, Gunnar is reminded of how he felt as a bed-wetting child. Relieved, warm, but ashamed of what just happened.

Embarrassed now, Gunnar slowly opens his eyes and looks down at his torso. It is soaked in fresh blood. Warm and dripping down him, the blood appears black in the shards of moonlight that penetrate the trees around him. Glancing around in confusion, Gunnar sees the dark-skinned warrior that has ended his life. He tries to speak, but only gurgling sounds escape his ravaged throat. As blood continues to pour down his chest, he slowly folds back into himself before collapsing to the ground. His body lands among the bed of fallen pine needles.

It makes no sound.

He looks skyward and sees the tops of the tall swaying pine trees above him. They seem so tall and thick to Gunnar. He raises his arms out and reaches toward them. As he does this, he notices the red blood covering his hands. It slowly drips down his fingers to his wrist, and he begins to cry. Through a blur of tears, Sassa's sweet, beautiful face comes floating down to him. She is hovering above him, smiling and gesturing for him to rise and be with her. He sobs out loud in his shame and his loneliness. How had he forgotten how much he loved and missed Sassa? As he looks up at her with pleading eyes, her face slowly fractures, breaks apart and is finally blotted out completely. Replaced by an aged and weathered face haloed by cascading white hair. Strange and unintelligible sounds were coming from this face. Gunnar's sight slowly fades. But not before he notes the downward arc of the old man's weapon as it descends upon his head.

The warriors form a circle around the butchered beast lying before them. The sight and smell of the slain monster make this simple feat a task in itself. The three torches that had been carried by the group are now lit and held aloft. The bright fires illuminated the scene of their hunt and their kill. The medicine man reaches down to retrieve the severed head, continuing the chant he has repeated since leaving their village. He turns and faces the mountain and begins to walk.

Marching up it once more.

Still dripping from its bottom, he holds the head by its long, matted hair as he walks. The warriors, having been instructed before they headed out, each grabbed hold of the headless body. Hoisting it above them, they, in turn, follow the medicine man to the clearing near the top of the mountain. Moving as one, they carry the remains of the thing they had finally caught and slain. Each somber and repeating the chant the medicine man had them memorize before starting this quest.

As they reach the clearing on the side of the mountain, they all enter the black cave that serves as the home of the monster. Wincing and gagging at the smell inside, the warriors nevertheless almost reverently lay the still dripping body down in the middle of the cave. They begin to eye the long, strange weapon and the other unknown objects scattered about the cave floor. The medicine man gently places the detached head next to the body on the floor of the cave.

The white-haired wise man then turns his attention to the

animal skin bag propped against the far wall of the rock cavern. Squatting down, he quickly and disgustedly rips the feather from the bag, slipping it under his clothing for safekeeping. He then ponders the container before him for long moments. Never touching it or looking inside the pouch. The long pause broken, he seems to make a final decision. Still never touching the bag, he instead unties his own finely made buckskin medicine bag from around his waist. He places this directly on top of the sack containing the strange black stone that had traveled so far. He then stands and quickly turns away to face the astonished faces of the brave men watching him. He nods and gestures at the headless corpse.

"Wendigo. A skinwalker"

Working together through the night, the warriors loosen the rocks high above the mouth of the cave. One by one, the rocks and dirt tumble down and slowly fill the entrance. At last, the largest boulder resting across the roof of the cavern comes crashing down as well. As if made for the opening or perhaps obeying the will of the medicine man, it lands dead center in what had once been the cave's opening. The gaping hole was now completely sealed by the multi-ton rock and the mountain debris. Leaving no room for air, light, or anything of this world to enter.

Or anything from the cave to gain freedom.

The headless body, the strange metal weapon, and the black stone encased in the side of the mountain looked as if the hole had never been there at all. Wearily, the group of warriors heads back down the side of the mountain. Knowing the horror that had befallen their people was finally over.

CHAPTER 27
PRESENT DAY

"I HAVE TO BE HONEST, Stander. I'm just not seeing it." Secrist looked up from the journal Stander had swiped from Ethan's room earlier that morning. "Believe me, I want to, and I think Ethan is disturbed and needs to be seriously looked at, but this journal's ramblings are no different than someone who watches all those serial killer documentaries on TV and maybe takes them a little too seriously."

"Are you fucking kidding me? This is not some moron obsessed with Norwegian death metal bands or hiding behind a keyboard in his parents' basement. This is a grown man describing, in vivid detail no less, how to dispose of a body."

Stander grabbed the journal off the table where Secrist had been reading it. He flipped back a few pages before finding the passage he was referencing. "Right here! He writes, and I quote, 'The body's disposal was very hard. You hear about acid, but even that leaves teeth and gallstones. And the amount of acid required is not reasonable to obtain. Burning was a nightmare as well, and I never got enough heat to actually melt the bones down. The stimulants all failed.' Then he goes on to list all the ones he tried that he says failed. How can you not see that? He is telling you how he destroys a body!" Stander couldn't understand his friend's lack of urgency.

"Listen to me. I am not saying this isn't important," Secrist gestured at the book in Stander's hand. "But it in itself is not a smoking gun that I can use to call in the cavalry. It is compelling, and, coupled with everything else we know about Ethan, it only strengthens my stance that he may be dangerous and needs to be questioned. But, even if Craig could use this, and now he can't since you illegally broke into Ethan's room and stole it, no law enforcement official is going to say this alone should get him taken off the street."

"But this is what proves it. It ties everything he was doing in the mountains together. I am telling you, this guy has had it all planned out from the beginning. You saw what he wrote about the first time he ever came to Marquette. How he longed to 'walk in the sacred paths bloodied and sustained by James Tathum and see what he saw,' blah, blah, blah... How he had spent time last fall and again this spring up at the top of Mt. Arvon, hearing the cave call to him and talk with him as it did Tathum. All the while carving on the boulder so he could 'commune with his god,' as he put it. What was it he called it again? Oh yeah, 'tending it,' he said. Give me a fucking break! He is a complete psycho! According to this," Stander gestured again to the little black book in question on the table. "He spent almost every weekend leading up to this summer looking for 'Tathum's lost children.' Whatever the fuck that means." Stander felt his anger rising. He hated being played for a fool and was mad at himself for not seeing Ethan's deception. "That son of a bitch probably unearthed and touched Sherry and then lied to my face. Pretending not to know anything at all about Skull Rock and letting me lead him up there to discover it for himself."

"That is why Craig is zeroing in on him. We knew a couple days ago things weren't adding up. But lying to people and talking with rocks doesn't get you thrown in jail...."

Frustrated, Stander opened another page and thrust the image in the retired detective's face. "Would you look at this? Just look, man, what do you think that is?"

Secrist looked down for the second time at the crudely drawn image on the last page that had been filled in. It was clearly meant to depict a macabre scene playing out on the ground in front of Skull Rock. A man, most likely meant to be Ethan, had a naked woman bowed down and facing the dramatically grinning, skeletal-faced boulder. She had been decapitated, and the caricature of Ethan had her head held high above him, blood dripping directly from the base of the severed woman's head into his mouth. The face of the woman did not have eyes or even eye sockets drawn, but instead, two "Xs" where the eyes should be. For some reason, that disturbed Stander more than the other pieces of the lurid drawing.

Secrist looked up at his friend. "What do you want me to say?" He shook his head, "You can't slap the cuffs on someone for creating bloody art that portrays murder. If so, we would have executed Alice Cooper decades ago…"

"I fucking know that. But this is the last page of a book that you and I know was written and drawn by Ethan. Now he has gone missing, Liz has gone missing, and her SUV was at his motel, where it had no reason to be. He may be up on that mountain right now, bringing this drawing to life. We have to get up there and stop him."

"Now you sound nuts, Stander! Listen to yourself. You just saw Ethan yourself yesterday morning. And this Liz from the university? She was with you last night, so that hardly qualifies as missing. If anything, I am more worried about the coeds that disappeared from Ann Arbor, somehow being wrapped up in all this madness." Secrist sighed and looked down again at the open journal in front of him. Looking back up at Stander, he continued, "But even that is just guesswork. Craig spoke this week with the detectives doing the investigation in those cases. There is absolutely nothing that ties Ethan to either of the college girls, and nothing anyone has seen, even you after breaking into his motel room, hints at them being hauled seven hours away here to Marquette. Or up the Huron Mountains, for that matter."

Stander resigned himself to the fact that he was simply not going to convince Secrist. He stood up and pulled his car keys out of his pocket. "Well, if you are not going to do anything, I am."

"What? What are you going to do?"

"Drive up there. My neighbor is still dog-sitting Frazier for me right now, anyway. So I have time to see if I can find Ethan or Liz. Maybe check that boulder out a little closer that he is so obsessed with. You can sit here with your thumb up your ass if you want. Just lock the fucking door when you leave." Stander turned and headed over to his door.

"Whoa, whoa, whoa there, cowboy. I'll go with you. But let me drive, so you don't kill yourself driving like an idiot."

"I thought you said you didn't see it like I did," taunted Stander.

"I just said I didn't see the journal you swiped as being reason enough to raise the alarm. But there's no reason we can't drive up there and enjoy some scenery, right? If we happen to run into him, well, all the better." Secrist gained his feet and pushed himself away from Stander's kitchen table, "And besides, maybe I can keep you from jumping him and getting yourself arrested for assault this weekend." The two men exited the loft apartment and walked for the second time that day down the stairway before climbing into Secrist's car.

Less than two hours later, they pulled into the gravel lot near the base of Mt. Arvon and parked beside Ethan's pickup truck. On the drive up through the winding country roads, the two men had agreed if they did find Ethan, that Secrist would do the talking. He explained to Stander he didn't want to spook the grad student or give him a reason to leave town prematurely. Before exiting the car, Secrist pulled the small firearm he kept locked in his glove box. After verifying it was in order and loaded, both men climbed out of the vehicle. Neither man called out for Ethan. Instead, Secrist put his hand on the hood of his truck and found it still warm despite being parked under the shade of a large oak tree. Even more of a surprise was finding the truck's cab was unlocked with the keys dangling from the ignition. Secrist opened the driver's side door while Stander climbed up and into the back of the truck.

Stander pulled the blue plastic tarp away that covered half of the pickup bed. Underneath was the GPR unit, some digging tools, and a large five-gallon plastic pail. The bucket was black and splashed with old paint, dried mud, and the thin steel handle was unattached on one side. He moved the wire handle away from the top of the container and pulled back on the lid until it snapped off with an audible pop that reverberated inside the mostly empty truck bed. Inside the big pail, Stander could see several hand tools. Their multi-colored grips stuck upright near the top of the bucket and were all clustered over to one side. On the other side were several dirty rags bunched together that probably had been kitchen towels in their previous life.

Stander pawed at the filthy cloth.

Underneath, he found a grinning human skull staring up at him from the bottom of the bucket. The teeth on the top and the bottom were perfect, and Stander could see the lower jaw had been wired and screwed in place as God originally intended it to be. But just above the front teeth, starting where the nose would have been, the bone had been chipped away up to the two eye sockets. The damage to the middle of the face of the skull gave it an other-worldly or less-than-human appearance. With the middle hollowed out, there now was an upside-down triangular hole in the middle of the skull's face. It looked like what you might expect to see if you unearthed the bones of a mythical cyclops creature from deep inside a Greek cave.

Stander didn't touch the creepy fleshless head, leaving it exactly as he'd found it inside the plastic container. He carried the entire bucket down with him to show the curious find to Secrist, who was still rummaging around the truck's front compartment. Stander touched him on the back of his shoulder and held the pail aloft silently for his inspection. Secrist peered inside, frowning at the grim victim that smiled back at him. He looked back up at Stander and nodded. Then he stepped aside and gestured for Stander to view what he found inside the truck's cab.

On the grey plastic dashboard was one partial bloody handprint near the middle of the dusty dash. The thumb and pinky of the print clearly outlining and defining the ends of the handprint's shape. Blood was also visible on each side of the steering wheel as if whoever drove the truck last had a wound on both of their hands. The amount of blood on the wheel and the dashboard was minor, and there was none visible anywhere else on the seat or on the floorboards. Even the door handles on the inside and outside of the driver's side door were dry and unmarked. But the site of the half-dried and coagulated blood made Stander's heart beat loudly in his ears. His thoughts immediately turned to Liz. Alarms went off in his head as he pictured her empty SUV parked outside Ethan's motel room door.

"What the fuck?" breathed Stander, his statement encapsulating the gruesome find in the bucket as well as the spattering of blood inside the truck. Adding more loudly as he handed the bucket to Secrist, "We need to find out where Ethan and Liz are right now!" He then turned to make his way up the side of Mt. Arvon towards Skull Rock before Secrist grabbed his arm.

"Just wait a second, will you," the retired detective started, "let me put this bucket in the trunk of my car and grab the truck's keys out of the ignition. They are still hanging there, and I'd feel better if we took them with us and locked the truck up until we know what that blood residue is. For all we know, Ethan is watching us now and will drive off once we get halfway up there."

Stander was anxious to get moving but waited as Secrist slammed his trunk and carefully secured Ethan's truck. As both men started up the incline, Secrist added, "Don't get all crazy about the skull and blood when we see him. Who knows how long ago or where he got that skull. He also could have just cut himself out here working…" Stander turned just long enough to give Secrist a "give me a break look" before moving forward in long, purposeful strides. Not running but moving quickly up the dirt trail that led to the newly discovered cave. Secrist struggled to keep pace, hobbled by his recently repaired foot.

The two men crested the steepest of the incline and separated themselves from a cluster of trees. Their sight automatically going to the eerie outline of the boulder and cave in the distance ahead. Skull Rock remained just as menacing as when Stander last visited the site the day before. For Secrist, however, the large rock's transformation was startling. He'd only been up this way once or twice in the past and hadn't actually laid eyes on the outcropping of the oversized stone in fifteen years or so. The boulder looked nothing like he remembered. His eyes were drawn to what both men now understood was more a manmade sculpture than a trick of nature. What was once only oddly shaped, weathered, and resembling a man's face or skull, was now a cruel visage of evil. To Ethan - and perhaps decades ago to Tathum as well - it was the face of a cruel god demanding attention and service. A protector or jailer of the dead once entombed behind it. The face meant, perhaps, as a warning no different than the Jolly Roger flag of a pirate ship.

Secrist scanned the area around the rock and the new opening of the cave as he hiked upwards. It appeared deserted. There was not any movement visible, and he began to think they were wasting their time walking up to the summit. His eyes stayed trained on the rock and area immediately surrounding it as he walked higher on the trail. Secrist, no longer paying attention to where he was stepping, suddenly yelped once like a kicked dog and collapsed in a huff behind Stander. Instantly grimacing in pain and clutching at his foot, he sat up after he hit the ground and tried reaching down, confused at what had happened and thinking something heavy had been dropped on the top of his foot. His sudden movement resulted only in a new wave of burning hot pain that made him wince. It felt like someone had taken a sharp knife to the top of his foot and sliced downward. Stander was instantly kneeling beside him, asking what had happened.

"Mother of Mary! It's my goddamn foot!" Secrist tried moving his toes on the injured foot but was unable. Searing pain streaked all the way up the front of his leg when he tried to move it. "I felt something inside pop when I stumbled." He gritted his teeth together, "I am going to kill that doctor!" Secrist clutched at the weeds beside him, muttering under his breath and cursing his clumsiness.

"Can you stand or move at all if I help you?" Stander reached for his arm, but Secrist resisted.

"No, just let me rest here and catch my breath for a bit. Give me a minute, and let me think." Secrist looked around him as if a wheelchair, crutch, or magic carpet might suddenly appear. He tried again to flex his foot but stopped immediately. He looked at Stander and could tell his friend was concerned for him but clearly itching to check out the carved boulder.

Secrist looked up at where the entrance to the cave would be. Still no movement. He couldn't help but wonder if Ethan was down below them somewhere in the forest, sweeping dirt off of Indian artifacts with a brush and a big bandage on his hand…

"Look, Stander, it doesn't seem like anything is happening up there." Secrist pointed to the landing in front of Skull Rock. "I'll stay here and get myself a little bit more under control before we head back down. I think I could probably make it with your help. Why don't you go and make sure Ethan isn't up that way. I can watch you from here. Once you are satisfied, get back down here, and we'll head back to the car and go from there."

Stander agreed without hesitation. Now that he was here, there was no way he wasn't going all the way to the top. Secrist was hurt, but Stander knew he was a tough old bird. A bad foot was hardly life-threatening. Stander turned and started making his way back up the remaining stretch of ground between where Secrist was, and Skull Rock lay perched.

Like Secrist, Stander saw no movement as he hiked up the remaining hundred or so yards. He soon reached the flat area and was relieved to find it empty. He glanced briefly at the gate securing the opening of the cave, and it seemed unchanged from when he and Liz had left yesterday. He turned back around and looked out across the valley and land below him, hoping to see the movement that would indicate where Ethan was at. After a few minutes of futile searching, Stander was about to head back down to help Secrist when he noticed the footprints in the dirt around him. The last footprints should have been his and Liz's walking away from the gate, but the depressions in the soft dirt by the gate were going the opposite way. There were two sets: one larger and one smaller. Stander moved closer and saw that, although the gate appeared closed as he and Liz had left it, the padlock was unlocked. He crept near and peered through the steel bars of the opening.

Secrist watched Stander from below. His hike up the trail was uneventful as he suspected it would be. The cop saw Stander move back and forth in front of the creepy boulder and then look out across the horizon around him. The shadows from the surrounding trees and mountains played tricks on Secrist's old eyes in the bright sunlight. Skull Rock looked alive and animated, almost as if it was watching Stander. Secrist had the bizarre thought the boulder at any moment would open its mouth wide and, leaning forward from the cliff, gobble Stander up where he stood. But the carved stone remained solid and as unmoving as it was.

A rock.

Soon Stander was turning and on his way back down. At the last minute, Secrist could see that something caught his eye on the ground near him. He felt a brief panic as Stander turned back around and made his way back towards the side of Skull Rock. He moved methodically until only the back of his grey-haired head was visible. Fifteen seconds later, that was gone as well. Secrist groaned.

Stander appeared to have been swallowed by the mountain after all.

CHAPTER 28
PRESENT DAY

THE INSIDE of the cavern was dark. At first, with his face pressed to the metal bars of the gate and looking in from the bright afternoon sunlight, Stander had trouble seeing anything at all. Gradually, his eyes adjusted, and the outlines of the rocky walls and the dirt floor of the cave came into view. Although the battery-powered lights were not lit, enough sunlight streamed through the opening of the cavity to provide some illumination inside. There, tossed casually along the ground near the entrance, Stander recognizes the dress and sandals Liz had been wearing the night before. A sick and sinking feeling leaves him hollow inside when he spies her pink panties in the dirt two feet deeper inside the cave.

A flurry of movement from the back recesses of the cave, however, gives him no time to ponder the significance of the discarded clothing. Stander strains his eyes and is able to just make out the outline of a figure scrambling on its hands and knees along the farthest wall of the cave. The outline groped silently in the near darkness with palpable desperation along the narrowing back wall. Running its hands across the dirt floor urgently, pausing only briefly to toss small rocks and handfuls of dirt out of its way. Finally, its hands grasped whatever it had been searching for, and the figure stood holding its treasure in both hands. The shadowy figure stumbled back to the center of the cavern and laid its find reverently on the floor before backing several steps away from it. The retreat revealing the treasure from under its finder's shadow, exposing it to the few rays of the sun able to punch through the cave opening and steel gate.

The filtered sunlight flashes off the shiny object, drawing Stander's gaze. His eyes focus on the find; a glimmering, medium-sized black rock or gemstone. The black stone contrasted dramatically with the rough brown dirt, sand, and gravel lining the rest of the cave floor. The color appeared translucent in the light reflecting off it. A reflection so bright it hurt Stander's eyes to look directly upon it. This trick of the light made the stone appear to have a white-hot halo circling the edges of it. What little he could see of the black rock appeared highly polished. Almost as if it had been cleaned and buffed out. Polished like a diamond. A black diamond.

A dawning recognition hit Stander like the slow roll of thunder. It was the same stone Liz had briefly shown him and later reported was missing. The rock they both thought Ethan must have swiped before leaving the site early yesterday. Now the rock had somehow found its way back into the home or prison where it had been bound for so many centuries. Stander felt an odd thrill at seeing the stone once more. Somehow relieved, it had not been selfishly taken far away.

He knew he wanted to touch and hold it.

With no regard for the unidentified figure whose movement he had witnessed inside the cave moments before, Stander opened the gate wide and stepped towards the black rock. The metal gate screeched loudly, the sound echoing all around the inside of the cavern. The surprising explosion of sound briefly breaks Stander's focus on the stone he longed to retrieve. Momentarily, he felt as if he were standing inside a large ringing bell. The sound waves reverberated all around him, causing him to sway unsteadily on his feet, his equilibrium off balance. Briefly dizzy, the sensation passed, and Stander realized he had somehow made his way near the middle of the empty cavity inside Mt. Arvon. The black rock still lay untouched on the ground, now mere yards away from his grasp.

An equal distance away from him, somehow unnoticed by Stander until now, Ethan was kneeling on the ground of the cave. His outline in the gloom matching the figure Stander watched searching the cavern moments earlier. Ethan, on his knees, was leaning forward and looking facedown at the dirt in front of him as if searching for a lost contact lens. His back faced Stander, but despite the peculiar posture, Ethan was still easily recognized by his shiny, nearly bald head. Strands of dark hair streaked across the back of it like varicose veins splintering along the back of an old woman's leg. The wire glasses pressed tightly to his skull, a dead giveaway that the unmoving man before him was the grad student. Stander recalled urgently needing to talk with Ethan but now had trouble remembering why. Stander's mouth opened and shut several times as if pulled up and down by a mute ventriloquist with a hand up his ass.

Stander idly wondered if he had somehow suffered a stroke.

But the memory of speech and language gradually returned, and words began to slowly form in Stander's mouth once more. Yet, before he could utter a single syllable, the sound died in his throat when he recognized Liz was also in the cave. Her form was barely visible in the shadow-filled cavern. The sun's filtered light barely penetrated the back of the cavity where she stood.

Liz stood in front of Ethan. The black rock on the ground between them both. She was motionless and nude, with blood splattered on her chin and across her chest. On one nipple of her breast hung a single drop of gore, suspended in animation as if afraid to take the plunge to the dry ground below. Liz's eyes were open but unseeing. Both arms were outstretched at her sides in a bizarre parody of the Virgin Mary. The blonde hair that rested on her shoulders appeared pink and hung straight down, weighted and mixed with some of the same thick, red blood splashed across her front.

For the first time, Stander tasted the blood in the air...

Recognizing Liz standing deeper in the cave, the avalanche of earlier anxieties and apprehensions all returned to Stander. Her appearance seemed to break the stupor he was sleepwalking around in. Awakened fully once more, he abruptly realizes how peculiar the scene unfolding before him is. All the recent fear and concern for Liz washed back over him, and he remembered again that Secrist was outside of the cave and down the hill waiting for him. The entire reason for him being in that cave all flooded back at once. Stander quickly refocused on Ethan, noticing his hands were tinged red, stained with blood, and dripping with gore. Stander looked over at Liz, covered in blood, just barely out of reach of the kneeling man in front of her.

Stander stepped forward swiftly and, after briefly gathering himself and crouching slightly, hit the kneeling man as hard as he could. Aiming for the side of his face, he was rewarded for his focus with a satisfying crunch that Stander felt reverberate all the way up his shoulder. Neither Stander nor Ethan uttered a sound as the blow was delivered, but the audible pop of the bone-jarring punch echoed inside the cave. Stander stood over Ethan, bent side-wise at the waist like a baseball batter swinging for the fences. A snarl pulled at the corners of his mouth.

The side of Ethan's cheek split like a warm watermelon. The wound appeared like a second mouth on the side of his face, but one without lips. Ethan's body went down hard, dropping as if from a great height. Yet soundless, the earth of the cave absorbing the shock as he was laid out. Blood flowed and pulsed from the new gash, but nothing else on Ethan moved. Nor did he make a sound. Stander barely looked down at the crumpled form lying in the cave dirt at his feet before rushing over to Liz.

Liz appeared to be in shock. Stander reached for her, and she flinched once at his touch before her legs gave away. Stander caught and fell with her. Both ended up side by side on their knees like two faithful believers praying together on hallowed ground.

Stander frantically searched Liz's body for the wounds where the blood came from. His hands ran all over her sticky and slick body. But the large amount of blood on her in the poor light made it difficult for him to see or feel anything. Stander felt briefly hopeful when he realized the skin on her back was free of blood, and there were no puncture wounds or cuts on her backside either. But without any previous medical training, Stander soon panicked again and cursed his ignorance when he was unable to determine the cause of her blood loss.

Grabbing her wet chin with one hand, he peered directly into her unseeing eyes. "Liz. What happened? Where are you hurt at?" Nothing. No response or recognition glimmered within. "Liz! Did Ethan do this? Where is all this blood from?" Stander peppered her with question after question. But whether from shock or loss of blood, she remained mute and unresponsive to his pleas for information.

Out of nowhere, stars exploded across Stander's eyes as his head was knocked violently sideways, his concentration broken. The cave floor and ceiling swam, and a loud ringing was all he could hear. He no longer understood where he was, and dizziness swept over him in wave after nauseating wave.

Stander tried to regain his feet but found his legs uncooperative. Still kneeling, he swept his eyes across his surroundings, searching for the cause of his pain and current confused state. Groggily, he lifted his right hand to his head and felt the warm trickle of his own blood pooling inside his ear. As he pulled his hand away, he tried to look but lost focus once more. Instead, his eyes flittered away and found Liz's left hand. In it was the black rock, and as he looked on, she raised it behind her head like a baseball pitcher about to release a fastball. Stander vaguely understood she had just hit him with the strange black rock and was about to strike him again. Uncomprehending, Stander fumbled at her rising arm, but the motion hurt his head tremendously. He suddenly felt woozy, sure he was about to be sick.

Stander somehow finally staggered to his feet, disrupting and avoiding the violent swing of Liz's arm in the process. He stumbled away from her and back towards the entrance of the cave. He tripped over the prostrate form of Ethan and walked directly into the cavern's wall. The sharp protruding edges dug into his shoulder, and the brief flash of pain helped revive him. Stander was able to finally right himself and plunge towards the exit once more. Slamming his body against the metal gate, it, in turn, rebounded and knocked him sideways as he spilled out into the afternoon sun. The bright light hurt his eyes, and nearly blind, he fell to his knees before half-crawling and half-rolling down the side of the weedy mountainside. Barely aiming himself toward Secrist, who was crawling forward to meet him.

"Hey! Stander! God dammit, what happened up there? Hey!" Secrist was shaking Stander, who, flat on his back, had either momentarily fainted or fallen unconscious. Stander's eyes flew open, and he was instantly awake once more. The side of his head hurt like a son of a bitch, but the buzzing was receding from his ears. He propped himself up on his elbows and tried to clear his head from the shock of the unexpected blow. The bright sun and fresh air seemed to aid in his recovery. Stander dimly wondered if just getting out of the queer cave itself was what revived him as much as anything. Secrist was still shaking Stander but less urgently now, "Are you OK? Where did all this blood come from? Stander!"

"I'm fine, I'm… Just give me a second." Stander rubbed at the expanding goose egg rising steadily at his hairline. He stuck a finger in his ear canal, and when he pulled it out, there was warm blood on it. His shirt was covered in blood, but he knew almost none of it was actually his. It was Liz's… Stander moaned and started to try and get his legs back under himself to stand.

"Jesus, Stander, just hold on. What the hell happened? Did Ethan attack you? Was he up in the cave?" Concern was etched across Secrist's face. He had drawn his gun when Stander stumbled out of the cave, and he still held it ready but down at his side. He looked from Stander's face to the mountaintop and back again. No one followed Stander after he tumbled, dazed, down the hill.

Stander took a deep breath and dabbed at his bleeding and sore ear. "I found Ethan up there, but I got the drop on him. Knocked him unconscious."

Puzzled, Secrist's eyes narrowed. "Why did you do that?"

"It was Liz. He had Liz up in that cave. She's hurt and covered in blood." The memory of her gore-drenched body made Stander moan audibly once again, and he started back to his feet. "It was dark, but Ethan had her pinned in near the back of the cave. I took him down and tried to get her out of there. I think maybe she was dazed or hurt. Didn't know what she was doing… I don't know… Must have thought I was Ethan. Probably scared to death… Anyway, she whacked me a good one with a rock. Just defending herself but fuck, man, she hit me solid, and I lost it."

Stander was standing now, and he reached down to help Secrist up. Both men stumbled. But for Stander, the worst of the dizziness had left him. Secrist leaned heavily against a small tree beside him, putting no weight on his injured foot. Stander continued, "Let me go get her. She needs a doctor." He looked across at his friend of twenty-plus years. "You may have to drag your own fat ass down this hill. I doubt I can carry both of you…"

"Don't worry about me. But what about Ethan? You said you knocked him out, but he'll come out of that just like you did."

"I am not worried about that motherfucker." Stander paused, trying to focus his foggy mind. He dimly remembered the blood on Ethan's hands and how easily he'd collapsed when he'd hit him. "Anyway, if he gets in the way of me getting Liz out, I won't be so gentle next time." Stander paused again, realizing he would have to leave Ethan to get Liz and Secrist the help they needed. "There is a padlock and gate at the entrance of the cave. I guess we'll lock his ass in that cave once I get Liz clear. When we get back to where the cell service works again, we can get someone to come up and grab him. By then, we'll know what he did to her."

Secrist nodded, and Stander turned and began jogging back up the hill. He had a massive headache but felt like himself once again. Barely dizzy anymore, he focused on getting Liz to safety and a doctor. At the cavern's entrance, Stander cautiously poked his head in just enough to make sure Ethan was still out of commission. Stander could see the grad student's boots and legs splayed out on the ground where he had left him, hopefully, still out cold. Once he identified where Ethan was, and the coast was clear, Stander entered and walked steadily and cautiously, not wanting to startle Liz. He called out to her calmly. As you would a scared child.

Liz was still on her knees in the cave but now was hunched over the horizontal form of Ethan. Her bare back was facing Stander as he approached them both. He could see Ethan had turned over and was now lying flat on his back. Stander was certain he had been faced down before, and this change unsettled him.

He called out softly again, watching for any movement out of Ethan, "Hey, Liz. It's me, Russell. It's Stander. Let's get you out of here, huh?" Stander moved several more steps towards them both, now just a yard away from where they were on the floor of the cavern. There was no response to his voice. The lack of reaction or movement by either one of them troubled him. He could now see Liz was hovering directly above Ethan, and Stander thought she may have been trying to revive the man. Perhaps doing CPR or mouth-to-mouth resuscitation. Again, Stander wondered grimly if he had miscalculated the severity of the blow he had dealt the grad student. It wouldn't be the first time that had happened... Had Stander killed him?

The air inside the cave remained still, and the coppery taste of blood lingered. Stander called out softly once more to Liz as he reached for her back. Trying to be gentle with her in the face of the trauma she had endured, most likely in this very cave, "Liz, come on now... Liz?"

Stander reached down, and his fingers brushed her exposed back. Soundless, Liz's head slowly rose from where it hung directly above Ethan's face. Her backbone followed the upturn of her head, and she sat straight up, knees and shins still resting on the ground of the cavern. She contorted and twisted her torso around to face Stander with a chest smeared in fresh blood dripping down between the valley of her breasts. Her chin was an obscenity of human gravy, and unashamedly it spilled off her, dripping to the ground. Her jaw worked in a circular pattern but never opened, not a sound escaping from it or from her.

Stander's mind raced to comprehend what he was seeing, initially believing there was an additional injury to Liz. In the shadow of her chin and in the dim light of the cave, the cascading stream of gore that ran down seemed to sprout from her throat. Stander's sight darkened. A loud buzzing filled his ears. He started to reach for the front of her neck as if his touch could stem the flow of blood he saw. He looked down at Ethan dumbly. Trying to process if the man on the ground held a knife and somehow slashed the throat of the woman kneeling over him. If so, how had Stander not seen it?

But Stander could not find Ethan. Where his face should be, there was nothing. He had been eviscerated from the neck up. White teeth were exposed in the absence of his lips, a dark wet hole where his nose should have been. One ear hung precariously by a strand of meat; the other ear was not visible on or around him. Unblinking eyes stared up at Stander. Eyelids were torn away, as were the flesh and eyebrows above them. Stander suddenly felt very hot, and his stomach threatened to empty itself.

What was once Ethan opened its mouth. The eerie sound constricted Stander's throat and instantly stopped the gurgling vomit. Stander, forgetting his sickness, focused once more on the man laid out on the ground. Ethan's wide-open eyes seemed to narrow and refocus on Stander as well. A single teardrop squeezed itself from the corner of each eye simultaneously. Then the white teeth and lipless mouth parted. A single word stretched out slowly.

"W…WEN…WENDIGO…"

At the utterance, Liz turned. Cat-like, she pounced back upon the wreck of the human being on the floor of the cave. Paralyzed, Stander watched as she tore into him and worked her fingers like tiny jackhammers. In seconds, she had removed both of Ethan's eyes with the swiftness of a practiced hand. Popping each in her mouth with the glee of an eight-year-old devouring buttery popcorn during a Disney matinee. Liz crunched both of Ethan's eyes inside her mouth and moaned as she had under Stander just the night before.

Finishing, she rose to her feet and faced the frozen man who came to her rescue. A smile cracked wide across her full lips, stained red and pink again as the night before. Her blonde hair, now splashed in crimson blood and gore, was tinged a pink, strawberry blonde. Stander's legs grew weak… Too late, he recalled the strawberry blonde hair he's seen in his earlier vision right inside this cave. The blonde hair hadn't been Sherry's. It had been Liz's!

Liz's smile broadened. She hissed out the name Ethan had used with his last breath, "Wendigo." Her green eyes shimmered and widened as Stander began to shake uncontrollably. Her face then opened ever wider. Her jaw unhinged like a snake swallowing an egg. As if to kiss him, Liz moved seductively to Stander's face. Her bare chest pressed against his shirt. She wrapped herself around him, lowering them both to the floor of the cave.

———

Later, when she was done with Stander, Liz picked up the shiny black rock from the cave floor in one hand. The rock rose and fell and rose and fell over and over until her arm refused to raise the dripping stone any longer. Underneath her was now unrecognizable as a man, woman, child, or even a human being. Where the head had been, there was only a circular, wide indentation in the cave floor pooled with blood. Shards of shattered bone and floating grey chunks of brain matter littered the puddle. The lifeless corpse resembled a man with his head buried in the sand or dunking himself face first in a deep puddle of thick, filthy, red waste. The bludgeoning of the black rock decapitating and annihilating everything from the neck up. The inside of the cave reverberated only with the sounds of Liz's heavy breath as she gasped in and out.

Her grisly work completed, Liz pulled the shirt off the headless corpse. She tenderly wrapped the dripping black stone inside the soft cotton, much as a mother would her precious child, before laying it back on the floor of the cave. She then picked her own clothes up from the ground and walked casually outside of the cavern, slick blood dripping down and off her nude body. The bright sun hurt her eyes initially, but she was able to make her way over to the stream that ran next to the entrance of the cave. She cleansed herself in the cold mountain spring, washing the bits of flesh, bone, and the worst of the blood stains from her face, arms, and chest.

When she was satisfied, Liz dressed and stood. As she turned, an older man she didn't recognize, awkwardly hopping on one leg, sweating and clearly in agony, crested the flat area in front of Skull Rock. He was leaning hard against a broken tree branch and held on to it with both hands to stay upright and balanced. Out of breath, red-faced, and panting, he managed to croak out a question.

"Where… Where is Stander? I saw, saw you come out… alone." Secrist swallowed and tried to regain his breath. "You washed up…Washed yourself? What I mean is, why would you?" He looked at the pretty blond facing him up and down, eyeing the faded but still visible blood stains on her hands, arms, hair, and clothes she had just donned. "Are you Liz?" Nothing was adding up.

Liz looked up at the man and smiled sweetly. Puzzled, Secrist squinted in the bright afternoon sun, more concerned with what was going on inside the cave than the strange blonde woman outside of it. Liz moved close to Secrist, almost casually, before lashing out and kicking the tree branch out from under him with her foot. Secrist toppled to the ground in a huff. The harsh fall knocked the wind out of him. Instantly, Liz pounced on top of the stunned man, straddling him and leaning over his face. She smiled down at him. Her toothy grin grew wider and wider…

Secrist managed to free his gun from where he'd tucked it under his belt while struggling to climb the last of the trail up to the cave. Bringing the weapon level with his attacker's face, he started to warn her of his full intention of using it when Secrist heard Stander's voice calling out from the entrance of the cavern.

"Yo! Hey! Look what I got here!" Stander stepped out from the cave, waving the black rock back and forth above his head. The strange stone in his hand glinted like a mirror as the bright rays of the sun reflected off it. "You were so hot for this. Well, here it is." Turning back to face the entrance of the cavern once more, Stander heaved the rock back inside the cave. "Go fetch, you fucking bitch!"

Liz, or whatever she had become, grimaced once as if struck, remaining motionless for several long seconds before shuddering and blurring before the two men's astonished eyes. Dropping her hands to the ground, she accelerated swiftly forward, scuttling on all fours with the nimble grace of one well practiced in the movement. In the blink of an eye, she dashed past Stander, leaving both men unsure of what they had just witnessed.

Stander slammed the steel gate closed behind Liz, quickly snapping the hanging padlock shut and locking it with the key sticking out. Pulling the key free, he jogged the few steps over to where Secrist was struggling to gain his feet, reaching down and helping him back up. Incredulous, Secrist's gaze never left the cave entrance.

"What the hell was that thing?" Then, looking directly at Stander, Secrist added. "I figured you were a dead man, and I was about to join you... How did you manage to avoid that...? Wait! What the hell was that thing?"

"That thing is still Liz, and I think she must still have some control over herself. When she pulled me down, I thought I was about to get swallowed whole. But at the last moment, before I passed out again, I saw something change behind her eyes. Next thing I knew, she had rolled off me and was pounding on Ethan." Stander looked down, "There ain't much left of him in there..."

"Jesus... Well, now what?" Secrist was looking once more at the cavern's locked doorway, wondering if it would hold whatever lurked behind it. Stander, still covered in drying blood but almost none of it his own, shrugged. Without a word, he offered Secrist his arm, and they both made their way to the steel barred entryway of the cave, cautiously peering inside the dim dark cave.

"Liz! Liz!" Stander, hearing no reply, brazenly put his two hands on the bars of the gate like a jailed man in a prison cell. "Liz! Can you hear me? What the fuck is going on?"

Liz, the black rock cradled once again in her hands, faced the two men from inside the cave. Her tongue was silent, and though her mouth was cruel, her eyes were soft as she looked directly at Stander. The black rock began to glow in her hands, the center or eye of the stone shining brightly. Within seconds, a blinding blueish-white flash illuminated the entirety of the cavern, and both Stander and Secrist were forced to look away.

When the blaze of white light subsided, Liz - or the thing she had become - was gone. On the ground where she'd stood, the queer black rock glowed a soft blue hue before dulling completely, becoming a simple solid black mass once more. Directly behind it, the headless corpse of Ethan lay unmoving on the floor of the cave where Liz had left it.

Stander turned to Secrist, mouth ajar. "Holy shit! What… What the fuck! Did you just see that? Please tell me I am not going nuts today, and you saw that too."

"Yeah… Yeah, I did. But who is ever going to believe us?" Secrist rubbed his eyes with one hand, but when he opened them once again, the result was the same. The blonde had disappeared right in front of him, and the rock remained. "Maybe… God, how am I going to explain this to Craig?"

"Maybe we didn't 'see'…" Stander started to make quotation marks with his hands in the air before stopping himself. He looked grimly once more at the inside of the cave where Liz vanished. "Maybe we just came up here and found Ethan's body. Let someone else try to make sense of it all. I sure as hell can't."

"Yeah, agreed… What about that freaky rock?"

Stander reached up and unlocked the padlock. "Oh, I'll take care of that," he said as he opened the gate and stepped inside. "Don't you worry…"

With Stander's back to him, Secrist could not see the widening, ear-to-ear smile on his friend's face as he bent down to retrieve the black stone. As Stander touched the warm rock, it weakly pulsed once as he repeated softly.

"Don't you worry."

-EPILOGUE-

SCOTTY, the local UPS driver that serviced much of the downtown area of Marquette, pushed open the front door of the bar. In his hands, he carried a single long and slender box. From behind the bar, Stander, washing glasses in the bar sink, called out to him. "Hey Scotty, how are you doing today?"

"Hello. Doing good, doing good…" he replied, nodding slightly. "Just one today." Crossing the otherwise empty tavern, he placed the delivery on the top of the bar and scanned the shipping barcode with his handheld device. "Looks like your putter came."

"Putter? Do you really think I look like a guy that would golf?" Stander, smiling, raised his arms out to his side in mock incredulousness. His black and red White Stripes concert t-shirt was the antithesis of golfing apparel.

"Sorry. No, not really…." Scotty was chuckling as he pointed at the box he'd just delivered. "But that's usually what's inside boxes like that. Titleist uses that style of shipping container for their orders." The UPS driver waved as he headed back towards the door. "See you tomorrow, Stander."

"Take it easy, Scotty," Stander noted the handwritten address tag was simply his name and the address for the bar done in block letters. There was no return address or any indication of where the shipment had originated from. Reaching under the counter, he pulled out a pair of scissors from beneath the bar's cash register and used them to slice open the packaging tape before pulling back the cardboard flaps and yanking out the loose packing material near the top. Inside he found a small note written on the same hotel stationary where Liz had stayed while in Marquette. The handwriting, although cursive and distinctly more feminine than the address label had been, was the same.

"Keep this close and find the others. In the end, you'll need them all. I'll see you in the next life. Unless you see me coming first."

Stander pulled the long sword from the shipping container. Badly corroded and difficult to see clearly, the metal blade was covered in a myriad of symbols. Though he couldn't decipher any of them, they were familiar. As Stander held the weapon aloft, he looked up at the sword's twin hanging above his bar. The one his great aunt had bequeathed to him upon her death.

"Curiouser and curiouser...." Stander whispered under his breath.

FOR MORE INFORMATION

Gritzmonster.com

Coming 2023

Book 2

Skulldiggery: The Quarry